NIGHT SHADOW

NIGHT SHADOW

A Novel

CHERRY ADAIR

BALLANTINE BOOKS

NEW YORK

Published in the United States by Ballantine Books, an imprint of The Random House Publishing Group, a division of Random House, Inc., New York.

BALLANTINE and colophon are registered trademarks of Random House, Inc.

Library of Congress Cataloging-in-Publication Data

Adair, Cherry.
Night shadow : a novel / Cherry Adair.
p.   cm.
ISBN 978-0-345-49973-8 (hardcover : alk. paper)
1. Terrorism—Prevention—Fiction.   I. Title.
PS3601.D348N54 2008
813'.6—dc22
2008038285

Printed in the United States of America

www.ballantinebooks.com

2   4   6   8   9   7   5   3   1

To my friend Karla Baehr, who loves to read, but has no desire to write. Not only do you make me laugh, you're also the most organized woman in the galaxy, and I love you for it. Thank you for all that you do to keep me sane (-ish).

NIGHT SHADOW

One

Blinking snowflakes off her lashes, T–FLAC operative Alexis Stone shot a quick glance down at the toes of her brand new, size eight combat boots as she teetered on the edge of the snow-encrusted roof. The excruciating headache that had plagued her for the last several minutes intensified. A headache was going to be the least of her damned problems if she didn't *move*.

Jump. Get it over with. Quick and painless.

What the . . . ?

Jump *across,* she told herself. Not down. *Across. Between* the buildings. A relatively easy jump, yet she hesitated. Terminal velocity wouldn't be in effect in such a short drop. She'd only fall about a hundred and fifty feet, not the four hundred necessary to pick up the hundred and thirty-five miles an hour to achieve terminal speed.

What was she *thinking*? Mouth dry, heart pounding, Lexi shook her head to clear it.

Mathematically, a falling object—*her*—increased its velocity by thirty-two feet per second as it fell. Acceleration to gravity—

Over. Not down.

She'd be on the ground in less than two seconds—

Over. Not down.

Jump. Do it now.

Hallucinations?

Crap. She blinked white out of her eyes, her breath coming hot and fast. The training simulations hadn't aptly portrayed what it felt like to be out in the field under hostile conditions. Not the cold, not the pressure, not the frantic tattoo of her heart. Not the irrational thoughts clouding her mind. One word summed up the experience.

Terrifying.

Focus. Fortunately, she was a pragmatic woman. Flights of fancy weren't in her DNA. Or hadn't been before tonight. She'd trained with the best of the best. Now she just had to put it into action. She could do this.

Do not *imagine being shot in the back.*

Do not *picture falling.*

Do not look down.

Her mouth was too dry to even attempt swallowing. She started counting, silently, to slow the rushing thud of her pulse which made it hard to hear and intensified the headache.

Her gaze climbed upward incrementally until she focused on the hotel across the alley. Only eight feet separated the two buildings.

Fifteen stories to the snowy ground below.

She'd never been afraid of heights before. Lights popped on in some of the dark windows as dusk fell like an unwelcome blanket over Moscow.

They'd followed her. She knew they had. *Jump!* her brain screamed.

Despite the bone-chilling cold, sweat beaded her face. Her entire body was damp and clammy beneath her black civilian clothing. The familiar weight of the Glock, all seven ounces of firepower, felt as heavy as a boulder in her numb fingers.

Running footsteps, crossing the roof behind her, sounded like a freaking herd of crazed wildebeests charging. Her galloping heart jumped into her throat. Too late. Her hesitation was going to cost her. She glanced down at the shadowy drop just beyond the tips of her boots, then back at the dark footprints just behind her. Easy to follow her trail when her steps were clear in the snow blanketing the rooftop.

She'd had a five-minute, eleven-second head start. They'd caught up. The men following her had scaled that blasted metal fire escape in record time. And probably without being terrified the thing would pull away from the crumbling brick wall as they scrabbled for purchase.

The high-pitched *whine-piiing* and yellow sparks of a bullet ricocheting off metal just a few feet away made her flinch. Close. Too close. *Do it, Lexi. Just freaking jump.*

No. Return fire. *Then* jump.

Cautiously, but as fast as she could manage, she walked backward in her own footprints. As soon as she felt the heated metal of a four-foot-wide exhaust flue against her back, she spun and dropped into a crouch behind the only cover for a hundred feet of flat white rooftop.

A dozen indistinguishable exhaust fans dotted the roof, belching unsynchronized clouds of foul-smelling steam. The steam and stink collided with the rapidly falling snow, making visibility nearly nonexistent in the pseudo fog the mix created. If she couldn't see them, they couldn't see her. She hoped.

Crouching to below their eye level, Lexi squeezed off a half dozen textbook-perfect shots. Night was falling as fast as the snow now, and the spare illumination was a thick, barely transparent charcoal. She knew exactly how to get to where she needed to be. Like a lodestone, she had ID'd the black shutters against the white-washed walls of the safe house seven buildings southeast.

Five men had chased her all the way from Belorussky Railway Station on Tverskaya Zastava Ploshchad, through the alleys and up onto this rooftop half a dozen blocks away.

Piiingpiiingpiiing. They weren't messing around. Sparks shot out like fireworks as a hail of bullets struck metal. The men were firing blind. A waste of ammunition, but pretty much a guarantee that one of the stray bullets would hit their target. Her.

Six. There'd been *six* of them, she corrected, seeing them come out of nowhere in her mind's eye. A mathematical mistake could very well bite her in the ass. One guy was way ahead of the pack, moving fast and low, closing the gap between them.

Shifting her trigger finger off the frame of the Glock, Lexi squeezed off a shot. The impact of the bullet hitting him square in the chest knocked the guy off his feet. With a brief look of annoyance he went down soundlessly.

Went down . . . and dissipated into nothingness before his body hit the ground.

Ducking out of sight, back flat against the warmth of the pipe, Lexi sucked in a startled breath. *Shit. My first kill shot. A wizard?* Her heart beat hard enough to block out the sound of running footsteps. She felt the vibration through the soles of her boots and took a chance, angling her head so she could see them coming. And there they were. Thirty yards and closing. Five men, dressed in black, their shadowy forms barely visible.

Narrow-eyed, she watched a second guy break from the pack,

coming at her flat-out, long legs closing the gap between them. Weapon raised, he stopped, head shifting as he searched the rooftop for her.

Two other men joined him, snow veiling them where they stood, warm breath thick in the air around their heads.

"Did she jump across?" the middle guy asked the other two in his native Russian, glaring down at the gap between the buildings. Lexi followed their gazes. Her footprints teetered right on the edge. Visibility was iffy, and unless they looked closely, they wouldn't notice the faint blurring of her double steps. She hoped.

She held her breath as two more men caught up, the murmur of the voices blending. One man indicated they separate, and they spread out on the roof.

Her pulse shot into overdrive, and her mouth went dry as a metronome ticked off the seconds in her head.

They'd find her in moments. And there was no wondering what they'd do to her if they got their hands on her. She freaking knew. She'd seen too much. And she was as good as dead unless she could make that jump.

As much as she wanted to plot things out to the last variable, as much as she wanted to calculate the exact trajectory necessary to leap the gap and how she should fall on the other side, Lexi literally took a running leap of faith.

The run, followed by an ungraceful jump had her body suspended over nothing but air for what felt like an eternity. Rapid fire, followed by shouts, accompanied her leap across the abyss. Too pumped up on terror and adrenaline to feel any pain, she landed hard on the other, slightly lower, roof, and stumbled into a low run.

Go. Go. Go.

Her breath led the way as she found the extra speed necessary to leap between the next two buildings, a jump of at least twelve feet this time. One foot skidded out from under her as she landed in wet snow on the other side. Sheer willpower pulled her upright and she kept running.

Go. Go. Go.

Chunks of cement exploded inches from her feet, sending bits of it stinging into her skin through her pants. She spun, returning fire. She knew she wasn't going to hit anyone; her aim was too wild, and she couldn't see a damn thing now that it was fully dark. Numb with cold, the snow was a soft menace as it landed soundlessly on any exposed skin. A stark black-and-white movie with her frantic heartbeats and sawing breath as theme music.

The whine and the hot slice of a bullet as it cut through her coat and into her shoulder made her curse under her breath. It would probably hurt like hell later. Well, no *probably* about it, but right now she didn't feel a thing. Lexi ducked behind the dubious protection of a small cement maintenance shed in the middle of the rooftop. Hat down, collar up, just her eyes visible, she scanned the area. The cold, and the vicious vise of the headache, made her eyes water and burn, forcing her to waste precious seconds blinking things back into focus.

There they were. Running, spreading out, determined to catch her. Catch her, hell. *Kill* her.

No CGI-generated bad guys. No drill. This was as real as it got.

Reaching into her tac belt, she grabbed a new magazine and wiped the sweat out of her left eye onto the shoulder of her jacket. *Let the training take over.* Deep breath in. Rapid reload. Pop the empty clip, slam in a new one. Thumb the slide-stop so the slide jacks forward and fire again. And again. Chest high, level and steady. Wrist firm, firing hand pressed securely against her opposing palm. Double-tapping in controlled bursts, tiny lateral movements to avoid creating gaps in the kill-zone.

Visualize the target; see the slap of the bullet.

She squeezed the trigger. A scream indicated she'd managed to hit one, even in the dark.

She heard the thud of his body with grim satisfaction. That one wasn't a wizard. Or if he was, he was a dead wizard.

Her weapons instructor would be proud.

Two down. Four to go. And six more buildings to navigate before reaching the safe house.

She couldn't lead these yahoos there. Four more kills, or a wild goose chase across the rooftops of Moscow. In the dark. God, what a choice.

Lexi tried to come up with a plan. Heart manic, sweat stinging her eyes, she leaned against the cement wall.

Think.

Easier said than done when an anvil pounded behind her eyeballs and every instinct told her to run like hell. Odds were she'd be shot within the next few minutes.

Take a deep breath. Center yourself. Think.

Somehow she had to circle around behind them.

Somehow.

Couldn't see them, but Lexi heard their voices. Whispered Russian, carried away on the light breeze, impossible to hear well enough to interpret. She prayed they'd conclude she'd managed to evade them.

For a moment a stray bit of light reflected off the snowy ground and she saw them. They'd gathered in a tight little group at the edge of the roof, a knot of dense darkness barely visible against the even bigger blackness of the night. Big mistake, boys.

Four shots. Rapid. No hesitation.

They wouldn't expect her to return the way she'd come— straight at them.

Pulling the extra fabric of her turtleneck over her mouth and nose, Lexi welcomed the few seconds of warmth. Good time for a tac-reload. Quietly, she slid the clip out of the mag well and replaced it with a fresh one, stowed the partly spent one in her belt. Then, blocking out the cold, she dropped to the ground. A shallow, twelve-inch-high wall ran around the perimeter of the flat roof. On her belly, using her feet and elbows to move her forward, she crawled up against the wall, the fully loaded Glock in her right hand.

One chance to do this.

One.

She could hear them more clearly the closer she got. Confused. Undirected. They weren't sure what to do next. *Good.*

Sucking in a breath, she squeezed off a shot. Another, and another. Three down. One to go.

The remaining guy fired back, yelling in Russian as he tried to pinpoint her location from her muzzle flashes. But she'd already moved. She was practically under his feet as he fired blindly into the darkness.

Rolling to her back, Lexi aimed for the underside of his chin. She let out half a breath. The big oaf looked down just as she squeezed the trigger.

In that instant, some of those training details that seemed so hard to memorize came back effortlessly. Nine-millimeter, 124-grain, plus-P rounds. For a Glock 19, that translated into a muzzle velocity in excess of thirteen hundred feet per second—

Her bullet punched into his gaping mouth and blew the back of his head off. His body instantly turned to a fine black powder.

Shuddering, she didn't pause to congratulate herself on her marksmanship or her mastery of weapon specs. There wasn't time. All the gunplay and shouting would draw the curious, or stupid, sooner or later. Lexi hauled ass and ran as if the hounds of hell were on her heels.

Stretched out on the narrow sway-backed bed, hands stacked beneath his head, Alexander Stone dozed lightly. Since the room was on the top floor, he opened one eye when he heard pounding footsteps on the rooftop just above the window.

Interesting.

Curling his fingers around the butt of the Sig Sauer lying on the mattress beside his hip, he lay still, just another shadow in the room. Seconds later, the window slammed back against the wall. A slight figure, dressed from head to toe in black, catapulted feet first through the opening as if jet propelled.

He could barely make out her slender form in the darkness. Hands on her knees, head down, Lexi struggled to catch a wheezing breath. "Shit. Shit. Shit."

Alex sat up, swinging his feet to the floor. "How was the play, Mrs. Lincoln?"

At the sound of his voice, coming as it did out of the darkness, she let out a startled yelp as she straightened. But damn if she didn't come up weapon raised.

"Turn on the light." Still out of breath, but her voice was strong.

"Hell, Lexi. I could've shot you ten times by now. Shoot first, ask questions later." Alex leaned over and switched on the light beside the bed. He immediately noticed the dark red wetness on her right shoulder. "But it looks like someone already beat me to it." Jesus. What the hell was Lexi Stone doing in Moscow? Bleeding? When the innkeeper had assured him his room was ready, Alex had had a moment of confusion. *He* hadn't already checked in ... Alex Stone. *Alexis* Stone. No relation. Not even third cousins five times removed—he'd checked.

Might be confusing for the accounting department, but he'd never expected to see her anywhere but HQ in Montana. Didn't make a damn bit of sense seeing her here.

She belonged at her desk in the research department. She was completely out of context in a shit-hole of a safe house in Russia.

Dove-soft gray eyes blinked at him, her expression a mixture of confusion and irritation. "What are *you* doing here?"

"Here in Moscow or here in our room?" He'd forgotten how

tall she was. He was used to seeing her hunched over her computer at her desk at HQ.

"It isn't *our* room. It's *my* room. My op."

Her . . . *op*? "Do you own Moscow as well, or is that up for grabs?"

Annoyed, she pulled a black knit cap off her head and stuffed it into the pocket of her coat. Well, hell. Her hair used to be a very pretty, glossy light brown. And long. She used to wear it in some sleek, complicated braid thing on the back of her head. She'd cut about a mile and a half off. Now it was chin length, fashionably choppy, and a sunny blond. "Cut your hair yourself?"

She raised a hand to her chin-length bob and didn't bother answering the obvious. "You're supposed to be in Paris." She touched the bridge of her nose.

Damn it to hell. She used to wear *glasses* as well.

"True." He pushed back on the edge of the bed to lean against the wall, dangling his hand off his bent knee. "You wearing Lock-Out under that jacket?" Hip-length black Thinsulate coat, black jeans, soaked to the hem of the coat, and the smallest damned combat boots he'd ever seen, carrying a Glock, and packing an attitude a mile wide.

With a fucking bullet crease in her shoulder.

Color crept into her already chill-bright cheeks. "I just went to—"

"Get shot?" he said dryly. "We'd better take care of that." He shoved himself off the bed in one lithe move, tucking his Sig in the waistband at the back of his pants. She backed up. "Did you manage to hit anyone?" Yeah. She was taller than he remembered. Her sunny hair would brush his lips if he were to hold her. Which of course he had no intention of doing. His gaze dropped to her lips. Mistake. She had the kind of soft mouth that would distract most men.

Didn't distract him. Alex concentrated on eye contact.

Up went the chin. "I was trained by Darius, what do you think?"

The best of the best. No need to ask further. "Were you followed?"

She shot a nervous glance over her shoulder at the open window and the night sky beyond. "I don't believe so."

Shit. Damn. And fucking hell. "You'd better be sure."

"I—" She wanted to tell him to go to hell, Alex could see it in the mutinous line of her lips. "I'm not sure," she admitted somewhat belligerently. Lexi. Honest to a fault.

He gave a lugubrious sigh and slid the Sig out of his waistband, not sure who else was coming through that window. "Get that coat off and go into the bathroom. Take a shower. I'll be right back."

"I'll go with you."

If he was any judge of women, and he was, the lady was about to puke or pass out. Possibly both. "How will I explain your bloodless body to your supervisor in the—What department is it again? Accounting?" She was the girl with the glasses and great legs in the research department.

A cool look from hot gray eyes. "I'm an operative now."

Alex cocked a brow. Recruitment had to be at an all-time low if they'd made her an operative. "Strip and get in the shower. Let's see what garbage you've left for me to clean up."

"I killed five men tonight." She sounded half proud, half repulsed.

Yeah. She was an operative all right. Not.

"Did you, now? And how many were on your ass?" He shrugged on his coat, pulling the collar around his throat. The windchill inside the damned room was below freezing.

"Six."

"You don't sound too sure."

"Six."

Reaching into a pocket Alex pulled out a cap made from Lock-Out, put it on and pulled the stretchy black fabric all the way down to his eyebrows. It would keep the cold out—and everything else.

"You don't believe me?"

Fuck. Now she was getting pissy about it. Of course with a first kill that was expected. The shock had to wear off, and then you either crashed or pushed through it and became a real operative. "Every word. I guess you could stand right there waiting for me to get back," he prodded when she didn't move. "But Muravyou is going to be pissed about all that blood dripped on his fancy carpet."

Rurik Muravyou was the corpulent, tobacco-chewing manager of the T-FLAC safe house in Moscow. He would no sooner trust the creaky elevator up to the twelfth floor, to see a *carpet,* than he'd ever be fit enough to be an operative again. He was eighty pounds, fifteen years, and apathetically past it.

"Thank you for pointing out that I'm bleeding. Don't you have someone to shoot?"

"Yeah, good thinking." He motioned for her to raise her arm, which would slow the flow of blood, then swung himself up onto the shoulder-high windowsill feet first. "Direction?"

"Northwest."

"Lock the window, close the drapes. Clean up. I'll be back to tuck you in and tell you a bedtime story."

Her lips tightened. "I can hardly wait."

Alex's lips twitched and he gripped the Sig tighter to focus his thoughts away from her soft, sassy mouth. "I promise, it'll be worth waiting for."

Two

A hot shower was going to make the bleeding on her throbbing shoulder start again, but Lexi was too cold to care.

First things first, however.

She locked the window, yanked the drapes closed, and raced into the minuscule bathroom. Still wearing her coat, she slammed the door shut and sank down on the edge of the rusted tub, burying her face in her shaking hands. If Alex hadn't been lying in wait for her, she was pretty darn sure she'd be throwing up right now.

Scratch that. She was absolutely certain she'd be puking. But it wasn't the *chase* that had shaken her to the core. That had been exactly what she'd imagined being on an op was all about. She'd been scared, but pumped by the danger and the huge surge of adrenaline that had kept her focused and on target.

No, the chase had been cool. Except for the getting shot part. What freaked her out and made her sick to her stomach was knowing how close she'd come to ending it all. The overwhelming suicidal thoughts—God, the feelings had come over her so quickly she didn't have time to examine why she had them or where they'd come from.

She rubbed the dull ache between her eyes. Out on that rooftop she'd felt like failure, a rookie about to lead the tangos behind her straight to the safe house and ruin T-FLAC operations in Russia. Why had she ever aspired to being one of the big dogs dressed in black? She'd failed before she'd even completed her first op. The only thing that could make it better, could possibly salvage the damage she'd likely already caused, was if she took herself out of the equation. It would be so easy. Just one foot over the edge.

The overwhelming desire to step off that damned building in a freefall to the ground below and the realization of how close she'd been, just a heartbeat away from acting on the impulse, now made her insides twist with revulsion.

Before tonight Lexi had never had a suicidal thought in her life. Thank God the dark thoughts were gone and she was back to her normal, pragmatic self.

What was up with *that*?

She'd had a psych eval a month ago. She'd tested sane, rational, and extremely well adjusted.

Perhaps the dark thoughts happened to all new operatives their first time in the field? Lexi thought that through, then shook her head. "Bull. There hasn't been *one* report, not one, of any such thing happening." Of course, an operative wouldn't broadcast their diagnosis, and the medical staff would get handed their heads on a plate if they divulged private information about a patient.

Still, she hadn't heard any rumors about new operatives being suicidal or *committing* suicide. And the research department heard just about everything, true, false, or rumor.

Logically, Lexi knew she had nothing to be concerned about.

An aberration, then. An aberration brought on by adrenaline, fear, cold, and the damn headache from hell.

It took a few minutes of deep breathing—in through the nose and out through the mouth—to collect herself enough to stand up and remove her coat. Adrenaline still surged through her system at breakneck speed. If operatives felt this way after every confrontation, it was a wonder they didn't all keel over with heart attacks before they turned thirty.

She leaned over and turned on the shower to get the water warm—research told her water was rarely *hot* in Russia—then went back into the room to hang up her coat in the curtained-off closet space and collect a change of clothes. Alex's black duffel, nearly identical to hers, was on the floor near the bed. The difference was, his bag was battered and beat up, hers was pristine and new.

God, just how pathetic had she looked to him, busting into the room, shot up without LockOut on? Mortified, she briefly squeezed her eyes shut, then told herself to buck up.

He'd taken a bottle of her water and consumed half of it, then left the open container on the table next to the head of the bed. The room smelled like him. Which was patently ridiculous; operatives used nothing containing fragrance for obvious reasons. Yet there was something indefinable about Alex that clearly left his imprint on the room.

Lexi lifted the lumpy pillow from its crushed position at the head of the bed and pressed it to her face, inhaling deeply. It smelled of fresh air and . . . Alexander Stone.

Asinine.

Her, not him.

With a curse, she tossed it back onto the rock-hard single bed, then stared at it. He'd know she'd moved it. She leaned over and tried to re-create the way Alex had smashed the pillow under his head. He'd claimed the only bed in the room. *And just where does he think he's going to sleep?* she thought, annoyed with her foolishness. *With her? Not in this lifetime.*

Section C, paragraph v, subsection 1 stated that *Operation team members are expected to share quarters as necessary to accomplish mission objectives when safe houses are in use.*

The room. Fine. But she'd be damned if that regulation would mean she'd share a *bed* with him too. *Really?* A little voice in her head taunted. *Disinterest is why I followed his every op. Why I learned languages he was learning. Why I know just about everything about him including his underwear choice and size? Boxers. Medium.*

A crush. A small case of hero worship. That was all. Proximity and her job would nip that foolishness right out of her.

Her shoulder burned like fire. She needed to tend to it and take that shower before he got back. She also had to get her story straight so she didn't trip herself up.

The lock on the bathroom door wouldn't keep out a determined child, so she took a straight-backed chair into the tiny bathroom with her. Not that he'd invade her privacy if he returned and found the bathroom door closed. He wasn't a man who had to go out of his way to pick up women. His thick dark hair, dark green eyes, and body, buff enough to make grown women weak in the head, ensured he was never lonely. Rumor of his conquests were bulletined all over the research department like a weekly soap opera update.

In her department, all the women wanted to date him, and the guys wanted to *be* him. Her coworkers thought Alex was *the* most charming, amusing, hot, dedicated operative they'd ever worked with. The women's emphasis was on the charming/amusing/hot portion of his program. They rhapsodized about his sexy mouth. His great body. His naughty smile and, oh God, those brilliant green eyes. They laughed off the fact that he was a rule breaker and a renegade.

Whatever. All he was to Lexi was a pain in the butt.

And the fact that she and Alex had names that were almost identical amused their coworkers as much as it confused human resources.

Lexi thought it all embarrassing, especially the part about their
names. He'd received her paycheck seven times in the last five
years. When she'd accidentally received his, *twice,* Lexi had put it in
his mail slot *unopened.* When he'd returned hers, he'd not only
opened the damn envelope, he'd written some irrelevant comment
across her pay stub. It was an invasion of privacy.

Just like now. He was here. Instead of Paris where he was supposed to be.

The man was annoyingly unpredictable. And in her neat, tidy
world, unpredictability equaled liability.

Lexi stripped as steam filled the bathroom. She suspected only the
frigid air had produced steam from water barely above room temperature. Using the single threadbare white towel, she cleared away
a circle on the mirror and tried to see how bad her shoulder was.
Hard to tell with all the blood smeared on her skin. She'd look again
after she washed it off. Right now, it felt as bad as it looked. The bullet had only made a four-inch furrow in the fleshy part of her shoulder. She shook her head as she tested the temperature of the water.

Only. Twelve hours on the job, and a bullet wound was *only.*

Feeling like a fool was a new and annoying experience. Alex
was right. She'd had no business not wearing LockOut under her
clothing. The T-FLAC Protocol Manual was crystal clear on the
matter.

*Chapter One Section viii, paragraph 1 on uniforms. LockOut suits
must be worn as appropriate on all T-FLAC sanctioned operations. Injury
resulting from the lack of a LockOut suit will result in disciplinary action.*

But I only went there to watch, *dammit. How was I supposed to know
what would happen?* Then she shook her head. It was her job to
know, to be prepared.

Damn. Not a full day into her first black op and she'd already violated one of the basic rules. Not good. Not good at all. The excruciating pain in her shoulder served her right. The write-up was going to feel worse.

Gritting her teeth against the pain that had grown into agony, she climbed into the tub, pulling the mildewed curtain across the opening. The thin spray stung her chilled skin and she shifted out of the way to adjust the temperature before stepping back under the three pencil-thin, limp jets of water reluctantly shooting out of the antiquated showerhead. The once-warmish water was now tepid.

She made it quick. One, she had no idea when Alex would be back. She didn't want to be in here, naked, when he was out there, knowing she was in here, naked. Two, she wanted to dress the bullet crease. And three, she'd run out of tepid water; it was now a few degrees above cold.

"How many did you say there were?" Alex yelled through the door just as she stepped onto the bare linoleum floor. No bath mat, and she wasn't going to use the only towel.

Lexi covered her breasts with one hand and her pubes with the other as if Alex had X-ray vision. Which he didn't. At least she didn't think so. It wasn't in his file. His powers were the ability to null psionic fields, temporal acceleration, and she'd heard rumors that he was amphibious. He might have several more improbable talents that she didn't know or want to think about.

All, as far as she was concerned, contributed to being a T–FLAC operative the *easy* way. The psi unit had so many tricks up their collective sleeves she wondered that they didn't rule the damned world.

There was the easy way, and then there was the right way.

She grabbed the ratty towel and started drying off. "Six." She didn't have to raise her voice; the door was hollow and paper-thin.

"I didn't see anyone, alive or dead. You say you got five of them?

Where are the bodies, and where's the sixth guy? Did you mis-count?"

Reaching for her panties, Lexi rolled her eyes. Blood dribbled down her arm and she had to mop that up before she put on a bra. "I don't miscount," she told him, making a pad out of the damp towel and laying it over her shoulder so she could pull on her tank top. "One . . . evaporated."

Silence.

Lexi pulled jeans over her damp skin. "Alex?"

"Evaporated?"

The vision of the men vaporizing into clouds of black dust against the white snow was clear in her mind. "More like disinte-grated."

"Which is it?"

"Disintegrated."

"Know who these guys were?"

God. She hated telling tell him this part, she really did. It was embarrassing. "They followed me from the railway station."

"*Belorussky* station?"

His voice was neutral, but she winced anyway as she moved the chair out from under the handle and opened the door. He was leaning against the jamb and she walked right into his hard chest. "Yes," she muttered shoving him with the flat of her hand. Surpris-ingly, Alex stepped back.

He wore black pants and a close-fitting black sweater over his LockOut. She saw the edge of it at the neck of his sweater. Well, big whoop-de-do. Give the man a freaking prize. For once, he'd followed the rules, which was all the more grating on her nerves as she held the towel to her bleeding shoulder. An injury she wouldn't have had if she'd done the same.

He followed her as she retrieved her duffel from the floor of the closet. "And you were there—why?"

She slammed the bag down on a rickety table, and yanked down the zipper. "I'm an operative now, if you must know. I went to *observe*." She took out her own personal first-aid kit. The one given to field operatives was excellent. Hers was better. Better if she could get the darn thing *open* one-handed.

"Here." Alex stepped in and removed the small soft-sided kit from her hand. "Let me do that before you break a damned fingernail. Sit."

Lexi parked her butt on one of two straight-backed chairs. The other one was still in the bathroom. She held up her hand. "As you can see, I don't have long nails to break, in accordance with Chapter One, Section viii, paragraph four on uniforms in the protocol manual, regarding personal grooming. If you'd just ope—"

"Got it. You talk. Start anywhere." Alex's green eyes glittered as he opened the kit and started assembling items next to her on the table.

"Actually," Lexi said smoothly, "I was on a T-FLAC jet en route to join you in Paris. In flight, we received intel that tangos were holding several hundred people hostage at the station. The plane was diverted here."

He removed the bloody towel from her shoulder. Lexi felt the heat of his body on her cold skin. She wanted to crawl into his nice thick sweater with him; for warmth, of course. That would heat her up fast. She imagined his face if she did something so uncharacteristic and nearly laughed.

Good God. What had gotten into her?

I need another psych eval the second I get home. Cold was tolerable. The renegade direction of her thoughts was not. As soon as her shoulder was tended to, she'd put on her identical black sweater and be as warm as toast. No body heat sharing necessary.

"Why were you joining me in Paris?"

She noticed his green eyes were darker around the rim, then glanced away, annoyed with herself for noticing. "I'm your partner on the bomb/virus op until a total threat assessment is completed. If it's warranted, you'll get a full team afterward."

That was the job T-FLAC had sent her on. The psi unit's Internal Affairs had sent her on another mission that had nothing to do with bombs or tangos, and everything to do with Alexander Stone.

Alex made a rude noise. "Hell. Are we short-staffed or something? Since when did we take people out of research and put them in the field?"

"Since I've been requesting a transfer to fieldwork for the last four years," she snapped, bristling. "Do you want to hear my report or not?"

He started cleaning the wound. It stung like fire ant bites. Not that she'd ever been bitten by an ant, fire or otherwise. But according to research it felt exactly like the searing, itching beelike sting spreading over her shoulder she was experiencing now. Lexi gritted her teeth and breathed through the pain. "The tangos had already locked down the railway station by the time I got there. My instructions were to secure any surveillance tapes and to wait for backup."

Alex was silent for another moment, giving himself time to tamp down the irritation building in him through her briefing. Instead, he inspected the shallow graze. "Doesn't need stitches."

Her skin was smooth and lightly tanned, and he was surprised to see the muscle definition in her arms as she braced her elbow on the table as he worked. The black tank top also revealed the upper curve of her breasts and the velvety valley between them. There wasn't a damned thing overtly sexual about her standard issue tank top, but he felt a surge of inappropriate lust nevertheless. Perhaps because he'd never seen her in anything other than business attire.

"Keep talking." He glanced briefly at her face, noting the tension. Her jaw was clenched so tightly she was going to break off a few teeth. Alex laid his hand over the wound and removed half the pain. Not all. She damned well deserved to feel some of it. Wearing LockOut was as basic as it got, rookie or not.

Clearly they hadn't told her that he was her babysitter on the Paris op. It was just a look-see. The team had already been in and done their thing. On her first op he was to ensure she didn't get herself killed. But that was supposed to be in Paris. Not freaking *Russia.* What fucking moron had sent a gung-ho new operative into a hostage situation for "observation"?

She was staring resolutely across the room. The bathroom door wasn't that fascinating, so clearly she was trying to focus on something other than him working on her shoulder. Fuck it. He took the rest of the pain. "You got there and they'd taken hostages," he prompted.

"They had the station locked down." She hesitated, took a breath, and then let it out and the lines between her pretty eyes eased as she felt the lack of pain. *His* frigging shoulder now burned like hell. Been there, felt worse.

Her rainwater-clear gray eyes met his. "Thirty tangos, five hundred-plus hostages. No one in or out."

Yeah, he knew. He was there. Too bad he hadn't known *she* was there. Someone's ass was going to be toast when he found out who'd sent a rookie in alone and left out that critical information for the rest of the team. "Where were you?"

"With security on the first floor. Watching everything on the monitors."

Okay, so she'd been out of the direct line of fire. He didn't have to kill anyone immediately. Perhaps just rearrange a few of their brain cells via a punch to the nose. But this get-your-ass-to-Moscow-ASAP had been a *psi* op. The regular operatives weren't supposed to be any part of it. And *she* was a reg. *She* was supposed to be in Paris waiting for him, dammit.

Alex crossed the few steps to the bed and retrieved the half bottle of water he'd left there, taking a moment to infuse it with a boost of energy to give her a lift. Handing it to her, he leaned against the table.

"Their demand was called directly to our hotline. Sixty million U.S. dollars or they'd kill everyone in six hours."

She nodded. "Exactly. The place was surrounded. A mouse couldn't have gotten through. A psi team beamed in. I couldn't see them of course. But I knew they were there because small sections of the crowd kept disappearing. It was slow going. But they were really making a dent in getting people clear of the building." She paused to take a sip of the water.

"I knew our team was doing their jobs, so I just kept my focus on the tangos." She ran a hand through her damp, choppy, sunshine-colored hair. "It was really . . . weird."

Alex moved to sit on the edge of the bed before he gave in to the urge to stroke her creamy, silken skin as he pretended to tend to her wound. "Weird, how?"

Her brows knit as she considered it. "First of all, all the tangos were *young*. Eighteen, maybe twenty. Possibly students. And they all had dark, almost black hair. Only thirty-two percent of the local population would have hair that dark. Ethnic Russians are from European stock, and tend to have medium-colored to light hair."

He almost laughed. "Hell, Lexi, tangos aren't just from this part of the world. You know that."

"I do. But *one* person could have blown up the station; they didn't need *thirty*. Statistically, the odds against that many tangos importing to Moscow just to blow up a single train station are *extremely* low."

She tapped a finger on the bottle of water she held, a move so unlike her characteristic stillness that he stared. "But not unheard of," he pointed out. "How do you know how old they were? Their faces were covered."

Her eyes narrowed. "And you know that how? Were you there?"

"Of course. Do you think I'm here because I particularly enjoy Moscow in February?" His laugh was genuinely amused.

She stiffened even more. "For all I know, you have a lovely Russian girlfriend."

"Several, but I came for the hostages. How do you know how old they were?"

She shrugged, clearly forgetting the furrow on her shoulder. "I just do. It was their . . . lack of *symmetry,* I guess. Like they hadn't grown into their parts. Feet, Adam's apple, hands." She rose. "They gave us six hours to get them the money and a plane to wherever. But they—" She scrubbed her fingers through her hair, making it stand on end. She looked damned cute for an operative. "I don't get it, Alex," she said earnestly, pulling a black sweater out of her bag. She yanked the standard issue garment over her head and tugged it down over her hips. Fit her a hell of a lot better than his fit him.

"Why blow everything to hell five hours *early?*"

"Not unheard of. These guys don't play by the rules."

"So you saw what happened."

No. He hadn't seen anything but the last fifteen people he'd managed to successfully teleport. His powers, lately on the blink, had malfunctioned, and he'd found himself back at the safe house, unable to teleport. He'd "sent" his bag there on his way to the op, but arrived himself only minutes before Lexi's dramatic entrance. "What happened?"

"I saw six guys go out a side door, and followed, but seconds before I left, the tangos all disappeared."

"Wizards, or Halfs." Except that if they'd been either, he and the team would have picked up on their Trace. There had been no indication that the tangos were wizards at all.

She shook her head. "I'll show you the last few minutes of the disk. You tell me." She leaned over and rummaged through her duffel, emerging with a small handheld device. "The disk's in my coat pocket." Retrieving it, she brought both items with her and sat on the bed beside him.

The bed dipped, making their shoulders touch. "Do you want to see all of this?" she asked as the image of the inside of the station came on the small screen. The scene was, of course, familiar. The black-clothed tangos were on one side of the station, their hostages on the other. Small pockets of hostages disappeared from the middle of the crowd as Alex and his team skillfully culled them from the group without calling attention to themselves, then shimmered them outside to safety.

"Skip ahead."

Lexi thumbed fast-forward.

"Stop." Alex took the viewer out of her hand to get a closer look. "What the hell . . ." He rewound, and looked again, enlarging the image two hundred percent as he zeroed in on two tangos standing side by side. Dark-haired, faces covered. Yeah. Young. He got that from their posture. One adjusted the blowback-operated MAC-10 submachine gun in his left hand. The long sleeve of his shirt rode up a bit. Running up the inside of his wrist was a tattoo of some sort. The image wasn't clear enough to identify it, but Alex would send it in for analysis.

But that wasn't what caught his attention. The two kids disappeared, all right. But they didn't teleport. What the . . . "They *disintegrated*."

"I told you that. So did the guys on the roof. It was as though they turned to dust and then blew away on the wind. Is that what happens when you wizard guys die? You turn to dust?"

"No." His sat phone buzzed. "Stone." He listened for a few moments while studying the images again on the tiny screen. "On our way."

Three

Taipei City
Republic of China
25 01 00 121 27 00 02 11 08

S he was going to throw up. No question about it.

Leaning against a wall, in a stinking alley . . . *somewhere,* Lexi pressed a hand to her roiling stomach and locked her knees so she didn't collapse at Alex's feet like a soufflé. Thank God it was dark so he couldn't see her weakness. Saliva filled her mouth and she had to swallow convulsively to keep her dignity.

"Where are we?" she demanded, putting strength in her voice and knees with considerable effort.

They had materialized between two blank-faced concrete buildings. The darkness stank. She held her breath for a few moments. Not breathing in the smell of old urine, rancid food, and God only knew what else, helped. A little. But it didn't do much for the disturbing feeling that she was going to fall over at any moment.

The slight breeze felt cool against her cheeks, carrying with it the stench of . . . whatever back alleys were filled with. Refuse and excrement cloaked in near blackness.

This is what you wanted, remember?

Despite the smell, and the unsettling sensation of having her hearing blurred by the dial tone she kept hearing, she loved the rush of adrenaline, loved the frenetic beat of her heart. Loved living on the edge. Loved being a T-FLAC operative out on an op. It seemed as though she'd wanted to do this forever. And here she was. *Wow.*

The lightness in her head was now two parts adrenaline and one part transport sickness. Alex had literally given her a two-minute warning after his Moscow call. Two minutes that included going back into the bathroom, pulling on her LockOut, redressing, grabbing her weapon, and bracing herself. He'd then given her an indecipherable look with those mesmerizing green eyes, shaken his head, and grasped her uninjured arm.

A blinding flash of white and here they were.

Teleporting gave her severe motion sickness, messing with her inner ear and tampering with her balance. And this was only her inaugural flight. She wasn't looking forward to repeating the trip.

"Taipei City." His eyes caught the dim lights from a distant building, a feral gleam in the darkness. The faint sound of music drifted tantalizingly on the breeze. "Specifically a quarter mile from the National Palace Museum."

Lexi glanced at the building beyond the alley, with its enormous glass skylights and four-story atrium brightly lit against the night sky. She recognized the museum from pictures. "We're on Taiwan?" She believed him, but she was trying to buy time before she had to move.

She didn't even flinch when something large ran over her right boot, but just managed to bite back her scream of surprise. Lexi remained silently propped against the wall, praying it would keep her upright a bit longer. "Why?"

"There was a grand ball earlier celebrating the acquisition of a priceless jadeite Tang horse." He continued to visually scan the area. "Life-size."

Thank God her equilibrium had started to return, and the accompanying ringing in her ears had dissipated. "I read about it. It has a saddle and bridle made of amber. Is someone trying to steal it?" *Join T-FLAC and see the world. How freaking cool was this?*

"Tangos are holding the guests hostage," Alex said grimly. "Sixty-million-dollar ransom, or they blow the place to hell."

Right. This was T-FLAC, not rinky-dink art thieves. These were terrorists. Terrorists with exactly the same demands made in Moscow. "How much time do we have?"

"Six hours, minus thirty-two minutes."

"If they're like the ones in Moscow, that means we can count out five of those hours, if that, which leaves precisely twenty-eight minutes until go time." Lexi pushed away from the wall, automatically removing her Glock from the hip holster. She didn't need to see it. She'd practiced fieldstripping the weapon in the dark until she had it down to eight seconds. From the pressure exerted by the fully compressed clip spring she confirmed a full magazine. Her heart skipped several beats as adrenaline surged. "Exactly the same MO."

"Exactly. Yeah?" he said, clearly speaking into his headset. He listened for several seconds. Then said "Fuck" quietly under his breath. "Reported." He was speaking to her this time. "A hundred and ten confirmed deaths in Moscow. Tangos released LZ17, then blew the railway station to hell and gone. The hostages we liberated were infected before we got them out. Dammit."

She hated to do it, but Lexi made a mental note to report that far from remaining at the scene to liberate the hostages, Alex had cut out early, and had been napping back at the safe house while his team members did what they could. She hated to even think it, but possibly, if Alex had remained at the station, there might not have been any deaths *to* report. Possibly his help would have gotten the people out before the coronavirus was released.

"You and the team managed to get seventy-seven percent of the people out." She had to credit him with that, at least.

"Twenty-three percent of them *died,*" he said tightly. "God *damn* it. This is overkill, and doesn't make any frigging sense. This is the same frankenvirus used in the London subway last week. Same as Paris yesterday. Where the hell are these people getting this shit? Who's making it? Who are they? What the fuck do they want?"

"Not the six mil, obviously," she responded, even though she knew the questions were rhetorical. "They aren't even making a pretense of waiting." It wasn't a *frankenvirus.* "LZ17 is that new, lethal coronavirus, right? Similar in effect and composition to SARS, but ten times more deadly." Really, he should call a spade a spade. Was he going to put *frankenvirus* in his report? He was irreverent enough. *Probably.*

She'd boned up on it during her flight, the *real* flight. On a plane. Not that there was much intel on how to defeat the new designer virus, just details on the gory effects. She caught the faint movement as he nodded.

"Impossible to detect until people present with horrific symptoms, and it's too late to treat." Lexi didn't have a very active imagination, but even she wanted to shudder at the idea of bleeding from every orifice while writhing in agony. Mentally pulling up her big-girl panties, she glanced at the brightly lit building beyond the dark alley, then back at Alex. "Are we going in alone?"

He tilted his left wrist to look at his watch. "Psi team rendezvousing here in . . . sixteen seconds."

Faster than a regular team, but still. Did every op have to be manned by *wizards*? Regular operatives managed to do their job with skill and smarts, without having to resort to hocus-pocus. "By which time, everyone could be dead."

"By which time, everyone could be dead, yeah."

She wanted to rub the chill from her arms. But under her clothing the LockOut suit kept her comfortable. Almost a second skin, it maintained an even body temperature of sixty-seven degrees. LockOut, invented by T-FLAC science guy Jake Dolan, was a modern miracle of fabrication and engineering. It was practically indestructible, kept out water and fire, was impervious to nicks and cuts. It was even self-healing if something did manage to tear it. If one *wore* it.

The injury on her shoulder itched just to remind her that it wouldn't *be* there if she'd followed the rules as she was supposed to. She shook her head in disgust and tuned back in to Alex's version of briefing. "How many guests?"

"Seven-fifty on the official guest list. Three hundred assorted staff."

Silence throbbed as they both considered what was happening inside the museum right that second. "The displays are rotated once every three months." Lexi said quietly, now preternaturally alert and itching for action. "Which means sixty thousand pieces can be viewed in a year. It would take someone *twelve years* to see them all. And in less than an hour a group of nut jobs wants to blow up over a thousand people and all those priceless artifacts?"

"Apparently so." He lifted his hand, using one finger to brush a snagged strand of her bangs off her eyelashes. He did it so absently, so casually, that she was shocked by her visceral reaction to the light touch.

She blinked hard. *Focus, Stone.* It was the chilly breeze making her entire body shudder, not his inappropriate physical contact. "You seem extremely calm about it."

"I'm not. But going off half-cocked isn't going to achieve anyth—Good evening, ladies," he said easily to the four men who suddenly appeared out of thin air. "Which of you has the schematic of the building? Daklin?"

Lord. Asher Daklin. A regular T-FLAC operative, although there wasn't anything *regular* about him. Like Alex Stone, Daklin's very presence commanded attention. Six feet plus of lean, broad-shouldered male with attitude. Lexi had supplied research on some of his ops. He'd always been polite, but guarded. And seemed solitary, not chatting to anyone after he'd requested information.

His hair was shaggy and way too long. The light and dark strands fluttering against his strong face in the fitful breeze should have made him look effeminate; instead, the movement of the strands made his face appear harsher and even more male. His fallen-angel mouth curved in a faint smile as his glance swept by her, paused as he tried to put her in context, then moved back to Alex. One brow lifted in faint question.

"We should shield," a swarthy man with a hooked nose and the eyes of a saint said softly, he too glancing briefly at Lexi. She recognized him as one of Alex's team from the file she'd been given to study on the flight to Paris. Ruben Ginsberg. A wizard.

Lexi had no idea if they were "shielded" or not, since everyone looked the same as they had seconds before. Maybe shielding meant no one else could see or hear them?

Barely two inches over five feet and rail thin, almost emaciated, the Chinese man in his mid-sixties standing next to Ginsberg produced a 3-D holographic image of the building cut into cross sections with a surprisingly graceful flourish of his hand. Lexi had to admit wizards had the coolest toys.

This had to be Li-Liang Lu. Also a wizard, he looked as innocuous in the flesh as he had in his dossier.

The sixth member of the team was Finar Kiersted, a stocky wizard with piercing light blue eyes, and—despite having just celebrated his thirty-ninth birthday—a brush of pure white hair, cut military short. He looked as though he'd been chiseled out of a block of unyielding stone.

Four wizards and two regs.

The shimmering blue image hovered in the air between them as they circled the hologram to see the best way in. She had a strong feeling she'd be the one standing in the cold outside. She couldn't teleport any of the hostages, so she was no use to them. But then, neither was Daklin. But *he* was here because he was a bomb dis-posal expert, so they'd probably take him inside with them.

No complaints from her. She was here. That's all that mattered. Experience would eventually get her closer to the action. Deter-mined to absorb everything she could and learn from these expe-rienced operatives, Lexi stepped in a little closer, memorizing the hallways and air conditioning vents. Her photographic memory would come in handy if any of the men became turned around once inside the building.

Her heart pounded, and her chest ached with suppressed excite-ment. Taipei. *Amazing.*

She looked like a frigging daffodil in a cactus patch, Alex thought, suddenly annoyed that he'd had to bring her along. This wasn't babysitting anymore. It wasn't as though he didn't work with women in the field. He'd been teamed with several female operatives. His favorite was Cooper. A crack shot and a dependable operative.

He never gave her sex a moment's thought, which was probably a good thing since AJ's husband, Kane Wright, was a friend. But having Lexi here—Shit. Nothing he could do about it. Alex had to trust she was as well-trained as the rest of them. If she wasn't, she wouldn't be here now.

She was just one of the guys.

A rookie.

With big gray eyes.

And bee-stung lips.

Hell.

"Daklin, walk us through the lower floor where the event's being held. Make it fast." A buzz indicated a call on the sat phone hooked up to his headset. Alex touched his earpiece.

"Make it fast," he told his new control, a woman by the name of Ellicott.

"Streaming you surveillance footage from the scene," she said in a naturally husky voice. She sounded sexy as hell, but was probably sixty and a chain-smoking grandmother. Or a man using a voice synthesizer. The image of the hostage situation came through his ocular implant and he projected it against a nearby Dumpster for the others to see.

The well-dressed patrons of the arts had been corralled like cattle to the far end of an exhibit area. Several glass cases and their contents were smashed on the floor. The life-sized Tang horse, the jadeite translucent, the amber saddle and bridle rich and fiery, stood in the middle of the space, its head twisted, its massive ears pricked forward as if listening to the terrified cries of the very people who'd come to admire its beauty.

Five men in tuxes and a dozen women in evening gowns sprawled on the floor. Even projected against the flaking paint of a Dumpster the blood was unmistakable. And no mistaking they were dead. Exsanguination. They'd bled out. Shit.

The tangos, forty or fifty of them, dressed in the same black garb as the bunch in Moscow, held the group at bay with MAC-10s.

"We're about to go in," Alex told Ellicott impatiently as he followed Daklin's pointing finger through the maze of corridors and back hallways to the exhibit hall where the hostages were being held. He and the three other wizards would shimmer inside and start snatching the hostages in groups. Daklin would defuse any bombs. Lexi would coordinate their efforts from outside.

Invisible, they'd teleport directly into the middle of the crowd as they'd done in Moscow. There were four of them. Taking twenty hostages each, they could liberate eighty people every four minutes. They wouldn't have time to get them all, but if they moved fast—

"Stand down." Ellicott's voice in his ear was cool and brisk. "I repeat, stand down. It's too late. They've already released LZ17."

"Medics—" Even while Alex knew their medical team, familiar with SARS and other viruses of this kind, were stationed nearby, there wasn't time to get them here, even magically. He cursed. Too little, too late.

The images on the Dumpster shifted and moved. Without warning, the tangos suddenly dissipated into black, swirling, powdery dust.

The guests crumbled to the floor en masse. It was a gruesome, bloody sight. Alex was grateful he could only see the screaming and not hear it. "Shit." He grabbed Lexi by the arm. She gave him a startled look. "Go. Go. Go!" he yelled at his team, then teleported the hell out of Dodge.

Except that he and Lexi didn't go anywhere. His damned powers were on the fritz. Again. Fuck. And they were alone in a stinking alley behind the National Palace Museum and now, it was about to blow. About to blow with God only knew how much LZ17 flying out with the debris.

With Alex's fingers clamped tightly on her upper arm Lexi braced herself. Three. Two. One.

No flash of white light, no sense of motion.

Maybe that only happened the first time?

"Damn it to hell," Alex said under his breath.

She opened her eyes. Same alley. She didn't need to see it to know they were still there. The smell was her first clue. "We didn't go anywhere."

"No shit, Sherlock." He ran the fingers of both hands through his hair. "S—" He grabbed her, wrapping his arms tightly around her body as he took them both to the ground. Lexi's breath whooshed out of her on impact with the hard pavement. Covering her body with his Alex rolled her over until she felt the immovable wall at her back. A large hand came up to cup her head as he pressed her face against his rock-hard chest.

An earsplitting explosion made the ground beneath them shake. A hail of debris rained down from the buildings around them. Though her ears rang with the percussion, Lexi heard distant screams and the dull *thunk-crash-thud-bang* of things falling around them, and while she braced for impact, nothing touched her.

It wasn't right that Alex was taking the brunt of it, but even if she'd wanted to, Lexi couldn't move. His steely grip on her was implacable.

It seemed like days before the noise subsided and things stopped crashing around them. "Can't b-breathe," she managed, trying to liberate herself from her squashed position between his body and the wall. "Of course technically I *can* breathe," she had to clarify. "Since there's no lack of oxygen. You're compressing my lungs making it *hard* to b—"

"Wait." Her hand was pressed between their bodies and she felt the hard thud of his heart in her palm. His breath felt hot against the top of her head.

Wait? She was going to asphyxiate in about five sec—The next explosion seemed to come from directly beneath them, buckling the ground like an earthquake. Their bodies levitated as the noise slammed into them. A double blow. Sound and motion.

Wrapped in Alex's arms, his legs twined with hers, Lexi felt weightless. A flash of white was the only indication that they'd teleported. But even then, she wasn't sure if that was Alex's power or a burst of light from the bombing of the Museum.

The following silence was deafening, filled only with the persistent ringing in her ears.

The men looked down as he and Lexi materialized in the safe

house on Taiwan. He gently released Lexi, who was clinging to him like a baby marsupial, then jumped to his feet, holding out a hand to pull her up beside him.

"Took you long enough," Ginsberg muttered.

It only took seconds for Alex to ascertain that Lexi hadn't been hurt. Fortunately, he'd been able to erect a protective shield, which had successfully deflected the falling debris caused by the explosions. Unfortunately, he hadn't been able to teleport when he'd needed to most. What the hell was going on with him?

He kept a supportive palm on her slender back until he was sure she was steady on her feet.

"Report?" he asked Daklin, who was sitting at a wooden table with the others. They all had monitors in front of them.

Kiersted held up a hand.

Alex glanced down at Lexi, her face was pale, her eyes dark. "Okay?"

"Of course." She stepped away from his supporting hand. "Why wouldn't I be?" She crossed the small room to grab one of the empty chairs, then keyed in her holographic keyboard.

"We have visual," Kiersted pointed out as all six monitors bloomed to life.

Alex took the seat next to Lexi, and keyed in his own keyboard. They were watching the security surveillance recording. "Let's work backward and see what we can see."

The explosion was fierce. Very impressive. It took out everything and every*one* in a five-mile radius. The local police, the bomb disposal unit, the medical teams, civilians, and press . . . all gone. Several hundred auxiliary personnel annihilated in less than two minutes. "Daklin?"

"Working on it. High explosive. Chemical components, but predominantly biological in makeup. A one-two-three punch. These bastards know what they're doing and damned if they aren't doing it extremely well."

Alex didn't even look up. "Don't sound so fucking impressed. So far they've killed upward of eleven thousand people on five continents. Lu, work with him on that analysis. Send everything back to HQ for further breakdown."

They watched the footage frame by frame, checking each image. Kiersted summoned sandwiches and coffee as they worked and the sky outside lightened as one or another of them rose to stretch or hit the head.

"Alex, look at frame seventeen three, ninety-two." Lexi leaned forward. "Run in sequence."

Alex went ahead a hundred frames as Lexi had done, then watched the footage in real time. "Well, I'll be damned. They're all left-handed."

"That, too. Watch the guy on the far left."

The tango, dressed in the same head-to-toe black as all the others, shimmered from his position against a pillar and reappeared in the middle of the confused, frightened crowd. He was there for less than two seconds before he shattered into the now familiar black swirling dust.

"Freeze," Lexi instructed the program. She leaned over to point to Alex's monitor. The people milling around the guy in black seemed oblivious to his presence. "Him, him, her, her and him, are the first ones on the floor a few minutes later. *He* was the biological delivery."

Alex studied the movement then replayed the frames. "Good work. Let's see if any more of his buddies had the same directive."

For the next fifteen minutes, they all watched the action in real time. A dozen tangos did the same shatter-and-dissipate. Seconds later, the people closest to them exhibited signs of a rapid biological attack. "Interesting."

Lexi glanced over at him. "Wizards?"

"No," Lu said flatly. "There was no Trace indicating they were wizards or even Halfs."

Scowling in concentration, Ginsberg peered at his monitor. "If not wizards, who or what else could shimmer like that?"

Lexi glanced around the table. "If it looks like a wizard, and acts like a wizard, it must *be* a wizard."

"Yes and no," Alex shot back. "Not everything is how it appears."

"That's illogical." Lexi swiveled her head to look at him.

"Yeah," Alex said, his eyes fixed and glittering as he stared at the monitor. "I know. That's the problem. They might have the behaviors and traits of a wizard, but they don't have a wizard signature."

"Don't know who or what these guys are," Daklin muttered, his fingers flying over the infrared holographic keyboard, "but you can bet we'll find out."

Lexi's heart clutched. "But how many people will they kill before we do that?" She knew that somehow, some way, T-FLAC *would* ID and annihilate these young tangos. But it felt as though a ginormous clock ticked over the team's heads as they tried to figure it out in time.

A clock that told you you had six hours, when really you only had one, perhaps not even that.

Four

Novos Começos Medi-Spa
Rio de Janeiro
22 55 43 12 09 03 08
Cabin twenty-three

A bead of perspiration trickled down her temple. Alex wanted to lick it off. Lexi, being Lexi, ignored it. Alex, being Alex, became fixated by the idea of licking his partner all over. Wanting to taste a fellow operative was a first for him.

He was stretched out on the wide, soft bed, arms folded beneath his head, bare feet crossed on the pristine white spread. Lexi paced. She was going to wear a damn groove in the floor.

Her eyes narrowed as she glared at him. Her lips tightened as if she could read his mind. Good thing she couldn't.

"The manual clearly states in chapter three on Logistics, section

H on Travel, subsection iii on Alternative Transportation: Operatives that are able to teleport may do so no more than *three times
within a twenty-four hour period*—"

She emphasized the time constraints.

*"Excessive teleportation can lead to operative impairment and malfunc-
tion, possibly rendering the operative unfit for duty at the level expected by
the Organization."*

It was ninety degrees outside, and she still wore LockOut and a
thick sweater. He pictured her in nothing at all. He bet if he looked
in the dictionary under *tenacious,* he'd see a picture of Alexis Stone.
"Do you have that damned book memorized?" he volleyed back.

She turned when she got to the kitchenette on the far side of
the room. "I have a photographic memory."

Of course she did. It was a damn good thing she was luscious,
because she was rapidly becoming a pain in his ass. "Look outside,
what do you see?"

The open windows and white wood shutters welcomed the
amazingly beautiful day into the airy bungalow. The turquoise waters of the ocean practically lapped at their doorstep, and there
wasn't a cloud in the sky. A picture-perfect day they were doomed
to waste sitting, or in her case, *pacing,* inside.

"All I'm saying," Lexi repeated doggedly, "is we can take a cab
just as easily as you can teleport."

"Ocean. Beach. Sunshine. Have you ever been to Carnival in
Rio?"

She crossed her arms. "Not while I'm working. No. Besides, you
have to buy tickets months in advance for the Sambódromo Pa-
rades or you end up paying a small fortune."

"We could watch from the street. Lucas won't be back for at
least six, seven hours." He'd gone to Montana to be debriefed and
take care of some personal business.

If possible, her jaw tightened even more. "That's the problem with teleporting. You can come and go on a whim, without regard for the rules."

He feasted his eyes on her. Even irritated and sweaty, she was hot. He was getting used to the cropped blond hair. It made her look . . . Not like a research clerk. "Rules are made to be broken," he said, because it was true, and because he knew saying it would needle her.

"Rules are made for the safety and well-being of oneself and others."

He flung an arm over his eyes, then raised his elbow to peer at her. "Did you grow up in a convent?"

"No."

She was making him dizzy with all that pacing. He covered his eyes again. "Well, if we can't go out and play, tell me how you grew up."

Pausing in her millionth circuit around the small bungalow, she looked out the window. "It's irrelevant how I grew up, Stone."

"Then we'll go for a swim while we wait for Lucas."

"That's the *Atlantic* Ocean out there. It's known to be rough, with strong currents. Lots of drop-offs along this coast. Tourists drown regularly. Besides, the water's not very warm."

"I'm a strong swimmer."

She waited a moment and he hazarded a glimpse to see why she was tongue-tied. Which made him study her mouth. Which only made him think about kissing her. Crap.

Her eyes narrowed. "Are you really amphibious?"

Wizards had varying skills and powers, but this one clearly seemed far-fetched to her. If only she knew. "Let's put it this way. I'm a *great* swimmer." His lips twitched.

"No swimming. We're *working*. We should walk up to the medical building and see if we observe anything suspicious." She turned and started back the other way.

"Do you know Lucas Fox?"

"Only by reputation."

"Is he a slacker? A moron? A bad operative?"

"No. Just the opposite. He's well respected for his attention to detail and the work he does."

Alex levered up on one elbow. "Then why do you think he'd leave a situation without securing it? Without turning over every rock and blade of grass for answers?"

Lexi shifted her weight. Interesting. She didn't like being on the receiving end of scrutiny. "According to his initial field report, he secured a warehouse. He's coming back to remove an entire floor of a medical building and tie up loose ends. What's left? If he's so efficient, what are *we* doing here?"

"A, because he and I both think this place has something to do with those dust bag tangos. B, because Ellicott *ordered* us to come. You wouldn't want us to disobey a direct order, would you?"

She shook her head and sunlight from the open window tangled in her hair. Her skin looked dewy, soft, incredibly *female.* Eminently touchable.

"That's what I thought," he said biting back a smile as she glared at him. "Want me to conjure a tanga for you?" He wondered how Lexi would look in the Brazilian swimsuit, which consisted of nothing more than a few brightly colored strands of dental floss.

She lifted her chin. "No, thank you."

"Can we at least get some lunch? I'm starving."

Her sigh was subtle, he would have missed it if he hadn't been admiring her breasts. "We'll walk."

He got off the bed and opened the front door, shimmering a change of clothes as he went. "Okay. We'll walk." He glanced back. "You might want to lose the sweater before we go."

Everyone seated at the outdoor restaurant wore as little clothing as possible. Dressed in black pants tucked into combat boots and a black tank top, her skin Montana-winter pale, Lexi felt like a fish out of water. Not an unusual occurrence for her. She ignored it, straightening her spine. And resorted to what she did best, categorizing the random bits of information that always floated about in her mind. Being a walking library with a photographic memory had its disadvantages. Like needing to file all the crap that came in, useful or not.

"Did you know that Brazil occupies almost half the area of South America?"

She was on an op. Didn't matter *what* she looked like. Right. *Focus, Stone.* Here she was, sitting under a white umbrella sipping freshly squeezed orange juice, looking at Alexander Stone, and it mattered, dammit. It mattered a lot.

"It's the world's fifth largest country." She shrugged off her irritation at herself. "Although just slightly smaller than the United States in area, Brazil's population is about forty percent less."

He looked at her, his eyes glazed. "Great."

Okay, so he didn't give a damn that she knew. She'd only told him because it was her way of—making conversation, a connection. As usual, it didn't really work. She sipped her juice. The waiter arrived with their food.

Alex's *Feijoada completa,* a simmered bean and meat dish of Bahian origin, looked and smelled delicious. Her seafood salad was . . . healthy. Beautifully arranged, but definitely not in the luscious category. In their line of work, eating a balanced meal at regular intervals was more about fuel than taste; her instructors had been clear on that.

The waiter asked her something. She had no idea what. Alex answered him in what sounded like perfect Portuguese.

She didn't know Portuguese, Brazilian or otherwise, which she would have made an effort to learn given half a chance. Hell, if she just read *Portuguese for Dummies,* she'd probably be able to acquire the language in less than a few days. In fact, if they'd flown here on the T-FLAC *Challenger,* she could have done some reading. But no.

Alex had insisted, *against the rules,* that they'd teleport. *Again.* This made the third time in less than twenty-four hours—that she knew of. He could have teleported off to see several of his Russian girlfriends before shimmering back to the safe house for her untimely arrival, for all she knew. And how the hell had he gotten to Russia from Paris? Another teleportation violation.

"Want sunglasses?" he asked, shoving Ray-Bans on his nose that he had somehow snatched out of thin air. He was slouched in his chair, feet propped on the seat opposite. Dressed in a lime green T-shirt with a surfer on it, purple shorts, and red flip-flops—all *uncoordinatedly* conjured before he left the bungalow—he looked, Lexi thought, annoyed, as though he were on vacation. Far too relaxed to be on duty.

"Sure. Do you have another pair—" He moved to pick them out of the air and her heart pumped up a notch. She darted a glance around the restaurant. *How in the hell did he think he could get away with that in public? People were bound to notice.* "You're going to hocus-pocus them? No thanks. I'm good."

Too good. Her full, sexy mouth was ripe for kissing. He wondered what factoid she'd have relating adversely to *that.* "You'll get little white crinkles beside your eyes," he told her, trying not to look too admiringly at the pale, creamy, velvety, *damp* swell of her breasts above the tank top. Not too much, not too little. Her breasts were damn near perfect, as far as he could tell.

Everywhere he looked he saw something about Lexi he wanted to touch, taste, smell. "Then you'll have to come back here for some painful treatment to get rid of them," he managed, sliding a pair of Italian designer glasses across the table. "Here. Put on the glasses. Who cares where they came from?"

She put them on. He was sorry he'd offered, because now instead of her soft gray eyes looking back at him, he saw himself reflected in the lenses. *No good deed goes unpunished,* he thought wryly. "Tell me about your family."

She tucked her hair behind her ear before picking up her fork and stabbing an innocent shrimp with the tines. "Why?"

She had cute ears. Had he ever noticed a woman's ears before? He didn't think so. They looked ... nibbleable. "Because it's a beautiful day and I don't feel like shooting anyone. Come on, Lex, let's just have a nice lunch and talk about something other than chaos and destruction."

"Exactly."

The waiter returned with the bread he'd offered earlier.

"Obrigado." Alex speared a pat of butter onto his side plate, then ripped off a chunk of hot bread. "Exactly?" He offered the piece in his hand to Lexi.

She shook her head. She'd had her carbs for the day. "You asked about my family, but you don't want to talk about chaos and destruction. Pick another subject."

Interesting. "Your family is chaos and destruction?"

"You're going to be like a dog with a bone, aren't you?" She took a sip of juice and focused on her salad. "My parents were in their midtwenties and pretty much hippies when I was born. I was an inconvenience. Oh, they loved me to death, but it was tough lugging a kid around, one step ahead of social services. We moved a lot. They had many creative and impractical ideas on how to make money. Note I didn't say make a *living.*"

She sighed a little. He wondered if she even realized she'd done so.

"They were, still are, charming, and persuasive, and God only knew how, always managed to talk some bank officer into extending them a small business loan. First it was the vegan restaurant in Denver. Of course it never occurred to them that they had no idea *how* to run a restaurant, nor about preparing food. Vegan or otherwise."

"How'd they do?"

"They loved it. But of course the health department closed that down within a month."

"How old were you?"

"That time? Seven." She paused to let the waiter refill her water glass. "Where were you at seven?"

He chewed a bite of food before he answered. "San Francisco. My parents had just died. My grandmother took in my twin, Victoria, but couldn't handle me. I went into the system."

"I used to *dream* about being in foster care," Lexi said dryly. "Are you and your sister close?"

Alex smiled. "We are. Tory and I have a great relationship. Her husband, Marc Savin, was one of T-FLAC's founding fathers, so to speak, and he and I were friends before he met her."

He could tell her eyes widened slightly by the way the smooth skin of her forehead moved. "Marc Savin is your brother-in-law? He's a legend."

Alex smiled. "His reputation is well deserved. They have a couple of great kids, and a good life. Things turned out okay."

"Were you ever adopted? Another dream of mine, by the way."

"No, but Mason Knight, a good friend of my parents', mentored me as I passed through the system."

"I'm familiar with Dr. Knight's reputation as a microbiologist. He's done some work for us in the past, and I believe Fox brought him in on these bombings, right? But why weren't you adopted?" She ate each bite as if measuring it for size and caloric content.

"How's your salad?" He stifled a grin.

"Protein, carbs, ten percent fat. Perfect."

Another rule apparently. He nudged his plate toward her just a little. "Want some of mine?"

"No thanks."

She was lean and fit, but then women were always talking about what they could and couldn't eat, which mystified him. "You don't need to be on a diet."

"I'm not. I choose to eat healthy, balanced meals. You weren't adopted, why?"

Dictionary. Tenacious. "Grandmother got some wild hair and refused to allow it."

Apparently, there was an invisible line down the center of her food. When exactly half—to the lettuce leaf—was consumed, she set her fork down and inched the plate away from her. "Sorry, but she sounds like a royal bitch."

"She loved Tory. That was good enough for me. What did your parents do when the restaurant closed?" *I'll see your Tenacious and raise you a Relentless.*

Her choppy bangs were a little long, and she blinked the golden strands off her lashes. He imagined doing the same thing with his lips. Too bad he had to chug cold water instead of the beer that would have made this meal even better. He could only imagine what she'd have to say about the consumption of alcohol while working.

"Dress shop in Charleston, where my father had a second cousin, twice removed, who lent them the capital. The shop hadn't even opened before they realized, because of poor planning, that they didn't have *enough* capital. We split in the night. I liked my cousin Sandra. I wanted to live with her, in fact. But that didn't pan out." She waved a hand, as if banishing the memories. "Okay. Enough personal stuff. Why don't you brief me on what we're supposed to be looking for here?"

"Right now, I just want to have a pleasant lunch with an attractive woman. Can briefing wait until later?"

She struggled to keep her mouth from dropping open and blessed the sunglasses he'd forced on her. He thought she was attractive? He hadn't thought she was attractive when her hair had been mouse-brown and she'd worn horn-rims. Then, he'd just come down to the research center and handed her whatever orders he wanted investigated. The only reason he'd hung around was to give her a hard time.

Propinquity. She was here. He was here . . . he just liked women. All women. Her head got that. Unfortunately, her heart didn't understand the game. Hell, her heart hadn't a clue how to *play* that game.

He wasn't going to give her instructions until he was good and ready. Lexi spent the rest of their meal giving him facts and figures about Brazil, South America, and Atlantic Ocean plant life. He stopped responding somewhere around sea turtles. She thought the information was both informative and interesting.

Obviously, Alex . . . didn't.

After a much too long lunch, Lexi walked beside him down the wide, flower-lined shell path toward Lucas Fox's bungalow and the beach. It really was paradise here. The sun baked her shoulders and the top of her head. And even wearing boots her step felt lighter. The air smelled sweet and salty, almost intoxicating to someone who'd walked out of the deep freeze of Montana two days ago.

The last thing she wanted to do was go inside the one-room bungalow and wait for hours for the other operative to get back.

And the absolutely last thing she wanted was to be in that one small room alone with Alex. Usually she was coordinated, but she felt like a bull in a china shop around him. Worse, she felt itchy from the inside out. Not a good way to feel about a fellow operative. She wasn't naïve. Lexi knew exactly what her problem was. She had to nip *that* in the bud, PDQ.

Turquoise water, capped with lacy foam, lapped at the sugary expanse of the beach for miles as they stepped off the path by silent agreement. It was as though she and Alex were the only two people left on the planet. "Did you know Brazil has over forty-five hundred miles of beach—"

Alex stopped, falling behind. "Lexi?"

She paused to glance over her shoulder. "Yes?"

"Shut up."

She hadn't seen him move, but he was right *there*. She glared up at him. "Don't tell me to sh—"

His mouth crushed down on hers, stunning Lexi speechless. For a nanosecond, she tried shoving him away, both hands flat on his chest. Then the thought evaporated like fog on a sunny day as the heat of his mouth made her brain turn to mush. All she could do was feel. And savor. And want.

His mouth was hard and demanding and tasted of the coffee he'd drunk after lunch. The flavor of him, the feel of his mouth on hers was everything she wanted, and everything that she didn't. Helpless to fight both him and herself, she met his tongue with her own and felt a rush of liquid heat surge through her body.

Their kiss was stunningly elemental. Male. Female.

Lost in the taste and feel of his mouth, Lexi freed her hands from between their chests, sliding them around his waist as he tugged her body flush against his. She fisted the back of his ridiculous lime green T-shirt, wanting to climb him. Wanting to . . . No. Wait— What—

She shoved at him—hard—until an entire *inch* separated them. Her mouth felt swollen and it took a few seconds for her eyes to regain focus. Every instinct inside her screamed to run like hell. The best she could do was stiffly uncurl her fingers from her death grip on the back of his shirt and suck in lungfuls of air and try to keep from falling over.

She had to be very clear in her reprimand at his unprofessional behavior. "That was inexusab—"

"Incredible." His eyes held hot green promise. She couldn't look away.

"Against the rules," she told him firmly. The rules were safe ground. Familiar ground. "Section C, part four-A, clearly state—"

His mouth caught hers again. Hungry. Aggressive. He nibbled her lower lip, making her whimper helplessly as she hung onto him as if her life depended on it. *No. No. No. No!* She tore her mouth from his again, her chest heaving, her breath raw. "Sexual harassment is defined as any loo—"

He took advantage of her open mouth, kissing her as if she hadn't said anything between one kiss and the next. She was sure she had. Hadn't she? His sneaky tongue made the heat in her belly spiral higher, and rational thought become impossible.

Squeezing her eyes shut against the agony of pulling her mouth away from his, Lexi sucked in a gasp of salt-laden air. The hard plane of his chest felt so damned good against her now-sensitized nipples. She wasn't fighting him. She was having a battle royal with herself. She had to win. *"Any look, comment or action with sexual overtone—"*

He blew out a breath, half exasperation, half laugh, then swooped his mouth back onto hers, combing his fingers through her hair, cupping the back of her head.

His kisses could become addictive. If she let them. Which she wouldn't . . . again, the thought dissipated like mist as he took a long, deep kiss that had her helplessly responding. When he lifted his mouth from hers this time, she followed him for a second before catching herself.

"Implication, subtext—" She was breathing as if she'd run a marathon. Her breasts ached for the touch of his hands. Moisture pooled between her legs. When his lips touched hers again, Lexi ripped her mouth from the onslaught, then pressed her face against the curve of his shoulder so she wouldn't kiss him again. It was too much. Too little.

"Or *intent*—" Her fists were locked on his shirt, holding him more tightly against the pulsing aches all over her body. She felt the bunch and stretch of his muscles as he tightened his arms around her and took her lips once more, giving no quarter.

She breached the kiss, sucking air into her starving lungs because when his mouth was on hers she forgot the unimportant things like inhaling and exhaling. "—makes an operative uncomfortable in the presence of another individual within the Organiza—"

She only had time for a quick indrawn breath before he tilted her chin up, and she caught a brief glance of laughing smoldering green before his mouth plundered hers again.

This time it was Alex who broke the kiss. Lexi felt groggy when he lifted his mouth from hers. Her knees dipped. His fingers curled against her bare arms, holding her up. She'd shake off his hold the second she got feeling back in her legs.

"Do I make you uncomfortable, Alexis?" he asked, voice smoky.

Breathing was difficult. Her lips were numb, her heartbeat manic as she pushed out one word, "Yes."

"Good." He brushed her bangs out of her eyes. "Because FYI? You make me damned uncomfortable, too."

Five

Lexi wondered if Alex and Lucas Fox knew how alike they looked. They were both tall, broad-shouldered, dark-haired, and green-eyed, the green of their eyes almost identical once the two men stood side by side. The odds against all of those physical characteristics coming into play were astronomical. Add the fact that the two men worked together, and had been brought up together . . .

She'd have to reference the percentages before she said anything, of course. But it struck her as extremely odd.

She suspected Dr. Knight had had more of a friendship going with Alex's *mother* than with his father. Same went for Fox's mother. And since Lexi wanted to be fair, she had to consider there was always the possibility the two couples had used an insemination process to conceive their children.

And then both chosen the same sperm donor?

She'd check the odds of *that* as well.

She and the men were walking through a small, empty warehouse on the grounds of the medi-spa. Since the forensic team had conveniently left their high-powered lights behind for them, the three of them could inspect every inch of the place at their leisure. Lexi liked that they were going over the site with a fine-tooth comb, even though their forensic teams had left with samples, as well as the two huge tanks.

She couldn't conceive of so many people, male and female, wanting to change their appearances. Sure, she'd cut her hair and had Lasik, but that was for her career. Everywhere they walked, people were sporting bandages on some body part or another.

She also couldn't imagine having some overpriced doctor wielding a scalpel on *her* body unless surgery was imperative and lifesaving. But to each their own.

After Alex left the bungalow she'd spent several hours reading Fox's report. Chatty, he wasn't. But she got the gist. He'd materialized three feet in front of her while Alex was out taking a swim. His sudden, unannounced arrival had surprised them both. They'd both frozen like deer in the headlights, with Fox recovering only an instant before she did. She made a mental note to report to IA that the members of the psi unit were clearly not following the teleport restrictions listed under Alternative Travel in the protocol manual.

She knew of Fox's reputation, but they'd never met before today. His favorite researcher was Carrie Anne Munroe, a close friend of Lexi's. Carrie Anne thought the man walked on water, and like Carrie Anne, Lexi liked him on sight. He was straightforward and very businesslike. But even though he looked so much like Alex, without the annoying irregularities of his behavior, her heart didn't do the kind of calisthenics it did when Alex was within a mile of her.

It made no sense, if she cared to analyze it.

She didn't care to analyze it.

This would not do. Not at all. First, she was trying to prove herself as an operative, not to get heatstroke from being near the most irritating man on the planet. Second, both the men she'd had long-term relationships with had been very much like herself. Organized perfectionists. Anything worth doing, was worth doing exceptionally well.

Alex Stone was—Lexi narrowed her eyes as he and Fox walked a little ahead of her. *The exact opposite.* He was a sloppy rule-breaker. With really bad taste in clothes.

Fox wore black pants, and a black close-fitting T-shirt. Alex was back to wearing the garish outfit he'd worn before his swim. *Perhaps he was color-blind?* Two percent of females were color-blind, and eight percent males. *No, he wouldn't be part of the Organization if that were the case.*

He desperately needed a haircut, she decided; all that dark hair would look very nice with a neat trim. Of course that didn't explain why her fingers itched to comb through the too-long, silky strands. Still, better to keep her attention on the back of his head instead of on his rather spectacular butt in those ridiculous shorts.

Lexi pulled her gaze away from the men and did a visual sectioning off of the warehouse, trying to picture it as Fox had described the scene before things had been moved.

He'd gone and called Alex in from his swim half an hour ago, and the two men had talked on the beach for eleven minutes, seven seconds. Effectively leaving her out of the loop.

Not protocol.

Annoying.

But it had given her uninterrupted time to observe their similarities. Well, she'd observed the similarities in the last *two* minutes, because she'd been looking at Alex for the first *nine*. With the exception of his behavior on the job and his innate ability to ruffle her feathers, everything about him appealed to her. Which was no excuse for her against-the-rules behavior.

And if kissing him back hadn't been enough of an infraction, Lexi was pretty darn sure practically climbing the man's body should be. Her cheeks now went hot with embarrassment, and she wasn't a woman who embarrassed easily. It had taken several seconds after he'd stopped kissing her for her to realize that she'd had one leg looped around his thigh.

Which had taken the "do not fraternize" rule to a whole new level of violation. Clearly, she'd spent too much time on the underground third floor at HQ than was good for her.

Damn, she really had to focus.

Since she was part of Alex's team, she picked up her pace to catch up with them.

"The two metal tanks were here." Fox indicated a pair of large stained areas on the cement floor about halfway back from the door.

Alex inspected a tangle of thick electrical cords hanging down from the ceiling. "Big guns," he observed. "Generator?"

Fox shrugged. "Could be. But I'm still running with my computer theory."

Alex tilted his head for a better look at the power-station-sized cabling. "At least a hundred, hundred and twenty-five kilowatts. That's a *lot* of power. Could be a mainframe. You mentioned in your report that you believed they were orchestrating the bombings from here. This amount of juice seems like overkill, don't you think? They could've done that with a laptop."

"And the bombings and dispersal of the viral agent haven't stopped, despite you closing them down. In fact, it's increased one hundred and sixteen point seven percent. So it's unlikely it was done from here," Lexi said, agreeing with Alex. Whatever they'd run out of here wasn't the simple computer they would have needed to do countdowns on the bombings.

"Walk us through the power grid that knocked you on your ass," Alex said, inspecting some of the cabling hanging from the ceiling. He had a very nice nose, Lexi thought, admiring the straight line of it.

Hey, Ms. T-FLAC operative! Focus!

Lexi shook her head and narrowed her eyes. Fox gave them the details of the effect of the do-not-disturb he'd encountered. Twice.

"Interesting," Alex said as the other man finished. Absently he reached out and grabbed Lexi's arm to prevent her from walking into a snake's nest of black cables on the floor. His touch literally felt like an electrical current shooting up her bare arm. His fingers were surprisingly cool against her warm skin. Instead of releasing her, he held her lightly tethered to him as he and Fox continued talking.

His thumb did an almost absent stroke up, down—pause—up and the little hairs all over her body stood at attention. It would've been less electrifying to walk into the wiring.

Lexi lost her ability to hear as she stood close enough to Alex to smell the saltwater on his skin. There was a distinct smell to him. A smell that made her feel dizzy and—God—*female*. Whatever it was, not soap or cologne or anything artificial, was something by which she'd recognize him in the dark.

I'm not a *female,* she reprimanded herself. I'm an *operative*.

She strolled away from him, breaking the hold and crossing her arms as she studied the floor again. "There were originally *nine* tanks." Lexi walked the perimeter of the bigger area. "You can see here where an attempt was made to clean the floor—"

"I don't see anything," Fox said easily, coming to stand beside her.

"It's very faint." She crouched down on her haunches to point, then glanced over at Alex, who'd come to stand next to Fox. "You said they were Type 304, stainless steel construction? Right?" Lexi shifted a bit and drew a circle in the air over the floor with her finger, tracing the outline of the mark. "Look. There was a flat-pitched bottom head tank right here, with an easy access drain . . ."

She indicated the faint square protruding from the wide circle where the tank had left a faint—okay, *very* faint—stain.

She glanced up at the two men when they didn't say anything. "I don't have superpowers, guys. This is as plain as the nose on my face. See the outline of the lifting and anchoring lugs here and here?"

"I see something," Alex said dubiously. "How do you know what kind of tanks they were?"

She glared at him. *Unlike you, I read the damn report. That's how.* Fox had intimated as much in his brief. The rest was logical deduction. "Fox wrote a description in his brief and looking at the size and depths of these stains . . ." She spread her hands and shrugged. "It's pretty obvious that these were repurposed wine storage vats."

Lexi jumped to her feet and dusted off her hands. "Highly polished stainless?"

Fox nodded.

"Insulated and fully welded stainless steel outer jacket? *Definitely* wine storage tanks. Damn, I wish I had a swab to test this area for any liquid residue the techs might have missed."

Fox shoved his hands into the pockets of his beautifully cut black slacks. "Forensics tested every inch of this place, Stone— Christ, that name thing is confusing."

"How many do you need?" Alex interrupted.

Fox shot him a glance and plowed on. "If there'd been seven more tanks I'm sure that would be in their report."

"Two—Thank you." She took the swabs Alex handed her, removing one from the protective cover. There'd been nine tanks. She didn't need to swab to know that the human soup concoction had been in more than two freaking tanks. The question was, why was Fox saying there'd only been two? Just because he'd . . . Settle down, she told herself. She'd do her own test.

"We know that'll show human remains. It was in my report," Fox pointed out as he hunkered down beside her.

"Yes. I know. I read it while Stone went swimming." She'd insisted on Alex conjuring the report so she could work while he improved his freaking *tan*. It was the least he could do to use his powers productively. She'd tried giving him the stats on skin cancer, but he'd merely put up his hand and walked out.

God. She'd been just about to mock his colorful choice of swimsuit when she'd gotten a look at his bare back—"I read the entire report ..." Lexi had to force herself to continue the conversation, because thinking about those awful scars on Alex's back made her want to throw her arms around him. And she'd already made a total fool out of herself doing *that*.

She knew he'd been *shot* several times in the course of duty, but it was the scars from his imprisonment in Italy that told their own tale of torture and unbearable pain. He'd been whipped. Repeatedly. Over weeks and weeks. How had he stood it?

"Fascinating reading." Lexi pulled her thoughts back to her job. "The question remains—Ah, just as I thought, tests positive for blood. No prize when it tests human blood. Nine tanks here for sure. The question remains," she continued her thought, "why would they kill the donors and make human soup out of them? To what purpose?"

"There *was* no purpose," Alex pointed out. "Other than an efficient means to get rid of the bodies of the donors."

She tilted her head so she could give him a skeptical look. At least she hoped it read skeptical instead of empathetic. "Efficient?" she scoffed. "Keeping the liquid in sanitary, temperature-regulated, and meticulously maintained tanks costing upward of a hundred grand a piece? In a warehouse protected by a massive wizardly do-not-disturb? That's just like the wiring; it would be overkill."

She shook her head as she walked around the marks again, visualizing the room when it had been filled with equipment. "No, these people were smart, resourceful. They wouldn't keep thousands of gallons of liquid remains here on the premises on the off chance that someone like Fox would manage to get in and see what they had. There are cheaper and easier ways to dispose of bodies."

"Don't ask her how," Alex told Fox dryly. "She'll tell you in excruciating detail."

Lexi replaced the swab in the tube, marked it with the pen she kept hooked in one of the pockets of her cargo pants and handed it to Alex. "Can you please send this to the lab?"

"I *can,* but is there some rule I don't remember that says it's verboten?"

He was hard to resist when his eyes twinkled like that. Really, the man was incorrigible. "Would I ask you to if there were? And please use the sealable biohazard bag to send it." She walked away from them, indicating vaguely that she was going to check the other side of the warehouse.

"Why have I never seen her before?" Fox asked as Lexi strode off with purpose.

Alex grunted. "They moved her from research into the field. She's a pain in the ass."

"Hmm. That why your eyes are glued to *her* ass when she isn't looking?"

"If my eyes *were* glued to Lexi's ass she wouldn't be looking, would she? Since she'd be walking away."

Fox shook his head. "Damn. Watch your back, pal. That one doesn't look like she takes any crap."

Alex knew Lucas Fox almost as well as he knew himself. And he'd read between the lines of Lucas's field report. There'd been a lot of detail about a Sydney McBride. Unless Lucas had switched teams, McBride was a woman. The same woman he'd taken with him to Montana for his debriefing a few days ago.

"Since when have I given *any* woman crap?" Alex asked easily.

"While you're working? Never, since I've known you, which is forever. But geez, man, what are you trying to do with that freakish outfit? Make her think I didn't teach you how to dress—" Lucas held up a finger in a stay command. "Incoming wizard."

A full. Alex felt it, too. In the split second that followed, both men had their weapons drawn.

"Good afternoon, gentlemen." Lark Orela's sexy voice and Scottish brogue were completely out of place in an empty warehouse in Brazil. Her black hair was a curling fall of gypsy silk down her back and she wore a black, off-the-shoulder top, a brightly colored tiered lace skirt, giant hoop earrings, and lots of bracelets. And high-heeled boots. She was the hottest five-hundred-and-thirty-two-year-old Alex had ever seen. He decided he preferred the long hair to the short spikes she'd favored for a while.

"And don't my two favorite operatives look handsome this fine day?"

"Hey, beautiful," Alex said with a smile, tucking his weapon back into the holster.

Lucas did the same.

Lark's appearance here didn't bode well. Alex shot a glance at Lexi across the warehouse.

"She can't see me," Lark told him.

Probably a good thing, Alex thought, amused. Lexi would have a freaking heart attack if she saw a Control wearing a dozen silver eyebrow piercings, brightly colored skirts, and black nail polish. Today Lark was a little bit gypsy with a whole lotta Goth.

"Problem?" he asked. Because Lark being there meant *something*. And it probably wasn't something good.

"Is Sydney all right?" Lucas spoke over him. He looked worried. Alex turned and faced him, lifting his eyebrows.

Well, well.

"She's fine, as far as I know." Lark conjured a red, Coca Cola imprinted bar stool, and hopped up on the seat in a swirl of lace. She cocked her head to look at Lucas through kohl-lined eyes. "Someone got her back to Kansas since you left her standing there without a viable means of transportation."

"Miami," Lucas corrected. "And I was a little busy trying to keep all my balls in the air."

Lark grinned. "Never good for a man to have his bollocks in the air, now is it? I hear you found a long lost sister," she murmured, untangling the dozens of silver bracelets circling her arm with a musical jangling sound of bells.

"Remains to be seen if she's my sister or not."

"DNA panned out—"

"Excuse me," Alex cut her off, not knowing about a sister, DNA, or anything else they were being so freaking cryptic about. He gave Lucas a hard *We'll talk later* look. "Do I need to stick around for this conversation? I have places to go and things to do."

Lark glanced over at Lexi, who was scribbling something in a small notebook, oblivious to the exchange a hundred feet away. "Well, so long as you aren't doing *her.*"

"Not my plan." It was a flat-out lie. But since he was a trained, accomplished liar, he made sure his blocks were fully engaged and neither Lucas nor Lark was any the wiser. "Did you come here to show us a new piercing, or do we have business?"

"You were a lot more charming the last time I saw you. I think the color of that shirt is affecting your disposition." Lark made a small moue with her scarlet-painted mouth and changed the shirt to black. "Better. I'm here merely as a courtesy, *boyo.* IA has someone watching your every move. Keep an eye out."

Alex barked out a disbelieving laugh. "Internal Affairs is keeping tabs on *me?* What the hell for?"

Lark shrugged, then sipped an umbrella drink that she pulled out of the air. Red lipstick marked the pink-and-white-striped

straw. "Just giving you a heads-up, as they say. Watch your back."
She disappeared, taking her drink and bar stool with her and leaving a cloud of expensive perfume in her wake.

Fox turned to face him. "Why would IA be looking at you?
What did you do?"

Alex frowned. "Not a damn thing. Unless they can read my
mind and know what I *plan* to do."

Six

If, as Internal Affairs suspected, Alexander Stone was a rogue operative, Lexi's directive was clear and specific.

Terminate.

She considered that irrevocable step as she turned her back to the deliciously hot pulsing shower to rinse conditioner out of her hair. The hot water stung the crease in her shoulder. But thanks to Alex, it wasn't as bad as it could've been.

Stone and Fox had gone up to the restaurant to have dinner and catch up. Since Lexi had nothing to catch up *on*, and an hour or two by herself sounded like bliss, she let them go without quibbling. A nice long shower followed by a little Internet research and an early night would serve her well.

Where the two men planned to sleep wasn't her problem. It was a nice night, the temp a balmy seventy-eight. For all she cared, they could sleep on the beach. She'd have that nice, big, white-draped bed out in the other room all to herself.

She'd killed six men her first day on the job. Killing someone she'd kissed was going to take a lot more balls than she had. She was going to have to deal with it.

"No more kissing." She rested her foot on the side of the tub to shave her leg. "No more kissing, touching, wishing to be kissed, or thinking about touching, Ms. Operative," she said, continuing the ongoing lecture she'd been giving herself for the last several hours.

If push came to shove, she was expected to kill Alexander Stone efficiently. Without hesitation. There was no rule that said she had to do it with no remorse.

"Next time I think about how incredible it feels when he sticks his tongue in my mouth, I'll think about shooting him point blank instead." *That* should give her pause.

She'd taken the job, accepting that proviso. Kill Alex if necessary. Killing people was part of the job. She accepted that. Killing Alex was a whole other ball game.

They'd told her his behavior in the past three months was suspect. He wasn't working up to his own high standards. He was disappearing in the middle of ops, and not returning until it was too late for him to be effective. Even given the nature of the psi unit, this behavior was still unusual enough to raise a few hackles.

It was as atypical as it was becoming consistent.

There *must* be more to it than this, Lexi thought for the hundredth time. Terminating an operative for being lazy, or lax, or whatever it sounded as though he were doing, seemed . . . overkill. Maybe he just needed a vacation. She was a show-me-the-facts kind of girl. Logical, methodical, by the book, especially when things were black-and-white. The problem was, there were too many shades of gray at the moment.

But she'd do it—she'd terminate Alex Stone—if and when she had the requisite proof that his elimination was unavoidable. The

fact that the man made her hot and bothered, and thrived on ruf-
fling her feathers, could have absolutely no part in her decision-
making process. Black was black and white was white.

Seeing him waiting in the safe house in Moscow was a case in
point, and highlighted his unusual behavior. He should have been
back at the train station getting people out as fast as possible. Instead he'd gone to take a nap or see a girlfriend or whatever had
happened. What the hell was *that* about? That dereliction of duty
was black.

Then there was the situation on Taiwan. He'd almost gotten
them both killed when he hadn't teleported before the explosion.
He'd told his team to leave, but stayed himself. Very un-Alex-like
behavior, since it appeared the man lived to teleport every-damn-
where. Why didn't he leave when it would benefit him most to do
so? A death wish?

Lexi frowned as she shaved her other leg. "With me?" If he was
suicidal, why would he want to take her with him? Why would he
have wrapped himself around her like a super-hefty LockOut suit,
keeping her safe? That was gray.

She didn't trust gray.

And *suicidal* reminded her of that terrifying, muddled, and powerful desire she'd experienced up on the Moscow rooftops. She
nicked her leg, the soap bubbles turning red from the small cut, and
her stomach knotted. She'd pushed that out of her mind to analyze
later.

And she would. *Later.*

Maybe Alex was sick. Maybe he was just sick and tired of the
never-ending parade of bad guys doing unspeakable things. Maybe
he liked being a bad guy better than being a good guy.

Maybe he *had* turned.

Hard to imagine someone like Stone turning, though. He didn't
appear to care about either money or power. What other reason
would there be to join terrorists? It was always either money or

world domination. Or fanaticism of some sort. Hmm. He seemed too laid-back to give a damn about any of that. But she hadn't been watching him long enough to know who he was, really.

Even though there was still plenty of lovely hot water, unlike the safe house in Moscow, Lexi turned off the shower and dried off in the steamy bathroom. Fox had offered her the use of a wardrobe filled with women's clothing. The woman in question was shorter, curvier, and a lot more fashionable than Lexi aspired to be.

She chose the most conservative thing she could find. Navy capris and a navy top with little green beads on it. Both a little on the snug side. But better than getting back into her sweaty work clothes.

After hanging the towels back on the rod to dry, she ran her fingers through her new short hair, then went into the main room of the cabana. She sat on the bed cross-legged and booted up the laptop Alex had hocus-pocused for her.

With her own special encryption, Lexi logged into the e-mail account for her reports to Internal Affairs. The report was short and succinct. She couldn't make a judgment call based on so little. She certainly wasn't going to terminate a fellow operative because he was . . . *lazy.*

After checking her personal e-mail—one from her mother, one from Carrie Anne at work—Lexi turned off the computer and put it aside.

There was nothing to read, and she wasn't in the mood for TV. What she'd really like was a swim. She'd made Alex believe she didn't like swimming, but that was just an effort to maintain distance from him. She loved the freedom of water. Made her feel as though she could fly. She got off the bed and went to open the front door, then stood there breathing in the refreshing smell of salt air.

The moon glistened on the water enticingly, creating a shimmering path to the horizon. The beach between the bungalow and the water gleamed white in its light. The lap of the waves and the susurrus of the water sweeping up the sand mingled with the faint samba beat of steel drums up at the main part of the resort.

There wasn't a soul in sight.

She had a crazy urge to swim nude, but quickly dispelled that notion. The idea of being naked anywhere near Stone was horrifying. Horrifyingly appealing.

After only a moment's hesitation, Lexi turned back inside and went in search of a swimsuit.

Bikinis and more bikinis filled one of the drawers of the dresser in the bedroom area of the bungalow. Not her style. She opted for the bottom of the most conservative suit, and her own black tank top. Grabbing a towel, and feeling like a kid let out of school early, she pulled the door closed behind her, then jogged down the soft sand.

Placing her towel and keycard aside in a clearly visible spot, she turned and ran into the water. The shock of cold against her warm skin was invigorating and she launched her body into an incoming wave, her spirit as buoyant as her body.

Lexi swam in strong sure strokes along the moon's path toward what looked like the edge of the earth. Fanciful, but what the hell. She was not going to feel guilty taking a few hours off. She hadn't taken a vacation in five years and seven months.

Estimating that she was about a mile offshore, she turned back in a leisurely backstroke so she could continue admiring the huge expanse of black sky. The millions of stars made her feel small and insignificant. Vulnerable and powerful at the same time. The concerns of the world seemed small compared to the infinite universe she lived in.

Letting the gentle swells of the sheltered sea of the harbor rock her, she felt the tension knotting her body and mind release her from its grip. This was almost like being in an immersion tank.

Completely relaxed, almost boneless, Lexi drifted with the

waves. One moment, she was almost in a trance, the next, hands grabbed her head, violently shoving her underwater. *Alex?*

Struggling against the implacable hold, Lexi kicked and bucked her body, clawing the hands clamped around her head with her short nails. The unexpected assault pissed her off. God damn it, if he kept this up, he'd drown her for real.

Her heart kicked into overdrive as she realized the person doing his best to drown her wasn't Alex. Hands and wrists were too small. A woman? No, those hands weren't that small and she felt the tensile strength of sinew and muscle in his arms—definitely of the Y chromosome type. Her vision blurred and her lungs struggled to sustain her last breath.

Underwater combat training had been an eighteen-hour course. She remembered every one of those one thousand and eighty minutes of drown-proof classes. She'd been top of her class. Straight As. She'd been trained in waterborne operations. Deep dives, diving physics, both day and night ocean subsurface navigation swims. She'd mastered drown-proofing. She knew what she was doing, and she could whip this son of a bitch's ass.

If she could only get one freaking deep breath before she got started.

Unfortunately, the guy knew that giving her a breath was going to give her the game. His fingers tightened around her head, digging into her cheekbones, his thumbs relentlessly squeezing the back of her skull.

The water was too deep to put her feet on the ocean floor, and she couldn't hold her breath much longer. Releasing a sip of air from her lungs to take some of the pressure off her chest, Lexi pivoted her body to bring her feet up over her head. Not much force because of the water, but she managed a hard enough rabbit kick to snap the guy's head back.

Bastard didn't release his hold on her head, however. He just took her with him as he jettisoned backward, shoving her deeper on impact.

Her bare feet hadn't encountered any sort of breathing device when she'd struck his face, so he was holding his breath as well. Good. She could hold hers for nine point three minutes. A record at the academy. *Let's see if you could hold yours that long, asshole.*

Of course, her adrenaline hadn't been pumping all the oxygen out of her blood in training, and she'd breathed in pure oxygen before the test . . .

In one fluid motion, Lexi twisted her body as far as she could against his unshakable grip on her head. As she fought for her life, she counted off the seconds.

Her lungs screamed, black blotches obscured her already limited visibility. She was contorted like a damn pretzel, but this time she managed to dig her nails into his arm. She managed to pry one finger on the bastard's hand back, loosening his hold. Tucking her knees under her body, she used his arm as a fulcrum and swung into him, kneeing him in the balls. Hard.

His rapidly released air bubbles caught a glint of surface moonlight. Suddenly, she was free. Lexi shot to the surface like a cork, gasping, filling her lungs with wonderful air. Blinking the water out of her eyes, she spun in a circle, looking for the guy. He'd be easy to spot in the moonlight. But there was no sign of him. She imagined hearing the soundtrack from *Jaws* playing in her head and shook it off.

Maybe he'd drowned?

She didn't think so.

She headed for shore with swift, sure strokes and powerful kicks. The guy was still in the water with her. Where, and how the hell he was maintaining his breath under the water, was a mystery. All she knew was that she'd be better able to fight him on land. Better yet if she could make it to the bungalow and her Glock.

Lexi's breath sawed like she was an asthmatic, her muscles felt like rubber, and the freaking shore looked like it was a million miles away.

Quarter of a mile and closing. *Focus, Lexi. Focus!*

Just as she thought she was going to make it, the guy popped up in front of her.

His tanned skin gleamed like polished copper in the moonlight as he stood, blocking her way. Lexi found her footing in the shifting sand as well. "Lexi . . ." His voice was so familiar, seductive. His large hands reached out as though he were her lover and was about to caress her face. She met his eyes. Green, sharp, familiar.

Alex.

But not.

Younger. Leaner. And dammit, meaner.

With an achingly familiar grin, his fingers closed around her throat, exerting gentle pressure on her windpipe. She stayed frozen, unable to move as she stared into the cold green depths of his eyes. The lightning-fast move shouldn't have shocked her, as he grabbed the hair on her crown, forcing her head back. She knew it was her fault. Instead of anticipating, and blocking his hold, she'd allowed it. She'd been *that* stunned to see a younger version of Alex.

Lexi didn't give a flying shit *who* he looked like. He *wasn't* Alex.

The water made it hard to maneuver. His fingers tightened, making breathing next to impossible and almost tearing her hair out by the roots.

The moonlight wavered as Lexi's vision blurred again. Using both arms she exerted enough upward force to break his hold, then used her leg as a pivot and pushed him backward.

She was already drawing her foot back as he bobbed up in front of her. Lexi flew at him, using his own weight to push him under. Grabbing hold of his hair, she pressed his head back, then used the side of her hand to chop his exposed throat. With as much power as the resistance of the water allowed, she head-butted him, striking his nose with her forehead and following it with a short-armed jab to the larynx.

His eyes went wide with surprise, and he made a horrible gargling noise as he started sucking water.

She sat on him, holding him under with everything she had. Body. Arms. Legs. Most of the time the waves rushed over her head, but she kept coming up for air. He didn't. "Turnabout's fair play," she rasped.

For several seconds he bucked and heaved beneath her. But Lexi wasn't letting the son of a bitch up until he was damn well good and dead.

"Sorry to commandeer your place," Alex said easily as he and Lucas strolled down the shell path back to the bungalow. It had been awhile since the two friends had had more than a few minutes' convo in months. They were going to go their separate ways in a few, and Alex still hadn't told Lucas what he'd wanted to tell him when he'd suggested dinner to "catch up."

"Like hell you are," Lucas's teeth shone white in the moonlight. "No sweat. Most of the bungalows are empty right now. I'll find a be—What the hell?" He pointed at two figures entwined in deep surf. "Looks like Lexi out there with some guy . . ."

But Alex didn't stop to hear the rest. He recognized Lexi's bright hair in the moonlight, and far from a lovers' tryst, she was battling someone with everything she had.

He tried teleporting. No go. Fuck.

Kicking off his shoes as he ran, he gathered speed until he practically flew down the beach. His Glock was in his hand as he hit the water. No point shooting yet. He'd hit her for sure. But he swam like a fish, underwater, close to the swirling sandy bottom, breathing easily.

He came up under them. Lexi and the guy entwined. Yeah. Looked like lovers. The guy was naked. She had her arms and legs wrapped around him. But the guy's head was under water, his hair a floating dark cloud around his moonlit pale face.

Alex's heart did a double tap. It was like staring into a mirror. Distorted, but no mistaking his own face. Jesus.

Lexi came under the water too as the guy twisted and turned until he was on top, Lexi on her back on the sandy ocean floor. Her eyes were open as she fought her opponent. For a second her eyes met Alex's, before the churning sand and agitated white water obscured her from view.

Alex grabbed the guy's leg to hold him in place, and started hauling himself upward. He could see the silhouette of the man's upper body above the film on the surface of the water. Without hesitation, he fired a single shot.

One moment he had living flesh gripped in his hand, the next . . . nothing. The guy was gone.

Reaching down he grabbed Lexi by the upper arm, helping her breach the surface. She came up gasping and choking. "Where is he? Where's the son of a bitch?"

He returned the Glock to the holster. "Thanks for saving my ass, Alexander. Oh, you're welcome, Lexi. Anything I can do to help."

She turned to glare at him, water beading like diamonds on her lashes. Her hair was slicked back against her skull. He noticed that her ears stuck out a little. Christ, she looked adorable. Sexy. Madder than a wet cat.

"My ass didn't need saving. I had him pinned—Oh, crap." She lifted her cupped hand. Water trickled between her fingers, sparkling in the moonlight and leaving a black, *dry* residue on her wrinkled palm. "This is him, isn't it?"

Alex examined her hand. "If soot can be called *him,* yeah. I'll send that to the lab."

She shuddered as he scraped the dry dust off her wet hand as waves lapped around his waist. "What *is* this thing?"

"No clue," he said grimly, thankfully managing to have the wherewithal to teleport the residue to Montana and the lab.

He attempted teleporting himself and Lexi, and this time he was successful.

Lucas was waiting inside the bungalow. Alex held onto Lexi's arms as she swayed and answered Fox's silent question. "We're good. But we need to talk. Which cabin are you going to bunk in?"

"Seventeen. Take your time." Instead of teleporting, Lucas strolled out, closing the door behind him.

"Okay?" Alex asked Lexi who was holding onto the doorjamb. Her pupils were jumping, indicating severe vertigo.

"Perfectly."

Alex coughed over a disbelieving laugh. "Tell me what happened."

"Can I grab two freaking consecutive breaths before I give you my verbal report?" She jerked her arm against his hold.

"Take three," he said magnanimously, inwardly glad she snapped, because it meant she was alive and feeling good enough to give it back to him. He loosened his grip on her upper arm slightly. When she swayed, he swooped her up in his arms and strode over to the bed. "Might as well lie down until that passes."

"Don't put me on the bed. I'm soaking—Dammit, Alex. I have to sleep on wet sheets now." She glared at him, pupils dancing, gray eyes militant as she tried to focus on him. "There's nothing wrong with me. I'm hungry, that's all."

He politely kept his gaze on her face, not easy since she was bra-less under a soaking wet black tank top. Her small, full breasts showed clearly through the thin material, her cold nipples hard little points poking against the fabric. She wore a black bikini bottom. The tank was rucked up under her breasts exposing her flat belly and skin that looked pale and baby soft, and so smooth Alex imagined it would taste like vanilla on his tongue.

Hell. "What do you want?" he asked gruffly. "I'll call room service." There were livid bruises on her throat; he could see individual finger marks on her pale skin. He gritted his teeth.

She shook her head and then pressed her hand to her eyes, as if to stop it from spinning. "Never mind. By the time they get here, I won't be hungry anymore."

He sat down next to her. "Lift your chin." She did as he asked and he rested his palm against her damp, cold skin and took away the pain, wishing he could kiss it away instead. "Tell me about your opponent out there."

"That's too . . . Thanks. That feels much better. I don't know who he was, but the freakiest thing is he looked just like you."

"That's a start. Lucas reported that one of the room service waiters here looked like me, too." He got up to grab a towel for her and her voice followed him to the bathroom.

"The guy looked exactly like you, minus a decade or so."

"I know, I got a quick look before I turned him into an oil slick." Alex dropped the towel over her head and gave it a quick, hard rub until she reached up and took over. "He must've been the waiter Lucas was talking about. Said the kid was my double. Which begs the question, were they one and the same, or two different . . . whatevers?"

Lexi shuddered and pulled the towel down to lie across the back of her neck. "You mean you think there might be more than two—" she waved a vague hand. "Doppelgängers? Sons? Spawn?"

"Lucas told me the kid was in his early twenties. Match with who you battled with?"

"Eighteen, twenty is about right, yeah." She sat up, pushing her wet hair out of her eyes. Her pupils and her gaze were steady now.

He nodded. "What else can you tell me?"

"He was strong. Determined. He came up on me totally unex-
pectedly. Didn't hear a thing."

"Teleported or swam up to you?" He watched her squeeze the
tank with the towel, getting some of the water out of it.

"I don't know. One moment I was swimming along, alone,
minding my own business, and then there he was." She frowned.
"Whatever, whoever he was, it's the same *whatever* as the guy in
Moscow, isn't it? The whole black dust thing. Spooky. Like a ghost
or something."

"I can assure you. That guy was no ghost."

She felt along her jaw. "He didn't punch like one either."

Alex laid his palm on her jawline, removing both the pain and
the developing bruise. Transference of the injury let him feel how
hard the son of a bitch had hit her. Feeling murderous, he ran his
thumb over her soft skin, skimming the firm outline of her lower
lip before dropping his hand. "Anything else?"

She blinked as if she'd been off somewhere else and suddenly remembered where she was. "He had some sort of marking on his
inner arm. Let me find a pen, I think I can draw it from memory."
She flung her long legs over the side of the mattress and padded
over to the table by the door, still trailing drips of water. Hanging
the wet towel over the back of a chair, she opened the drawer and
took out a hotel pad of paper and a pen.

She came back and sat on the wet cover beside him. Her skin
was starting to dimple with goose bumps and he wanted to dry her
off, warm her up . . . with more than another towel. Ah, man.

Keep on task, pal.

"Like you, he was left-handed. And I don't need to point out
that—"

"All the tangos we're encountering lately are left-handed as
well," he finished grimly.

"Yeah." She started drawing. "Did you know that less than ten
percent of the world's population is left-handed? Or that statisti-

cally, left-handed people have more home accidents because most everyday items are designed for righties. The most dangerous being a knife, they—"

Watching her mouth move had him thinking about how soft and warm her lips had been when they'd kissed. What the hell was wrong with him? He'd never been this—distracted. With anyone. "More drawing, less talking."

"Right," she said, then stopped and held the pad up at arm's length so they could both look at her half-finished sketch. Lexi glanced up at him. "What's this look like to you?"

All other thoughts stopped dead cold. "What the fu—It's a god-damned *bar code*."

Seven

Los Alamos
New Mexico
35 53 28 106 17 52 02 12 08

"Los *Álamos* is Spanish and means the Cottonwoods," Lexi informed Alex as they drove into town from the private airfield. "But *alamos* in *modern* Spanish actually means *poplar,* not cottonwood. The ancient Spanish who first colonized here spoke an archaic dialect. And the cottonwoods were so spare and distinctive the name stuck."

She paused. Not to gather her thoughts, Alex was sure, but rather to take a breath and roll onto the next page of the encyclopedia lodged in her cranium. "It's the best educated city in the country, did you know that? Sixty-eight point six percent of the over-twenty-fives hold an associate degree or higher. Fascinating, isn't it?"

"Uh-huh," he muttered noncommittally. For a moment he was profoundly glad his powers didn't include a photographic memory. God knows if he had had the random bits of information stuck in his head that Lexi apparently did, there wouldn't be room to focus on their current mission, let alone try to figure out why his powers were on the blink.

She hadn't asked why they hadn't teleported, and he didn't tell her it was because he fucking well *couldn't*. Dammit to hell. He took the sat phone out of his breast pocket as he drove, and thumbed in Mason Knight's main number. He had to find out what the hell was up with his fluctuating powers sooner than later. Hopefully, Mason would know and be able to fix it.

But what the fuck was it? A type of wizard flu? Hell if he knew. Whatever it was, he wanted it fixed yesterday. He was sick of his powers not working without warning. Fluctuating? How about totally FUBAR?

He put the phone on speaker, holding it against the steering wheel as he drove. It rang enough times to tell Alex that Knight wasn't going to answer. Without waiting for the recording he went straight to voice mail. His dear old mentor needed a freaking assistant.

"Mason. Alex. Call me ASAP. Thanks." He glanced at Lexi from the corner of his eye.

She sat upright in the passenger seat, belted—of course—the shades he'd given her perched on her nose. She wore a black T-shirt tucked into black jeans. Alex's lips twitched as he noticed her highly polished combat boots. For such a tall woman, she had small, delicate feet. And hands. And small, plump breasts, and a succulent lower lip just begging to be kissed.

More than his powers were FUBAR. Try his sense of timing, his ability to focus, and his knack for understanding women—all of it. FUBAR. Especially around Lexi.

"Los Alamos National Laboratory is one of the world's leading research institutions," she told him, adjusting the vent to suit herself. The sun shone from a bright cloudless blue sky, but snow lay thick on the ground and cloaked the trees along the road in a pristine cover of stark white.

Rio to New Mexico.

Hot to cold.

Well, hell, that described just about everything happening to him around Lexi. Would've been nice to spend a couple of days back in Rio helping Lucas. With Lexi. In a bikini. Or nothing at all. Forget the helping Lucas part. Fuck. Maybe whatever was screwing with his powers was turning his brain to mush, too.

"Their advanced technologies are very twenty-first century," Lexi informed him. "Even though the primary responsibility of the Laboratory is, of course, to maintain the effectiveness of the nation's nuclear deterrent, they also work on hydrogen fuel cell development, supercomputing, and applied environmental resear—"

"Nice pre-tour, professor, but we aren't visiting the Laboratories," he said, cutting her off. Just because the woman was a walking encyclopedia didn't mean he wanted to hear everything in that photographic memory of hers. A man needed quiet to think. Shit. As if he could think of anything but her in nothing but a tan.

With a frown she turned, tilting her sunglasses down to look at him over the dark rims. Her long-lashed eyes were the color of baby rabbit fur. Soft. Gray. Gentle. What in God's name made her want to be in the field where every drop of softness, every atom of gentleness would be smashed out of her in a heartbeat? Or worse, kill her.

"We're not?"

"Not at this juncture in our investigation. No."

"Isn't this something you should have told me *before* we left Rio at the freaking creak o' daybreak?"

Staying in sunny Rio hadn't been an option when he'd had a lightbulb moment at five A.M. "You were half asleep when we drove to the airport." Half asleep, and damned sexy, all ruffled and heavy-eyed.

Maybe he should pull over, yank off his clothes and roll around in a snow bank until his dick went back to normal and his hormones chilled out. Sounded like an excellent plan. Much better than the ice cold shower he'd had earlier.

"My hearing was just fine," Lexi assured him in that pithy tone that made him want to haul her into his lap and kiss her until she shut up. "If we're not going to the Lab, where are we going?"

"Team is meeting us at a warehouse west of town."

"I heard you giving the instructions before we left Rio," she told him dryly. "I thought that was just a meeting point."

"I have a theory."

She paused several seconds. "Okay. I'll bite."

Fuck. Yeah—he wished. *Tangos, blood, broken bones,* anything but thinking about her mouth and what he could do if she let him. "I'll fill you in when I brief the rest of the team."

"Hmm. Do you think we might visit the lab? Because I know things you might want to know about it."

The corner of his mouth tipped up in a lazy grin. "No. But if I think of anything I don't know, I'll be sure to ask."

Her lips twitched. "Smart-ass."

"Better than being a dumb-ass."

Lexi snorted back a laugh and pulled her legs up on the seat, sitting cross-legged as though it were comfortable.

"Do you do yoga?" The thought of her in some of those asanas was enough to turn him on. He just liked the name Downward Facing Dog; it conjured up all sorts of erotic images.

"Yeah, I do." She gave him an enigmatic look that made Alex

want to pull the car to the side of the road and kiss her. Hard. And for a long time.

"Did you read my personnel file?"

"Absolutely not," he said with just enough emphasis for verisimilitude. Hell yes, he'd read it. Every damned word. Her parents currently lived in Barrow, Alaska. As far north as they could manage and still be on the continent. Their finances were a shambles. Yet somehow they'd managed yet again to convince a bank, this time to back a mail-order cupcake business. *Cupcakes* from Alaska? There might be a more stupid business venture, but Alex couldn't think of one off the top of his head.

They might have loved her as much as Lexi thought they did, but their behavior indicated otherwise. They'd been selfish, irresponsible, and oblivious to the lifestyle they'd forced on their only child.

Lexi had gone to seventeen schools, a few steps ahead of collection agencies and child protective services, before she completed high school with straight As at age fifteen. Her academic record, and her photographic memory, had earned her a scholarship to Stanford.

Humanities and Sciences had been her field, and she'd gobbled up the courses in linguistics and philosophy, piling on letters after her name as if she were hoarding them for an educational famine. In only five years, she'd earned dual bachelor's degrees in philosophy and history, a master's in English and linguistics, and a damn Ph.D. in linguistics with an emphasis on French and Italian. Her dissertation on similarities in modern comparative romance languages was presented in English, French, and Italian.

At nineteen she'd taken her first lover, a twenty-nine-year-old science major, name of Frank Hinton. The relationship had lasted eight months. At twenty she'd been recruited by T-FLAC. She'd worked in the research department in Montana for eight years.

Alex adjusted the visor to ward off the blinding sunlight bouncing off the snow on either side of the road. He slid his gaze over to her gray, assessing eyes. "Reading someone's personnel file is against the rules. Isn't it?"

"It is. But that's never stopped you before."

Alex put a hand over his heart. "Alexis. You wound me."

"You are so full of crap." She looked out of her side window. "There's some great desert hiking here. I'd—"

"No."

He heard her teeth grind. "I was about to say I'd like to come back here sometime on *my own,* and do some hiking through the Bandelier National Monument wilderness area. I love hiking, how about you?"

"I like to *read* about hiking," he said, just because getting her goat was so freaking entertaining. He enjoyed anything to do with the outdoors, although it had been awhile since he'd done anything like that just for the fun of it. When he was hiking, it was somewhere inhospitable as hell with jagged razor-sharp rocks or deadly snakes, and usually with bad guys on his ass, chasing him, guns blazing. Fun where he could get it.

"You don't like communing with nature?"

"I like communing with a cold Coors and a hot redhead." Forget the beer. He had decidedly warm feelings toward a tall, cool-eyed blonde, with a luscious, kissable mouth.

"I thought gentlemen preferred blondes."

She was table dancing in dangerous territory. "I'm no gentleman." He shot her a quick glance as he turned down a side street heading west. "Is that why you went blond?"

"Absolutely," she told him cheerfully. "Blond hair is like catnip to guys. I have to beat them off with a stick."

He knew she was kidding. But for some reason the idea that guys were all over Lexi pissed him off. Lover number two had been three years ago. An ex-jock, and a clerk in T-FLAC's legal division. That relationship lasted eighteen months. Rumor had it Mike Love had wanted to marry her. Bad. She'd declined. Somehow they remained friends. Alex couldn't begin to imagine that having slept with Lexi, they'd be friends if they ever "broke up."

"T-FLAC's a close-knit community," he said, sounding a lot like her pastor, and feeling a lot savage thinking about her with another man. "You shouldn't pee in your own pond."

"That's a disgusting analogy. And I don't date people I work with."

Apparently six foot six, black, ex-football player Mike Love didn't count. "Then who *do* you date?"

"None of your damned business. Isn't that Daklin waving his arms like a looney-bird over there?"

Yeah. It was Daklin all right and he didn't look happy. The warehouse was beyond a row of rental storage units about three hundred yards ahead. Alex slowed the car, and shot Lexi an amused glance. "Is a looney-bird a real bird?"

"Certainly," she said straight-faced. "The looney-bird is found exclusively on the Galápagos Islands. They're from the order *Sphenisciformes,* family *Spheniscidae.* It's twenty-six inches tall, and similar in shape to a female penguin. Most of them are mild mannered, even docile. But the white-winged looney-birds are *very* bad-tempered."

Alex laughed as he stopped the car. "You just made that up."

This was the first time Lexi had seen him really laugh. God. He was already irresistible, but when he threw his head back and roared with amusement, her heart did more than just calisthenics, it prepped for the Olympics. She kept her thoughts off her face. "Are you sure?"

"That's the problem. I'm not sure." Still grinning, he rolled his window down as Daklin jogged up beside the car. A blast of frigid air swirled around the previously toasty interior of the car. "What's up?" he asked the other man, all humor gone.

Daklin opened the back door and climbed in, slamming the door behind him. "We have trouble in River City."

Alex turned to look at him blankly.

"A 1957 musical, then a movie," Lexi enlightened him. "*The Music Man*? Never mind. What's the problem?" she addressed Daklin, whose face was flushed with the cold.

"Apparently your wild woo-woo guess was right on the money," Daklin told Alex. He rested his folded arms between the two seat backs.

"What woo—" Lexi cut herself off. Perhaps better not to know Alex's every ability.

"The building, as you suspected, is locked down tighter than a—" he glanced at Lexi. "Tight," he finished. "Lu went ahead of us. Knocked him on his ass. Unconscious. Pulse thready. Serious burns to his face and chest. Ginsberg teleported him back to medical."

"Shit. Kiersted and Ginsberg?"

"In unit one eight six. Still puking their guts out while sitting on some little old lady's circa 1970 Naugahyde sofa. In the dark. With no heat."

"Poor delicate little flowers," Alex said unsympathetically. "You sick, too?"

"Hell n—Yeah," Daklin admitted. "Big time. Had me on my knees wishing for death for about ten minutes."

"Fuck."

Lexi's shiver had little to do with the cold. She shot a glance down the row of identical blue-doored storage units to what she could see of a cement building some three hundred yards away, at the end of the driveway/alley. The narrow slice of the warehouse she could see was blank. No door, no windows.

"Same as the warehouse in Rio?"

"Yeah," Alex said, clearly thinking. "There was only the one door. Probably same goes here."

"Didn't see even that," Daklin said shuddering. "How the hell did you even know the place was here?"

"The guy Lexi tangled with in the surf last night had a tattoo on his left wrist. Lexi drew it out for me. Photographic memory, ya know? Didn't make sense until I slept on it."

"We got that it was a bar code," she told the other man. "But I don't get what that—God. The *numbers*! I only remembered part of them—35 53 28 106 17 5—Ah." The lightbulb went off. "That's the longitude and latitude of Los Alamos, isn't it?"

"Enough of it to make an educated guess. Yeah."

She fell against the back of her seat. "Wow. You *are* good."

His grin was sexy as hell. "Intel is looking at the footage of all the bombings in the last six-month period. Checking to see if all the tangos are about the same age, left-handed, and have tattoos on their wrists."

Lexi's heartbeat sped up with excitement. "Bet they do."

"I'll take that bet and raise you a thousand bucks," Asher Daklin said grimly. "But what does that give us?"

"A mystery wrapped inside an enigma." Alex opened his door. Iced wind howled straight through Lexi's clothing, but that wasn't what made her shudder. There was no T-FLAC training, no simulations, for what they were up against.

"Come on, children, let's go find ourselves a powerful wizard and whip his ass." Glock in hand, Alex waited for Lexi and Daklin to join him.

"This is totally insane, you know," Lexi told him, shrugging into a jacket made from LockOut and keeping up with his long strides in the crisp snow. Her lungs burned and her eyes smarted, but her blood pumped hard and fast in an excited race. "I do *not* want to be down on my knees puking up wizard doodoo."

"Suck it up, Stone," Alex told her, picking up his pace. "This is what us macho operatives do."

"Give me a number to call when it flattens you on your ass and stops your heart." She said it half joking, but Lexi didn't find this situation at all amusing. Exciting. Scary. Not funny.

"Call Mason Knight. His number's on speed dial on my sat phone. He can call my sister if necessary."

Lexi grabbed Alex's forearm. His skin was warm although he wore only a T-shirt over his LockOut. She was so cold her teeth were chattering, and her body felt tense enough to shatter as her muscles locked against the cold. "Don't joke about this. Whatever is held in that warehouse can kill you. Us. Let's call in reinforcements."

She wasn't a coward, nor was she stupid. And not being afraid of this situation would be damn stupid. And risky. And utterly against the freaking rules.

Assess. Plan. Execute—basic as it got. Going in without backup when whatever it was had already taken down three operatives was insane.

She walked between the two men. All three had their weapons drawn, and plenty of room between them should they need to maneuver. Training manual page three hundred and eight. Not that a freaking bullet was going to do anything against a force, a power, none of them could damn well *see*.

For all intents and purposes Alex was her superior officer. She had to follow his command. Even if she thought he was out of his mind for going anywhere near the building.

What stunned and pleased Lexi was that Alex was treating her no differently than he treated any one of the team. He hadn't said go back and wait in the car. Or stay right here until I check to make sure you'll be safe, little lady.

He didn't slow down, just kept walking. It was sort of like three cowboys, guns drawn, walking down Main Street and the Big

Shoot-out. Lexi, instead of being one of the saloon girls, was one of the big, brave cowboys about to whup the outlaws' butts.

Felt good. Made her walk taller.

"I don't feel anything." Daklin frowned.

"Nothing here now," Alex agreed. "The power grid's gone."

"Does that mean the bad guys are inviting us inside?"

"Looks like." Alex indicated a blue, garage-style door ahead that was up a few inches. Daklin nodded. Alex raised his voice. "You girls in there doing your makeup? Wanna go to a party?"

The door magically opened, and Ginsberg and Kiersted emerged. Other than his scarlet nose Ginsberg was dead white, his eyes watering with the cold. Kiersted's white-blond hair was tipped with ice and his skin was a pale, sickly green. They both looked terrible, and Lexi felt a surge of sympathy, which she quickly squashed. They were working. Shit happened.

"Think we need to call in the Wizard Council on this one," Ginsberg said flatly, hunching his shoulders against the bite of the wind howling down between the low buildings.

"Think Duncan Edge should come in and save our butts?" Alex asked mildly as his eyes tracked the area around them.

God, he was good. Lexi wanted to be just like him. A fantastic operative, fearless, assertive. A leader his team would follow any-where, anytime.

Kiersted nodded. "Council has to be brought up to speed on this thing."

"Agreed," Alex said softly. "Let's see what we're dealing with here first." He took in the group. "Feel anything? Anyone?"

Cold? Scared? Excited?

Lexi wanted to experience the strength of the force field. Not the hurling part of the program, but she wanted a *sense* of menace. There was nothing other than the marrow-gnawing cold, and a few swirling snowflakes as the clouds rolled in and started lower-ing to dump several inches of snow on them.

They all agreed there wasn't a damn thing *to* feel.

"Let's go in," Alex told them, and they approached the building. "Headset and lip mics."

Lexi suspected they all expected to be struck down at any second. Alex touched her arm. Just a slight brush of his fingers near her elbow. Lexi paused to see what he wanted. "Stay by me, rookie," he said for her ears only. His green eyes looked translucent in the false dusk of the approaching storm. "Don't go off half-cocked." His mouth was a tight, grim line. "Understand?"

Of course she did. But then Alex knew that. He was worried about her. The "rookie" was to remind both of them that this was her first op. The "stay by me" was because he wanted to protect her.

Lexi's heart swelled. Appreciation for who Alex was tangled with what had started as hero worship and was rapidly becoming something a lot less manageable.

She held his gaze, the adrenaline drip starting to make her senses more acute. *This is not a drill. Repeat. This. Is. Not. A. Drill.* Her heartbeat started to race, and her skin felt sensitized even though Alex touched her through her LockOut gear.

"I'll follow your lead." There was more she wanted to say. A lot more. But even if this were the time and place, Lexi wasn't sure how she'd say it, or the actual words required to do what she felt justice. "I trust you," she told him just as quietly.

He touched his ear to activate the mic. "Let's crack this nut and find the weevils inside. Daklin, Kiersted, Ginsberg stay together. Take east. Both Stones west. Meet you in the middle. Go." He motioned her to hug the wall and keep moving.

Lexi hesitated. "Don't you want one of the others with you as backup?"

"I have you," he told her calmly. "That's all the backup I need. Keep moving, Stone, I'm not getting any younger."

Eight

It started snowing in earnest. Big, heavy flakes that stuck to the dirty, windblown mounds piled against the side of the building. There was a door—*somewhere.* The single-story structure was as big as a city block. Alex didn't sense the presence of any wizards or Halfs. But *that* didn't mean anything. He and his team were cloaked. Any bad-guy wizards in the area would do the same thing.

The arctic breeze sliced through the cotton of his T-shirt. Lexi walked directly behind him, her light footfalls crunching in the snow. Alex liked hearing her even, steady breathing in his ear. He'd purposely left her channel open. Her respiration was up a little, just enough to keep her sharp and focused. She was turning into a good operative. He had no right, but he felt a ridiculous surge of pride in her.

She was bright and funny, and sharp. On her toes and willing to listen and learn. Dammit to hell—he *liked* her.

He'd been in love once. That sure as hell hadn't panned out, but then, he hadn't expected it to, right from the start. He'd enjoyed the heightened awareness, he'd enjoyed the heat he and Kresley had generated in each other. They'd been good together. In bed. Out of it . . . not so much.

A trial attorney, she'd been an intelligent, beautiful brunette, as aggressive in the bedroom as in the courtroom. They'd seen each other for two years. Alex couldn't even remember why they'd stopped seeing each other. The relationship had just petered out without fanfare.

He'd been in lust plenty over the years, but *like*? He considered it as he visually scanned the seamless wall of the building for ingress.

Using the tetrabyte image-capture feature on his headset, he transmitted pictures directly to Montana for analysis. Not that there was much to see. White snow, gray concrete wall. But those techs could find a gnat's ass in an image when push came to shove.

He mentally blocked the cold. Lexi wore a LockOut jacket. She'd be warm. At least from the thighs up.

Looney-bird. His lips twitched. Jesus.

Had he ever been in like with a woman he lusted after?

No. This was a novel experience.

Preternaturally aware of Lexi directly behind him, Alex heard her foot slip on the ice and shot his hand back to grab her arm before she fell. He didn't turn and only waited a couple of beats before he released her.

"Okay?" he asked only loudly enough to be picked up by the mic near his mouth.

"Terrific."

No argument there.

His heart kicked up. Suddenly a door appeared in the wall ten feet in front of him. A door that hadn't been there seconds before.

But there it was.

Come on in, said the spider to the fly.

Slowing his pace, Alex touched the control on the headset to include the others. "Single door. West wall, midpoint. Teleport fifteen feet north of my coordinate."

Less than two seconds later the other three men joined them beside the titanium door. Lexi came up next to Alex, her weapon held steady in her black-gloved hand. White epaulets of snow decorated her black jacket, and splotches of white dotted the LockOut cap she'd pulled over her bright hair and down to her eyebrows.

Her gray eyes were huge and filled with banked excitement as she gave him a half smile.

The urge to kiss her chill-reddened lips was ridiculously strong. Alex resisted and turned back to inspect the door.

The titanium steel vault door—twelve inches thick and reinforced to withstand the assault of a tank, or a more powerful wizard—stood ajar. There was no door handle, and he couldn't see any hinges. The sucker was rock solid and unless one knew how to get in, impenetrable.

Whoever had installed it had been determined to keep everyone out.

Now, apparently, they were being invited in. The hair on the back of his neck rose.

Fuck.

With abbreviated hand gestures, Alex indicated where he wanted everyone to be positioned. He wanted Lexi back in Rio, but assigned her a position with the men. They were all locked and loaded. Staying out of the fatal funnel, he nudged the bottom of the door with his toe.

It swung open soundlessly.

Warmer air spilled like liquid out of the opening. The interior was unnaturally dark. No lights. No illumination from the dusk-like exterior, indicating that other than the door there were no other ways in or out. Maybe.

While he didn't pick up any wizard signature, Alex heard—no, felt—the faint mechanical hum of large machinery. He didn't even want to hazard a guess what the hell could be inside.

He signaled to the other two wizards that he'd take point, with Kiersted and Ginsberg behind him. The two non-wizards, Lexi and Daklin, would bring up the rear. Alex made eye contact with Daklin. The other man nodded, then fell into place behind Lexi.

At his gesture, everyone turned on their Maglites simultaneously and stepped into the darkness.

Lexi wasn't crazy about the dark. It wasn't a phobia, it was just that she didn't much care for unpredictable. And dark was pretty damned unpredictable. She'd actually gone to one of the T-FLAC psychologists to try to work through it. Because there was *nothing* about being an operative that could possibly be interpreted as *predictable*. She had to get over her need for order, and aversion to chaos, and embrace the fact that it was the nature of the beast if she'd wanted to be an operative.

The air . . . hummed. A low-pitched sound seemed to be conducting through her body, turning her into a giant tuning fork. It didn't hurt, but it felt odd, and a little uncomfortable.

There was a strong smell of ammonia and another chemical smell she couldn't quite ID. Whatever it was, the combination was strong enough to make her eyes sting and tear up.

She walked with the men, shining her flashlight, scanning the immediate area. There was nothing to see. Gray cement walls, ceiling, floor. A big warehouse. A big, dark, empty wareh—

"Get us some light." Alex's voice came softly in her ear out of the darkness. Lexi hung onto the calm rationality of it. He wasn't talking to her. The only way she could make light was if there was a light switch attached to something.

"Working on it," Ruben Ginsberg said just as quietly. Suddenly the place lit up like Dodger Stadium.

"My God—" Alex said softly, stopping dead.

Lexi blinked into the brightness, then her eyes widened as she stared, slack jawed.

"Holy shit." That was Daklin.

Kiersted muttered, "Fuck me swinging."

"Well I'll be damned!" was Ginsberg's contribution.

The place was *filled* with neat rows of clear plastic incubators.

"There must be a thousand of them," Daklin observed quietly.

Lexi thought considerably more.

The isolettes indicated newborns, but as far as she could tell there weren't any babies here. But it did explain the smell. And the low hum of machinery was explained by the powerful clusters of electrical cords running from each incubator up into the ceiling. The same electrical cords she'd almost tripped over yesterday in the warehouse in Rio.

"Spread out and report anything unusual."

"You don't think a thousand-plus empty incubators is unusual?" Lexi asked dryly.

Alex's hot green eyes touched her. It was so fleeting she was sure none of the others noticed. But she felt it like a caress. "Anyone have a frame of reference for any of this shit?" he asked. He still had his weapon drawn, so did the others.

The men all gave him the negative.

"I do," Lexi said quietly, walking up to the closest isolette. She rested her hand gently on the clear plastic dome as Alex walked up beside her.

"Now why doesn't that surprise me?"

She shrugged. She had a lump in her throat. "What, because I know things?" She felt his gaze on her, but kept her attention on the familiar gauges and tubes inside and outside the isolette.

"How do you know about this in particular? Interesting article you read in the *Journal of Modern Medicine*?"

"No. My mother had a baby boy . . ." Lexi absently stroked her thumb back and forth across the cool plastic. "Hal was in the

NICU—Neonatal Intensive Care Unit—for three weeks." She imagined his frail little body inside the incubator, his transparent lids taped shut, tubes running in and out of every orifice. He'd been so small. So helpless. "He died."

"I'm sorry." Alex stood very close. Not touching her, but close enough for her to get comfort from his presence and his body heat. "How old were you?"

Lexi wanted to turn into his chest. Like a physical ache, she *yearned* to feel the strength of his arms wrapped around her.

But that wasn't going to happen.

"Thirteen and three quarters."

"Your mother must have been devastated too."

"Yeah. She was, when I managed to get hold of her." Her mother had stunned Lexi by crying on the phone. She'd never ever heard her mother cry.

"What do you mean, get hold of her? Where the hell was she?"

"Oh, she and my father had to vacate the hotel where we'd been staying, so they were in Tijuana."

"And you and the baby were ..."

"New Orleans. I joined them after ... After."

"You were *thirteen* and you stayed in New Orleans *alone* for three weeks?" He sounded so savage that Lexi turned to look at him with surprise. "Who took care of *you*? Where did you sleep? What did you fucking *eat*?"

Bemused, she stared at him a moment. "I didn't need anyone to take care of me, and I stayed at the hospital with Hal, of course." It had taken a bit of ingenuity to keep the staff from knowing she never left. But she'd been an ingenious and determined girl.

"Of course." He dragged in a breath. "Tell me what we're looking at here. Every setup is identical."

Lexi glanced at the row behind her. She frowned. "Yeah. They are. Weird, because this many infants would have *different* needs. Okay. Here's what we have." She indicated each as she explained to Alex what was what. "Cardiac-Respiratory monitor. See the green, black, and white wires right there? Those are chest leads. Those are taped to the baby—To the baby's chest to monitor heart rate, rhythm, and respiration."

Lexi explained how the CPAP delivered oxygen, paired with nasal prongs for the "better breathers," and the endotracheal tube, which would be inserted in the baby's windpipe and attached to a ventilator to keep the little airway open and deliver oxygen for the babies less capable of breathing on their own.

She was familiar with every tube and wire involved, because she'd sat beside Hal for twenty-one days watching him fight valiantly for life.

There was the radiant warmer to regulate the baby's body temperature, and suction devices to vacuum secretions from his nose and mouth. The arterial umbilical catheter, which allowed someone to draw blood and give fluids without sticking Hal every time. He'd been too weak to cry. He'd broken Lexi's heart.

Alex rested his hand on her shoulder and squeezed. "Okay. I get the gist." His hand remained there, close to her face. Warm, solid, and comforting. "So we're talking premature infants and/or babies who are sick?"

Lexi nodded, seeing movement out of her peripheral vision as the others came back.

"As instructed, the techno geeks, lab rats, and assorted other CS teams are on their way," Ginsberg told them, wiping his nose with a square of blue-and-white-striped fabric. Lexi had never seen anyone actually use a hankie. He blew his nose, then shoved the handkerchief in his pocket.

Ew. Lexi shuddered thinking of the rapid bacteria multiplication.

"We checked every container," Daklin told Alex. "No kids in residence."

Alex removed his hand from Lexi's shoulder. The spot cooled

rapidly and she put her hand where his had been to hold in the warmth for one more second.

"Educated guess says when you guys first arrived, these cribs were full. The force field was in full effect keeping you out while they teleported them . . ." Alex shrugged. "Somewhere else. Then they left the door open so we could see how fucking goddamned clever they are, and possibly to scare the shit out of us."

He turned and faced his team. "Now the questions are: Where did they get a thousand premature or sick babies? Why were *they* chosen as opposed to viable *healthy* babies? And where are the babies *now*?"

"I have another one," Lexi said. "These babies weren't here alone. They had to have specialists taking care of them. Where are the neonatologists? The nurses? The respiratory specialists? The lab techs? Neurologists? A *cardiologist*?"

"Know what we have?" Alex said grimly. "A riddle inside an enigma inside of a giant fucking question mark."

"An isolette was found in the warehouse in Rio," Lexi said, shoving both hands into the front pockets of her jacket and hunching her shoulders against the cold. She didn't understand how Alex could stand there in nothing but a short-sleeved T-shirt and jeans without turning blue. She wanted to touch his bare arm so badly her stomach clenched as she resisted the powerful urge to close the gap between them.

His jaw was shadowed with a sexy as sin five o'clock shadow. Lexi wanted to rub herself against his rock-hard body like a cat. She wanted his big, tanned hands on her naked skin. Preferably in a sun-warmed room. She wanted to see those sharp green eyes haze as he looked at her.

She wanted to keep her job as an operative.

She flipped up her collar to keep the cold from going down her neck. Concentrate, *Stone*. Not on Alex. On the job at hand.

"Were there originally as many infants in Rio as there were

here?" she asked the others. "Having read Fox's report, and seeing a similar setup at *that* location, I suspect there were."

"Yeah. So do I," Alex said flatly. "Same electrical power source, et cetera."

"What are we saying?" Kiersted asked. "That originally there were a thousand babies in Rio and they—what? Moved the kids from Brazil to New Mexico? Why?"

Frowning in concentration Daklin looked around the vast open space. "Or they moved *those* babies and *these* babies to a third location."

"Where the hell did they acquire two thousand infants? And for what purpose?" Alex glanced over at a large group of men and women in T-FLAC gear who'd materialized several hundred feet away. He raised his hand to acknowledge they were there, and indicated he'd be right with them before turning back to his team.

"Ginsberg, find a secure location we can use as a command center, then check in and see how Lu is doing. Daklin, get an update on the latest bombings and have them shoot us all the film footage from every incident. Let's find the pattern. Stone, check with research. See what it can tell us about the tangos, the tats, and any other detail we might have missed on the security tapes. Kiersted, if we don't have at least fifty percent of the same personnel here that were in Rio, fix that. I want the same people working both ops." Alex scanned the room as if looking for something they'd missed. "Let's get a step ahead of these bastards instead of half a step behind."

Berlin
Germany
52° 27' N 13° 18' E

Alex felt as though someone had a hand clamped firmly around his dick, and was leading him—*somewhere.* Somewhere he fucking

well didn't want to go. The only fingers he wanted on that particular body part anytime soon were Lexi's. There was something—
hell, he couldn't define *what*, about this op that had his well-trained
instincts on high alert. It felt personal. Which was ridiculous. *Nothing* about this op was personal.

Babies?

He knew nothing about kids.

He'd never had a child, didn't know much about them. Frankly,
he didn't much care. He supposed that would change if and when
the situation changed, but until then there was nothing *personal*
about babies in general. There was nothing personal about several
thousand small beings being transported from pillar to post for reasons that had yet to be identified.

He glanced up from the report he was reading on his handheld
and met Lexi's eyes. She sat at one end of a long leather sofa, he at
the other. Daklin, Kiersted, Ginsberg, and the returned Lu were all
seated in the vast room of the safe house. Even though dawn was
breaking, they were each focused on an element of the op, and intent on reading the intel on their monitors.

There'd been little conversation for the hours after the meal
Daklin had volunteered to cook. Lexi had offered to prep whatever Daklin needed. She didn't complain by word or deed that she
was doing scut work. She'd chopped, Daklin had cooked. Kiersted
kept the coffeepot filled. Alex cleaned up afterward. Everyone had
done their part.

Alex continued to feed the fire, and through it all, tried to figure what the fuck it was about *this* op, at *this* time that made the
back of his neck itch.

A short time later, the smell of strong coffee, and dinner's grilled
steak and onions, mingled with the scent of the hickory logs crack-
ling in the fireplace. The scene appeared peaceful, relaxed. Yet the
very air sparked with tension as the team tried to match ill-fitting

pieces of the puzzle together into a cohesive picture that might indicate what the master plan was.

If he reached out, Alex would be able to stroke the arch of Lexi's
bare foot, which rested tantalizingly on the leather sofa just a few
feet away from his hip. Wearing light gray sweats the exact color of
her eyes, she was stretched out, her neck against the rolled arm of
the sofa, her bare feet crossed at the ankles, a laptop perched on a
cushion on her lap. Her cheeks were flushed from the warmth of
the fire.

Even though there was no fragrance to the soap in the bathroom where they'd all taken turns showering earlier, he could
smell her skin. Not floral, nor fruity, something uniquely Lexi. Alex
could almost taste her flavor on his tongue. He rubbed his hand
around the ache in the back of his neck.

What in God's name was he missing?

"We should call it a night," he told the others. "Tackle it fresh in
the morning with fresh eyes."

Seated at the dining room table with two laptops, a thermos of
coffee, and the last quarter of a steak sandwich he'd built an hour
after dinner, Daklin glanced at his watch. "It's practically morning
now—Holy crap! Stone, take a look at this."

Alex and Lexi rose simultaneously. Daklin's gaze connected with
Alex. He shook his head and smiled. "The name thing saves time."

"Doesn't it though? What do you have?" He sat in a chair beside
the other man. Daklin turned the monitor of one laptop so Alex
had a better view.

"Wait. I want to see as well," Lexi said, pushing in to stand
beside Alex. "Hang on, can you move—Yeah. Okay. Now I can
see."

"Do I need to get up?" Ginsberg asked, not removing his eyes
from his monitor. His fingers flew across the keys and he chewed
an unlit cigar in the corner of his mouth. Lu had his unlit ciga-

rettes, Ginsberg his cigars. Some habits were hard to break. As long as Alex didn't see a match near either, he was fine with it.

"What are we looking at?" he asked as Daklin manipulated the keys on his keyboard to share a split-screen image with him.

"The first screen is a still shot taken right after the London bombing. Who does this guy look like to you?"

"Alex," Lexi answered excitedly. "He looks exactly like a younger Alex. Holy shit. He's the same guy I fought in Rio."

"Or was *this* the guy in Rio?" Daklin keyed in another screen. The second doppelgänger was dressed identically to the first. They weren't mirror images. They were indistinguishable.

"Same guy," Alex said grimly. "Ditto," he said as a third image came up.

Lexi leaned in, putting a hand on his shoulder for balance. Silky strands of her bright hair brushed his face. Her hair smelled of honey. Her low "Hmm" shot hot and straight to his stomach like a slug of tequila.

Not the time for this. Not the fucking time!

"I would have been pretty damned precocious if I'd started having sex and making children at fifteen or sixteen." His voice was gruff. He was as aroused by Lexi's nearness as if they'd been having foreplay all day. Damn good thing he was seated. It was going to be uncomfortable all around if he had to stand anytime soon. He was as hard as the table.

"Zoom in." Her warm breath smelled of the coffee she'd been drinking. Alex wanted to taste it on her tongue.

Daklin's finger hesitated above the keys. "Faces?"

When she shook her head filaments of her hair clung to the bristle on Alex's cheek. He froze, his heart careening around his chest as if she were the first girl he'd ever been aware of.

"See how close you can get to their left arms." The *tattoo*. Of course. Alex's sense sharpened as Daklin manipulated the three images until they could see the guys' left arms and the series of lines and numbers.

"Please, please don't take us back to Los Alamos," Lexi whispered under her breath.

"Jesus," Alex said, stunned as the three images came into sharp focus.

All three of the bar codes were different.

Not one doppelgänger.

Three.

Nine

Lexi chose the smallest bedroom on the opposite side of the house near the kitchen. It had probably been servant's quarters originally, more a closet with a bed in it than an actual room. The guys had all offered to switch, but there was something comforting about small spaces, so she'd declined.

Three of the men had gone to their rooms to catch what little sleep the night offered. Given the implications, this op had the potential to blow sky-high. The question wasn't if, but *when*.

On the way back from the bathroom, she heard the low hum of voices from the living room.

She recognized Daklin's low tones, but she didn't need to *hear* Alex's voice to know he was close. Her body seemed to have developed Alex-dar, a sense of his location that shimmied through her in palpable waves whenever they were within a mile of one another. The closer he got, the more she . . . pulsed.

Lexi glanced into the room as she passed. The fire had died down to red embers, and most of the lights were off. Just the pendant light still shone over the men's heads as they sat, talking quietly at the dining table. The computer monitors were dark, and the men didn't look as though they were talking business. Just two friends, drinking coffee and shooting the breeze in the early hours.

A ridiculous twinge of jealousy seized her as she passed through the dark kitchen and opened the door to her room. She wanted to be the one talking with Alex in low tones in the loneliest part of the night. While she wanted to dismiss the fatal attraction she had for the man as an adrenaline overload from her first op, Lexi rarely lied to herself. Her memory was too powerful to let her get away with it. The truth was, she was halfway in love with him, no matter how foolish, or ill-advised, or against T-FLAC guidelines it might be.

"Dipshit," she whispered to herself as she undressed in the flickering red neon glow bleeding through the flimsy curtains from the hotel sign across the street. Maybe she was like some stupid ingenue in a play, falling in love with her leading man? Actresses did it all the time.

No. She was too pragmatic and sensible to believe for a moment that she could ever change and become flighty and irresponsible just because the man she worked with was physically appealing. Her attraction to Alex was one thing, acting on these feelings another. She was a brand new operative on her first assignment. She'd do nothing to jeopardize that.

And she had to report any questionable behavior to IA. Instead of being neatly black-and-white, her interest in him colored this situation in a never-ending palette of grays. The linoleum floor was cold under her bare feet. The room was just as chilly and she rubbed the goose bumps on her arms as she hung her clothes neatly over a straight-backed chair in the corner.

She was a bit like a dog chasing a car. Yeah. That was a better analogy than the moonstruck young actress idea.

Stripped down to men's boxers and a tank top, Lexi crawled between the so-cold-they-felt-damp sheets in the narrow twin bed and curled into a ball. She preferred sleeping nude, but over the course of her training she'd learned that naked wasn't conducive to leaving at a moment's notice. And working with a team—usually consisting of mostly men—meant that any one of them could and would haul her ass out of bed if she were needed. She had to be ready for anything.

She'd considered drawing the blackout curtains beneath the others, but if it was too dark, she'd sleep too hard. Lexi sighed. Rolled over. Curled up. Straightened out. Sighed and turned over the other way.

Red blink. Flicker. Red blink. Blackness. Red blink. Flicker. Red blink. Flicker. Argh! Damn neon. She pulled the pillow over her head. She had to get some sleep to be fresh for whatever happened next.

She rolled over. What were Alex and Daklin talking about? They'd closed down the session half an hour ago after contacting the techies in Montana. Alex had requested a program for an algorithm to analyze and extrapolate information from the partial bar codes on the three men's arms. The tech department guys would work all night, which gave the team a few hours of shut-eye they all badly needed.

Lexi tried to unclench her muscles and relax. Too much coffee. Too much adrenaline. Not enough Alex. And a cold bed. The sheets would warm up in a few minutes and she'd—Was that a soft knock at her door? Her heart lurched hard against her breastbone. She bolted upright, the pillow over her face sliding to the floor as she tossed the covers aside and jumped out of bed.

And he was there. A large, predatory male, teleported two feet in front of her as if she'd made a wish upon a star. Lexi stopped dead in her tracks as hot and cold shivers ran through her body. For a moment, the red neon light illuminated Alex's unyielding features. His need was palpable. She saw his desire, his hunger in the taut planes of his face, and she forgot how to breathe.

Wordlessly, he closed the gap between them in one long stride. He plunged his fingers into her shower-damp hair with a rough sound of passion. Lexi's body slammed into his as he drew her up on her toes, bringing her mouth up to his in a punishing kiss that sucked the air from the room and left her ears in a vacuum. He didn't ask, he took, his mouth hot and ravaging as his tongue sought hers. Lexi whimpered, head spinning, heart ballistic.

He tasted of coffee and a stark hunger that mirrored her own. Her fingers fisted in the front of his T-shirt as his tongue dueled with hers, hot and hard. She felt the hard thump of his heart pounding beneath her hands as she met and matched him in fervor. Still kissing her, he shoved her against the wall with a hard thump, even though the bed was mere feet away.

Lexi wrapped a leg around his hips to hold him close, grinding her soft, damp core against the hard length of his erection. She almost came right there.

He freed one hand from her hair, sliding his palm down her throat and across her chest, then curled his fingers around her breast. Cupping the full weight in his palm he pinched the erect nipple, making Lexi arch her back as pure sensation flooded her entire body. He lifted her as if she weighed nothing. She whimpered as their lips were roughly pulled apart. She reached for him, grabbed hold of his broad shoulders for balance as he buried his face between her breasts, then turned his head and closed his mouth over her nipple through the thin cotton of her tank top.

The hard, hot pull as he sucked caused a shudder of pleasure to travel from her head to her toes in rippling waves. Her nails dug into his skin as his teeth closed over her hardened nipple. She shuddered with the sharp pleasure of the small pain.

She realized that he was suddenly naked. She wanted to be the same way. But she didn't want him to stop what he was doing.

The seam of her tank top gave way as he ripped the material to get at her breast. The barely controlled violence of the act made being half-dressed, while he was naked, even more erotic. Lexi wrapped her legs around his waist as he shifted her from the wall to carry her to the narrow bed.

The pulsing red light filling the room reflected demonically in his eyes as he lay her down, then kneaded her thighs apart, ripping off her boxers like a magician, then making them disappear before he lowered himself between her thighs. Lexi's hands gripped his shoulders, and she slid her knees along his sides, opening herself wider. Welcoming him inside her.

His entry was hard and fast. Her entire body bowed with the exquisite sensation as the heat of him filled her. He slid his hands down her back, cupping her bottom in both large hands, his fingers digging into her flesh as he brought her impossibly harder against him. She lifted her legs high, tightening them across his upper back as her entire body shuddered with the impact of each stroke.

Alex. Alex. Alex.

Slick with sweat, their bodies rose and fell in counterpoint as coiled tension built unbearably, causing her body to arch and shake.

If he was insatiable, so was Lexi. She grabbed his face, bringing it down to hers so she could kiss him as he plunged deeper. The muscles in his back bunched and straightened, and she dug in her heels, holding on tightly as he drove into her. His jaw was rough, his tongue slick and hot as his hips pounded against hers in a rhythm that took them over, drove them in this wild erotic dance.

The first climax hit her so hard she had to tear her mouth from his and bite her lip to prevent herself from screaming. A soft, keening sound escaped her and she almost bucked him off her as her body bowed with excruciating pleasure. But Alex wasn't going anywhere. He kept thrusting, and the second climax, higher and stronger than the first, rolled right over the tail end of the last without giving her time to catch her breath. She bit his shoulder as her entire body clenched around him.

His body shuddered, stiffening over hers as he gave a guttural cry, his hips jerking powerfully with his release.

The sound of their harsh breathing filled the small room. Lexi couldn't move. She didn't want to move. She loved the feel of his weight on top of her. Loved that he was still hard inside her. Loved—

She pressed a kiss to his shoulder, knowing her bite had probably left marks on his skin. His fingers tightened on the globes of her ass, holding her possessively in place. As if she wanted to be anywhere but exactly where she was. They lay pressed together, sweat gluing their skin as both fought for breath.

She felt him getting harder deep inside her and tightened her knees against his sides, locking her ankles in the small of his back, feeling the taut muscles bunch and gather.

This time, some of the urgency was gone as he moved deeply inside her. Lexi combed her fingers through his damp hair as the pressure inside her built quickly and with such intensity she had to grit her teeth so she didn't scream out loud and wake the whole damn house.

She licked his nipple as he surged against her. He groaned as she nipped him not so lightly with her teeth. Dizzy with lust, she surged against him as his thrusts became even deeper and more powerful.

They climaxed together and Lexi swore she saw fireworks of red burst behind her closed lids.

Alex shifted so that they lay side by side, still joined. Lexi opened dazed eyes as he trailed his fingers over her shoulder to the slope of her breast in a lazy caress that gave her goose bumps. Neither had said a word the entire time.

"Jesus, sweetheart," his voice was thick, low, rough with emotion when he finally spoke. "Did I hurt you?"

She shook her head. And inside Lexi thought, *No. But you will.*

Sydney
Australia
33° 51 35.9"S 151° 12' 40"E

Only one of the tangos had a bar code legible enough to read. The close-set black lines went from inner wrist to his elbow.

33 51 35 09 151 12 40 02 14 08

Latitude. Longitude. The last three pairs of numbers might be a date. Or it might mean bugger all. They'd got the call from Intel half an hour before.

So here they were in Sydney, in the safe house on Macleay Street. The nondescript exterior of the three-story office building looked pretty much like dozens of others in the neighborhood. The name of the company, embossed on a classy plaque beside the double glass doors, was 1788 Exports, homage to the first vineyards planted near the Sydney Harbor Bridge in that year. The business was real, employing several dozen T-FLAC auxiliary personnel, and maintaining the secure safe house on the top floor. Ironically, their business cover was in the black, and doing quite well exporting excellent Australian wines around the world.

The location, hidden in plain sight among newly renovated upscale retail outlets, good restaurants, and service businesses, was centrally located between downtown Sydney and the harbor.

"Hey. Did you know the Sydney Opera House was made a UNESCO World Heritage Site in mid-2007?" Lexi asked the others as they sat around a table.

God only knew all safe houses looked alike by now. The round table, circled by high-back chairs, the long, low couches that doubled as sleeping space when numbers were high. They were field-stripping their weapons and waiting for more intel.

Lexi went on. "It was one of the twenty finalists for the project—"

Ginsberg's head jerked up and he scowled. "Who gives a shit?"

"Easy," Alex said mildly, purposely not looking at Lexi who sat to his left, stripping her Sig Sauer with the precision of a neurosurgeon. He'd never seen anyone strip down and reassemble a weapon that freaking fast. Last time he'd looked, like twenty-two seconds before, she was still a little green around the gills from the teleport from Germany to Australia.

"Have you been here before, Ruben?" Lexi asked, picking up her Glock. She held the weapon in a safe direction and pulled the trigger, then held the slide back, all while looking at the man across the table.

"*Ginsberg*," Ginsberg emphasized. Alex knew it would just make Lexi call him by his first name to annoy him. "Couple of dozen times over the years. Yeah."

"Excellent," she said cheerfully, then pulled down the slide lock on both sides of the weapon simultaneously.

Alex watched her slender hands, fascinated by her dexterity and speed as she pushed the slide forward until it fully separated from the receiver, pushed the recoil spring slightly forward, and lifted it away from the barrel. Once the barrel had been removed, she started to clean each piece carefully, then reassembled the weapon with blistering speed. She hadn't looked at her hands once.

"Then *you* can tell us something about the city," she told Ginsberg smoothly. "Since we're here, and not going anywhere for a few more hours at least."

Ginsberg stared at her, disbelief etched on his face. He pinched the bridge of his nose. "Do I look like a fucking travel guide to you, Lara Croft?"

Lexi shot a brief glance his way to let Alex know she could handle it and set her weapon down while looking the other operative dead in the eye. "No, you look like a guy who doesn't play well with others. Don't like working with a woman? Tough shit, Ruben. I'm here to stay. Suck it up or ask for a transfer to another team."

Since she'd finished stripping five weapons to Ginsberg's two, and they were fully loaded and lined up inches from her fingertips, Ginsberg wisely shut the hell up.

Daklin tried to hide a smile. Alex did a better job of hiding his annoyance.

Daklin had casually mentioned the night before that Ginsberg had complained to anyone who'd listen that he didn't like working with female operatives. Too fucking bad. T-FLAC was training more and more women to work in the field. All of them good.

Lexi had handled him just right. Didn't mean Alex wasn't going to sit on him and bend him into a pretzel if he got out of line again. Too bad. Ginsberg was a good operative, Alex had worked with him before. He was usually a pretty even-tempered guy, and now that Alex came to think of it, had worked with AJ Cooper on that op. He'd had no trouble with Cooper. What was it about Lexi that got his goat?

Whatever it was he'd better get his shit together. Alex would not tolerate friction between team members when they were working. Period.

He'd been damned fortunate he'd been capable of teleporting both Lexi and himself to Australia from Germany. But he couldn't put off reporting this any longer. When his power outages affected only himself he'd convinced himself that reporting the "illness" wasn't necessary. But since the occurrences were coming closer and closer together, and now involved Le—an entire *team,* he couldn't be so cavalier.

They might, of course, relieve him of his duties and send in someone else to lead the team. He was man enough to be okay with someone else taking over; if they would do a better job, then he deserved to be released. What he *wasn't* man enough to take on the chin was some other guy being around Lexi.

Christ, he had it bad.

Hyperaware of her sitting just a foot away, he smelled her skin. It smelled like honey. Her taste—

"How long do you think before we mobilize?" Lu asked, leaning back. He talked around the white plastic filter of an unlit black cigarillo. He'd never seen the man laugh, but Alex couldn't miss the amusement in Lu's black eyes as he flicked a glance upward.

"Why? Want to go sightseeing?"

He shook his head, and the cigarillo changed sides. "Stone can give me a travelogue, right?" Lu's gaze switched to Lexi.

"Don't stir the pot," Daklin told him, folding his cleaning cloth and putting it away.

"She knows things, right?" Lu followed suit. The exercise, even for the rest of them, hadn't taken up more than a few minutes. Boredom was a big part of being on an op. Hurry up and wait.

Lexi clasped her hands behind her head and tipped her chair back on two legs. "Right. I'm a font of useless information."

"Ginsberg might not be interested in the construction of the opera house, but I am," Kiersted assured her. "Tell us what you know."

Alex bit back a smile as Lexi launched into the planning, history, construction, blah, blah, blah of the landmark building. She was a good storyteller, weaving facts and numbers into a lively monologue. Daklin and Kiersted looked interested, and Lu egged her on. All of them doing it to piss off Ginsberg.

Clearly irritated, Ginsberg inserted earphones from his kit, and without a word, ignored them all.

"Back off, guys," Alex said in an undertone. "We'll be going out in a while, and we still have to work as a unit."

The secure buzzer rang, indicating someone downstairs. "Dinner. I'll go." Lu offered.

"I'll give you a hand." Lexi rose, automatically holstering her Glock before following him out to the elevator. They'd opted for take-out Chinese while they waited for a call from Montana.

When they left the room, Alex turned to face the sullen, earplugged operative.

"What?" Ruben Ginsberg demanded belligerently, yanking out one plug.

Alex lifted a brow at his tone but kept his own voice low. "I didn't say a word. But you know damned well you were out of line with a fellow operative. You're lucky she didn't hand you your ass."

"Not only do females have no business in the field, she isn't even a fucking wizard. What's she doing on our team anyway?" Ginsberg reassembled his weapon clumsily, swearing under his breath as he misaligned the barrel.

"Hey," Daklin said mildly. "*I'm* not a wizard, and I'm on the team, what's your beef with us regular personnel, Ginsberg?"

Ginsberg shoved his chair away from the table. "Fuck you both."

"Maybe it's his time of the month," Kiersted offered, watching the other man storm out of the room. Daklin grinned.

Alex didn't find the exchange amusing. Ginsberg was a blowup about to happen. "One goddamn warning, and his ass will be replaced. I won't tolerate that kind of behavior from any member of my team. As for you guys—you'd better cool it as well. Here." Alex tossed the sat phone across the table to Daklin. "I'll be back after I've reamed him a new one."

He attempted shimmering to intercept Ginsberg. Couldn't teleport. "God damn it."

Kiersted, who'd moved to an easy chair and a three-day-old newspaper, glanced up. "What?"

"My powers are FUBAR. Just tried to shimmer. Can't do it."

The newspaper was put down, as Kiersted gave him a narrow-eyed look. "You're shitting me. Why not?"

Alex shrugged. "Anything like this ever happen to you?"

"No, thank God. Has it happened before?"

"Has what happened before?" Lexi asked, arms laden with white paper bags. She headed to the table, followed by Lu, similarly burdened. Alex's mouth watered at the savory aromas of the food.

Christ. He hadn't wanted to make this public knowledge—but . . . What the hell. "My powers are flickering."

Lexi's head jerked up, her gray eyes concerned. "What does that mean? Does it hurt? Is it serious . . ."

"I don't know how serious it is," Alex admitted. "I wasn't actually going to fill you all in on the situation while we're here. This has been going on for the past several weeks. Not just my ability to teleport—Remember when we were outside the National Palace Museum? Tried to shimmer before the explosion. Couldn't do it."

He stuffed his fingers into his front pockets. "I've had problems off and on with invisibility, too, of course. Every power is apparently short-circuiting to some degree. Turned down an op in Greece because my amphibious powers didn't work at all for a while. Yet I was able to make use of a small amount in Rio. Unpredictable, to say the least."

"What about your Temporal acceleration?" Kiersted asked with a frown. This revelation had more impact on Kiersted, a fellow wizard, than it would have on either Lexi or Daklin.

"Hasn't worked—at all—" he admitted. "Not even a flicker for three weeks."

"Holy hell." Kiersted slid his chair back. "Think this is contagious?"

"Not that I know of."

Lexi hadn't moved from her position on the other side of the table, but he felt her empathy as if she were physically touching him. "Alex, what are you going to do?"

He blew out a deep breath. "I sent a message to Duncan Edge, Head of the Wizard Council, when we got to Germany last night.

I was hoping this would pass, but it's—Shit. It's getting worse, not better. I can't depend on my powers."

Her brows puckered. "Do you have a—wizard doctor of some sort?"

"Yeah, there are doctors who are wizards, and of course I'll consult someone. *After* I talk with Edge and see if anyone else has reported this anomaly. Also left a message for Mason Knight. He might be able to shed some light on this." Alex shook his head. "Look, let's eat. My power outage won't be resolved here, and we could get a call and have to mobilize any minute."

"How will you mobilize if you can't teleport?" Lexi asked reasonably.

"Same way you and Daklin do, if I can't manage it." He could practically hear her agile brain working as she finished hauling take-out boxes out of the bags.

Her eyes were clear and direct as she asked, "Want me to go and tell Ginsberg the food's here?"

"No." Alex pulled out a chair for her. Out of sight, he brushed his fingertips across her back as she sat down and was rewarded by her small shiver. "He was sent to his room without dinner as punishment for being an ass."

Turning to look at him over her shoulder, Lexi grinned. "Bad Ruben, bad *bad* Ruben, no *Ling Mung Gai* for him."

Her smile did something weird to Alex's insides. His heart double-clutched and an unfamiliar warmth seemed to permeate his entire being.

He was so fucked.

Ten

D aklin, their bomb expert, was off inspecting nooks and crannies with his toys, hunting traces of any explosives secreted away. In what amounted to eleven acres of floor space, including six thousand seats in five theaters, several restaurants, rehearsal halls, sixty dressing rooms, extensive plant and machinery rooms and all the admin offices, it was a monumental task.

Good thing he had a large chunk of Sydney's police force and a dozen bomb-sniffing dogs, as well as the building's excellent security people, working with him.

Lexi stood with the rest of the team in the back of the Concert Hall, watching the people and dogs scattered across the building scurrying around like ants. She shoved her fingertips into the front pockets of her baggy black cargo pants. "I don't want to sound pessimistic," she said soberly. "But even with all that manpower, I don't know how they'd find an explosive device in such an enormous structure. This building is packed with thousands of hiding places."

"No idea if the tangos already planted an incendiary device, or not. But I sense the Trace, indicating the presence of a large number of Halfs. And recently. They weren't visiting to hear the symphony. Still, it's a challenge," Alex said dryly.

No shit, Sherlock.

"A wizard can go through this place in less than half the time," Lu told Lexi, obviously reading her skepticism. "And we have about a hundred wizards with the Sydney PD. If anything's here, they'll find it. Quickly."

"Or the whole fucking place will blow, and the city will lose a landmark. But there won't be any people killed," Ginsberg said, rubbing his forehead as if he had a headache. "That's gotta be a plus."

Lexi didn't think Australians would be quite so blasé about their precious Opera House being reduced to rubble. She gave Ginsberg a considering glance. He was an ass. She hated to complain, but if he kept on the way he was going she was going to take him aside and have a serious operative-to-operative chat. Maybe Alex hadn't been able to give him an attitude adjustment yet. Or didn't want to. She figured she could give it a shot.

Through the doors opening into the outside lobby Lexi heard several of the dogs barking. Bomb-sniffing dogs. The place was being gone over with a fine-tooth comb. And then again with an even finer comb that could cleave a nit's ass in half.

"Possibly, they want to demolish a world landmark, not the people inside." Kiersted rested a hip against a seat back. "The planet would definitely sit up and take notice if the Sydney Opera House went bang."

Lexi frowned. "It seems like being here's a stretch. It doesn't fit their MO—"

"Nothing's a stretch as far as tangos go," Alex said curtly, cutting her off.

"Everywhere else they've hit has seen extensive property destruction *and* massive collateral damage. Something doesn't fit." A persistent itch was building on her neck.

She was still surveying the activity when Alex muttered something in his sat phone, then clipped it to his belt.

"Ginsberg. Stone. Go help get them out of here." Standing in the middle of the tiers of velvet-covered seats in the empty Concert Hall, Alex indicated the Copenhagen Royal Chapel Choir rehearsing onstage. The kids and adults making up the group were here an hour ahead of schedule, Lexi knew. The place was supposed to be empty.

Alerted by Alex to the potential terrorist threat, in-house security had called in reinforcements to assist the team with evacuation of all personnel and performers as quickly and quietly as possible. Uniformed police officers and Opera House security personnel moved with purpose through the auditorium. Weapons and bomb identification equipment were everywhere.

Lexi ran her gaze over the men searching each row of the large theater, the people milling about in the aisles, the choir still in rehearsal, and apparently—so far anyway—oblivious to what was going on beyond the lights onstage. No one moved quickly. No one was panicking.

She frowned. This was way too laid-back. Way too easy.

Dealing with tangos was never this clean and neat. She'd studied enough data to know that. Had their conclusion been wrong? They'd had the bar code on the guy's arm. No mistaking the longitude and latitude. That was all they had to work with. The Sydney Opera House was an international landmark . . . She saw the logic in the Opera House as the possible target, but the pieces didn't match. It was like looking at a jigsaw puzzle where the pieces all fit, but the images on top weren't lining up correctly. The picture just didn't make sense.

Evacuating a couple of hundred people in six hours was nothing. Yet her stomach and her gut told her not to dilly-dally. Lexi trusted her instincts. The same instincts had served her well as a kid. They'd warned her hours before her parents made a middle-of-the-night, one-step-ahead-of-the creditors run for it. That sixth sense had allowed her time to grab up a favorite toy, or article of clothing in the nick of time.

One part of her was sure that she and Alex and the team were in the wrong place at the wrong time. The other part of her wanted everyone out of the building ASAP because something unimaginable was about to go down. And why was Alex sticking her with Ginsberg when he knew they were having issues?

Was he trying to have them tough it out or put her in her place as a rookie? Perhaps the amazing, illicit sex in the early hours of the morning had fractured her brain, because none of it made sense.

"Got a problem, Stone?" Alex asked, shooting her an indecipherable look. He looked tall and grim as he addressed her. Like the rest of them, he was dressed in black, his weapon holstered in plain sight. At least the Glock was in plain sight. His other weapons were more discreet. And not all of them had been issued by T-FLAC.

They might both be all business, but having Alex's hot green gaze focused on her made Lexi vividly and viscerally remember where his hands, his mouth, and his penis, had been mere hours before. *Got a problem?* Hell yes. She did. But since she couldn't figure out what her problem *was,* she shook her head. Ginsberg was way ahead of her and close to the orchestra pit, while she was forty rows back trying to analyze her screwed-up instincts.

Focus, Stone.

"No problem. I'm gone." She hauled ass to follow the other operative, her steps accompanied by the young soloist singing the "Breton Fisherman's Prayer" up on the stage. Still oblivious to the activity around him, the boy's piercingly sweet treble soared over the voices and shouts in the enormous auditorium as he stood, eyes closed, completely transported by his music.

Taking the stairs two at a time, Lexi jogged down to the front of the theater. The afternoon performance wouldn't start for six hours. Logically, the tangos would have timed their strike for the sold-out evening performance when all two thousand, six hundred and seventy-nine seats would be filled. And that was just in this one theater. There were several more venues in the Opera House scheduled to hold evening performances that night. So potentially upward of five thousand theatergoers would be their target. That's when the frankenvirus could do its worst.

But that wasn't going to happen. There was plenty of time to evacuate everyone with time to spare. Plenty of time to cancel performances. Plenty of time to cordon off the streets and surrounding area. Plenty of time. And that was precisely what bothered her.

Tangos didn't do black-and-white, they did red all over. A hit here would grab worldwide attention, but not if everyone were evacuated. Tangos weren't above picking a secondary target if the primary was a bust. What if this was a decoy? What if the Trace they'd followed on the Halfs was just a planted trail to lead them astray?

What if Alex was wrong about the target? They didn't have sufficient intel to back this up definitively as the target. But orders were orders, and she was going by the book. Stone had ordered them here to do a cleanout. Not a bad idea, erring on the side of caution.

She'd do it, even if she had to do it with Ginsberg at her side. The notes of the child's voice faltered to a discordant halt as the stage was swarmed by uniformed security personnel. Lexi jumped up onto the apron, and started issuing instructions with the authority of a drill sergeant. Even the guards moved as she indicated where she wanted people to go.

Alex had given everyone their instructions on the ride over. There was no need to remind them to expect the unexpected. Lexi rubbed the tingle on the back of her neck as she reassured the members of the choir in passable Dansk that this was no more than a drill. Cool and calm, she still made sure she hurried people along.

She had a talent for languages. She'd learned Danish when Alex had been in Denmark on an op three years ago, so she could read the transcriptions of his reports, and the language had stuck. The fact that she'd learned a language because an operative had been posted there for several months was something she'd kept to herself. There was no need to have mastered the language while she'd been buried in the research department. It certainly hadn't been a part of her job description. Still, it came in handy here and now, halfway across the world in Australia.

Out of the corner of her eye, she watched Ginsberg as he pointed a group of adults and kids toward an exit. There was no reason to feel a shudder of revulsion travel up her spine. The fact that he didn't like women in the field, and her in particular, shouldn't bother her. And it didn't.

What bothered her was that he'd seemed pretty innocuous a couple of days ago. Now he . . . *wasn't*. He made the hair on the back of her neck rise. Every instinct she had said not to trust him. Yet he'd done no more than be rude, and not even particularly rude at that. She rubbed her temples, which were beginning to ache. And while she was casting stones, Lexi considered her own childish behavior in baiting the man.

Where the hell had that come from? He hadn't really annoyed

her enough for her to goad him as she'd done. Not only was it an overreaction, it was unprofessional. That entire exchange at the safe house, brief as it had been, was a bit odd. She needed to give it some thought when she had a moment, after she'd assessed Alex and made another report into IA. She was overdue reporting in as it was.

She absently rubbed her temples again, then turned away from Ruben Ginsberg's soulful black eyes to go back to herding kids. It took less than an hour and all non-security personnel had been removed, and the building secured. Lexi went to the front of the stage, shading her eyes, looking for Alex. Even though the house lights were up, she didn't see him, but Kiersted was about fifty rows back and happened to glance up. Lexi indicated she was going backstage to check for stragglers. There was sure to be some kid who'd just had to go to the bathroom. Kiersted nodded and went back to his study of some handheld device. She walked into the dimly lit hallway behind the main theater.

There wasn't anyone around backstage. Half an hour before, Lexi had ferreted three boys out of a bathroom down a long hallway, and she headed back down that way once more.

The sat phone at her hip vibrated, revealing a 411 code, meaning IA was calling. Lexi glanced around to make sure she was alone.

"Stone here."

Control answered. "Pass code?"

"Beacon." She waited for the affirmation.

"White." There was a pause as the control cleared the line so the call would not be monitored within T-FLAC except by the IA recorders. "All clear. The director is on the line."

"Your report is twelve hours late, Stone."

She turned and looked down the hallway as she answered. "Yes, sir. I'm still investigating the current mission. We've had some complications and I'm not certain Stone is the rogue. I need more time."

"Negative. We don't have more time. Whoever is leaking information is making T-FLAC look like a fucking triage patient with all their limbs blown off. That's how bad we're bleeding intel. I need answers and I need them now."

"I'll have a report to you by midnight."

"You better, Stone, or I'll pull you from the field and stick you in the filing room so fast it'll make your head spin." The call ended with an abrupt click. She winced. "Ass."

"Stone." The whisper came from directly over her head as she paced under a fly walk. Shit! She glanced up. Ruben Ginsberg stood in the shadows fifteen feet overhead.

She snapped off the sat phone. What exactly had he overheard?

"Come on down," Lexi told him, backing up a little so she could see him better. "We're heading out." As she spoke, she backed into the deep shadows near the wall. Whatever Ginsberg was up to, it wasn't good. She didn't trust him further than she could spit. And she couldn't spit that far.

Suddenly he was right *there,* so close she had to take a step back as he shimmered directly in front of her. "Busy taking orders from somebody other than Stone, bitch?" He smelled of nervous sweat and dust as he moved in. Lexi took another step back. He was almost on top of her. The meager light backstage suddenly glinted off the dull metal of the Ka-Bar in his hand.

Shit. Lexi reached for her weapon. It was gone. "What are you playing at, Ginsberg?"

"You annoy me, Stone. Annoy the fucking shit out of me. Especially when you're crawling off behind our backs, just waiting to take Stone down for IA." He waved the knife in front of her eyes.

"I'm sure I annoy a lot of people," she told him, forcing herself to speak evenly. "But they don't come at me with a knife." Her heartbeat was rapid enough to make her dizzy, and an alien panic was taking hold of her so that she was almost frozen in her tracks.

Lexi shook off the overwhelming feeling of pee-her-pants fear.

Focus, Stone. Her Sig Sauer was strapped to her ankle. He'd slice and dice her before she could free it from the holster. He had weapons, and he had his wizard powers. She had her wits, but she was too frightened to think rationally.

He's one man.

One trained, experienced operative with a terrifying look of determination in his black eyes as he stalked her closer and closer to the wall. He started tossing the large knife from hand to hand like some B-movie villain.

Back and forth. Back and forth.

She made herself maintain eye contact, but she could see every movement as the knife went from hand to hand. Hand to hand. Sweat stung her eyes as she felt the wall at her back.

"Are you threatening me?" Seeing movement out of the corner of her eye, she shot a quick glance at the two young men standing just beyond the dim lights. "In front of witnesses no less?"

"What witnesses?" Ginsberg sneered as the two guys disappeared into the shadows. "You're so certain your own shit doesn't stink that you're willing to take down a decent operative. You don't even realize what's going on with him, do you?"

Lexi tried inching along the wall, and instantly, faster than a normal human being could move, Ginsberg was in her face, nose to nose with her. He smiled. "I'm not going to let you fuck this up. And if he won't take care of your ass, I will." A demonic, unnatural smile that didn't reach his eyes twisted his face as he reached up and sliced her cheek. The knife was so sharp it took several seconds for her to feel the heat of it.

Strangely, it didn't hurt. She used the back of her hand to dash away the blood as a red wave of anger rolled through her like a noxious cloud pushing aside the fear as if it had never been. She'd never experienced anything like it.

Anger was bright blood red. A pulsing, blazing fiery crimson.

With a wild cry she struck back, knocking aside the hand holding the knife. They went down hard. She landed on top, straddling his chest. Forgetting every single lesson in hand-to-hand she'd learned and excelled at, Lexi punched, bit, kicked, heaved, and head-butted. Most of her defensive and offensive attacks hurt her more, she thought in the sane part of her mind, than they hurt him. But the fury rode her. She was too overwhelmingly furious, too blindly incensed and panicked to let the rational run the show.

Grabbing the short hair over his ears, she slammed his head down *hard* on the wood floor. Once. Twice. He bucked and heaved her off his body with a grunt, the knife, his whole arm, moving faster than she could see it. He straddled her this time, his considerable weight pinning down her legs, crushing her to the floor. Obsidian eyes gleamed with pleasure as he brought the Ka-Bar down.

She twisted, felt a hot slice on her upper arm. Again on her thigh. Didn't hurt and she didn't give a shit. He'd disposed of her LockOut. She was going to beat the son of a bitch senseless, then kill him with his own knife.

"What in holy hell is going on here?" Alex's voice. Ignoring his running steps, Lexi hauled back her fist and punched Ginsberg in the face, reveling in the crunch of bone and cartilage as his nose broke under her fist. Her heart soared with satisfaction. She tasted blood, and punched him again. This time he dodged and the blow landed on his bicep. He sliced her again, and her throat was on fire.

She barely heard Alex cursing. "Christ. Both of you. Stop right now. What the fuck's gotten into you?"

Lexi managed to shove Ginsberg farther down her legs. Far enough so that she could bring a knee up and strike him hard in the balls. He didn't make a sound. And even though she knew she'd put most of her weight behind the blow, he didn't even flinch. His eyes gleamed like malevolent onyx as he raised his arm, his meaty hand curled into a fist.

Alex teleported Lexi out from under Ginsberg seconds before

the other man's fist connected. His weapon was drawn and he slammed the muzzle of his Glock hard against Ginsberg's temple for emphasis. "I want an explanation, and I want it now. What the *fuck's* going on?"

Two things happened simultaneously. Ginsberg sliced out with the Ka-Bar, almost jettisoning the Glock from Alex's hand, and Lexi, enraged and bleeding, flew across the space separating her from her opponent. Launching herself onto him, she sent them both skittering across the floor in a tangle of arms and legs and flashing knife.

What the fuck?!

Puzzled and exasperated, Alex instantly removed Lexi, encasing her in a protective shield twelve feet away. He immobilized Ginsberg, one hand raised to stab Lexi, one foot braced against her attack, his expression a rigor of hatred.

Jesus.

He strode over to Lexi. Her eyes were wild, and blood dripped down her cheek. She had a bloody gash on her arm, another on her upper thigh and across her collarbone. Her face was filthy, and already starting to bruise. She looked ready to tear someone a new one. Alex had never seen a woman so completely enraged. "Want to explain yourself?"

She didn't spare him a glance. All her attention was on Ginsberg. Large gray eyes glittered dangerously, and her pretty mouth was held tightly as she bit out a terse, "No."

She was bleeding. Where the hell was her LockOut? "Bullshit, Lexi. This behavior is unconscionable."

"I'm going to kill him." She rose to her knees and rocked a little, resting on her hands.

"Apparently, he has the same agenda." Alex reached for the headset in his back pocket and attached it over his ear. He touched the control, keeping his attention on Lexi as she staggered to her feet and started pacing, testing the confines of her invisible prison with her balled fists. She was manic, feeling the air in a circle around her, trying to find a way out.

"Lu?" he said into the lip mic. "Kiersted? Backstage, my coordinates. We have a situation."

Lu arrived first. "What—" His gaze went from a pissed off, snarling, imprisoned Lexi, to a paralyzed Ginsberg. "Good God."

Kiersted materialized beside Alex, weapon drawn. He took in the situation with his usual equanimity. "Want me to shoot one or both?"

"Take Ginsberg back to the safe house. Find out what you can. Keep him in that state until we know what the hell went down here. Lu, find Daklin, fill him in. I want to make sure everything here is secure. But I have to get Lexi calmed down and cleaned up before I get her to tell me her version of events."

"Good luck with that," Kiersted said dryly, before teleporting himself and Ginsberg back to the safe house.

"Want me to hang around?" Lu asked.

"No. Find Daklin."

The man nodded, then paused, studying Lexi. "I wouldn't've taken her for a woman who'd lose her cool over nothing."

"Neither would I," Alex said, watching Lexi pace her confined space like a caged wild animal. Her eyes were glazed, her jaw rigid as she swore a blue streak; she seemed oblivious to her injuries. And oblivious to himself and Lu standing six feet away. This wasn't the woman he'd made love to. Alex didn't recognize this frenzied, wild-eyed woman in front of him.

"Ginsberg must've instigated this, given his earlier behavior, but I'm blown away that she reacted so violently." He was puzzled as hell. This entire bizarre situation didn't make any sense at all. "Usually she's got a pretty cool head."

"Yeah, well, I guess everyone has their breaking point." Lu shot Lexi a glance, then gave Alex a sympathetic look before teleporting to join Daklin.

As Alex approached the shield surrounding her, he glanced at his watch to see just how much time had passed since he'd last seen Lexi up on that stage, the lights shining on her blond hair like a tracker beam. Just over five minutes. Yet in that short amount of time she and Ginsberg had managed to leave each other bleeding, battered, and half dead.

Not what he'd expected when he'd absently sent them off in the same direction. Shit.

Face flushed, eyes snapping gray fire, Lexi pummeled the shield with her feet and fists, her beautiful features a rictus, contorted by fury. He'd never seen a woman so angry. A spark of fear coursed through him as he observed the tendons and nerves standing out beneath her skin. At this rate she'd have a damned heart attack if she didn't get her shit together.

"Take a deep breath and calm down so I—"

Suddenly he was standing outside on a curb in the brilliant sunshine. "—can . . ." he trailed off. Eyes narrowed, he took in his change of location. "What the fuck?" He was in a suburban neighborhood. Neat houses, kids riding their bikes. Sprinklers lazily arcing sparkling drops of water on lawns. He smelled freshly mown grass and cooking burgers. Heard a dog bark, music, kids laughing.

An orange-and-white school bus filled with children passed, leaving him in the wake of hot exhaust and the smell of diesel fuel. Alex's heart thumped as he looked around. Tried to figure out where he was. Why he was. Jesus . . . Just as rapidly he returned to the backstage area.

Now the light was dim, the air tainted by the scent of blood and dust.

On red alert, his fingers tightened on the trigger of the Glock as he scanned the backstage area. What the fuck?

Just himself and the imprisoned Lexi.

He shot another quick glance at his watch.

Barely two seconds had passed.

Had he imagined it? Something so freaking clear and vivid? Why here? Why now?

"...So I can see to those cuts," he finished the sentence as if he'd merely paused. Which he had. To take a fucking *field trip.*

One thing at a time.

Blood soaked, black and shiny, into the neckline of her T-shirt where Ginsberg had attempted to cut her throat. Christ. It looked deep, but if the man had sliced the carotid she'd have bled out by now. Bad, but not fatal. Scarlet dripped down her arm, and there was a large, wet patch on her left thigh. Alex hesitated as he debated sending her to T-FLAC's crack medical team in Montana or trying to patch her up here. Here and now was faster.

Decision made.

She threw her body hard against the shield. Hard enough to bounce. She came back at it in a frenzy. Already bleeding and bruised, she was going to break something if he didn't restrain her.

"Alexis! God damn it." He blew out his breath and consciously gentled his voice. "Honey, look at me. Ginsberg's gone. Lexi, do you hear me? Ginsberg's gone."

A second passed. Two. Her head swiveled toward the sound of his voice. She blinked, eyes glazed. "What?" Her voice sounded thick, almost drugged. Her fists opened, and her fingers splayed beseechingly, to slide down the invisible restraint separating them.

Alex released her and shot forward, catching her as her eyes rolled back to white, and she collapsed, a dead weight, into his arms. He lowered her to the floor, transferring her wounds to his own body. Jesus, it hurt like hell. How'd she been capable of standing with the kind of pain she'd been experiencing?

He'd had worse, and sucked up the sharp, familiar agony of three instant knife wounds slicing into him. Ignoring the pain, he materialized a first-aid kit and a large bottle of water. Since he now wore her injuries, cuts as well as all her bruises, he had only to wash away the blood on her skin, and see if there was anything he'd missed.

He heard the slide of a boot against the wood floor and glanced up. Two men stood watching. Great. They looked vaguely familiar. Twins, he thought absently, going back to tend Lexi when the young men didn't come forward and offer their help. People usually didn't want to get involved in a violent altercation. He didn't blame them.

As he rinsed the blood off her throat he realized just how scared—no, terrified he'd been when he'd realized she was out of control. What if he'd arrived too late?

Magical abilities aside, Ginsberg outweighed her by seventy-five pounds. Bad enough. But the male operative had twelve years more experience in the field than Lexi did. *And* the son of a bitch had a Ka-Bar. And speaking of weapons . . . Where were hers?

He did a visual search along her body. No weapons. He knew Lexi. She'd never leave home without strapping on every bit of firepower she might need. Not when she was working.

Ginsberg had magically stripped her of them, then come at her with a fucking fighting knife. As soon as Alex had assumed her injuries, the color had returned to her face, and the manic pulse at her throat slowed back to normal. But he didn't like that she was still unconscious. Maybe she had internal injuries? His heart leapt with fear. He tapped her cheek. "Wake up, honey."

"Hmm." Eyes closed, Lexi lazily rolled her face into his palm. He felt the flutter of her long lashes on his skin as she opened her eyes to look at him drowsily. "Hi."

"Hi," he returned dryly, scanning her eyes for serious injury. Heavy-lidded but her normal beautiful soft gray. "How're you feeling?"

"Still sleep—Oh my God, Alex!" She struggled to sit up, and he shifted to help her. Frowning, she gently touched his cheek with her cool fingertips. "He *hurt* you!"

"Who?" He realized what he must look like since blood still dripped sluggishly down his neck. He shrugged. He healed fast. In a matter of minutes there'd be no evidence that he'd taken her injuries onto himself. "No. Not m—" Alex's head shot up as Kiersted materialized a few feet away. "That bastard better be secure."

Lexi couldn't have inflicted nearly the amount of pain Alex was going to when he and Ginsberg came face-to-face again.

Kiersted ran his hand over his brush of white hair, his light eyes shadowed. "You are not going to be happy about this."

Alex pushed Lexi's bangs out of her eyes, magically eliminating a smear of blood in her hair. He narrowed his eyes, looked at the man over Lexi's head. "What now?"

"Ginsberg's dead."

"What the hell do you mean, he's *dead*? He was alive when you left with him five minutes ago."

The other man nodded. "Yeah. I was there. And during the teleport he ended up with his own fucking Ka-Bar lodged hilt-deep in his heart."

Eleven

Lexi paced the empty living room at the safe house. The men were still searching the Opera House. *She,* however, had been teleported back here, without even a see-you-later. Why, she had no freaking idea. Well, yes, she did. Guilt. She'd seen something she wasn't supposed to have seen, and now Alex didn't know what to do with her.

She was going to have to report him. Simple as that. But this situation wasn't freaking *simple* at all because she'd made a huge error in judgment by giving in to her needs instead of going by the book. Not going by the book had come up and bitten her in the ass. Again. But damn, it had been worth it.

Internal Affairs shouldn't have had to call her to ask for her report. Protocol dictated that she report in every twelve hours. She'd missed two reports flying hither and yon—she *was* on an active op. But that was no excuse.

Her job was to watch Alex for any suspicious behavior, and his behavior had just crossed the line from suspicious to criminal. Even she couldn't believe what her own eyes had witnessed.

Not midnight for her report.

Now.

But didn't he deserve the benefit of the doubt?

As her lover? Of course, he did.

As a fellow operative? No. He'd proven today that he was no longer playing for the T-FLAC team. Lexi couldn't imagine what had happened to make Alex switch sides.

Something profound . . .

Don't try to justify it, she warned herself. *Don't make excuses for him. That's not my job.* IA had given her the Golden Ticket to be a field operative. She wasn't about to screw up her first assignment because . . . because she'd been foolish enough to fall for the very man she was supposed to be watching.

No. Not fall for. She wasn't that stupid.

As much as she lo—*cared* about Alex, the security of T-FLAC was more important. Of course it was. Absolutely. If it came down to either her lover or the organization that kept the world safe . . .

No contest.

Except her heart ached, and dammit, Lexi wanted to talk to him. Hear his side of the story. Hear his rationale for his actions. Blasted man. Why did he have to go and have feet of clay? "And then the son of a bitch grounded me." Which stung. "Dammit to hell." She'd already tried the doors and the windows. They wouldn't budge. Magically sealed shut. She strode toward the fireplace in ground-eating strides. "Damn. Damn. *Now* what do I do?"

"About what?"

The unexpected sound of a female voice made Lexi jump, then spin around. An exotic-looking woman perched with one hip on the arm of the sofa, her boot-clad foot casually swinging. She smiled.

Lexi scowled, reaching for her Glock, then realized that Alex must've taken it before he teleported her back here. She wasn't in the mood to be friendly to some strange woman who looked as though she was part of a punk rock group.

"Who are you, and what do you want?" Wizard, Lexi realized, not feeling particularly warm and fuzzy toward wizards at the moment. She was fed up with wizards in general. And Alex in particular.

"Ooo. Touchy, are we?" There was a faint lilt to the words, and an annoying I-know-what-you-did-last-night twinkle in her eyes. In her early thirties, she was quite beautiful in a Black Irish, pierced and tattooed kind of way. Her long, curly black hair complemented her white skin and dark eyes. She was dressed in skintight leather— black again—from top to toe.

She wore no blouse under the formfitting waistcoat cut down to there. And those painted-on pants would give her a yeast infection for sure, Lexi thought, feeling catty because she didn't want to believe the woman actually *did* know what she'd been doing. Those FM boots must give her a nosebleed, they were so freaking high. And what was with the eyebrow and nose piercings, and the tattoos running up and down her milk-white arms? Did she really want to live with that crap defacing her body forever?

"I'm not touchy," she snapped.

"Mmmm. Now I wonder what could have gotten your wee knickers in a knot?" The other woman twisted a waist-length curl around her finger.

"That," Lexi said through her teeth, "is none of your damn business. If you flew in to meet up with a boyfriend, forget it. He's working." Didn't matter which of the men this sexy Goth princess was looking for. They were *all* damned well working. Except *her.*

The woman jumped lightly off the arm of the sofa. Despite the heels on her boots, she was a head shorter than Lexi. "I'm Lark."

"Great. Want to leave a message?" Holy shit. The thought occurred to her that this woman could feasibly be here to see *Alex*. Lexi's heart did a little hop and skip of annoyance. Of course she could be here to see any of the men. But Alex was the most obvious. He was the most intelligent, the best looking, and damn him, the sexiest member of the team. What woman wouldn't want him?

What woman would consider betraying the organization she worked for to keep her lover's secrets?

She narrowed her eyes as Lark bent over the coffee table to pour tea from a fat white teapot painted with purple pansies into a matching, gold-rimmed cup. The tea service, the plate of cookies, and the silver milk and sugar servers hadn't been there a second before.

The wizard straightened, holding out the translucent cup and saucer. "Tea?"

"I don't dr—" She paused as Lark raised a pierced eyebrow. "Sure." Lexi took the saucer, a little bemused.

"Oh, this outfit isn't suitable for tea, isn't suitable at all." Lark was suddenly wearing a flouncy, gossamer sheer, freaking baby-pink party dress. She'd kept the knee-high black boots. Pale pink feathers, woven into her long hair, wafted around her head like the snakes of Medusa as she moved.

Lexi sank into an easy chair with her unwanted tea. "The team is working," she told her visitor curtly. She had things to do and problems to resolve. And a report she didn't want to make to be made. She didn't believe in procrastination. Putting things off was a waste of time and counterproductive. She took a sip of the steaming tea and burned her tongue. She hated tea. It tasted like wet tree bark.

She set the cup and saucer on a nearby table. As much as she'd like to put off her report until midnight, she knew she had to call it in now. She had no choice.

"I'm not here to see the men. I'm here to hear your report,"

Lark told her, reaching out her hand. A cookie, on a doily-covered plate, materialized on her palm.

"Shortbread," she told Lexi, her teacup hovering within easy reach while she took a bite. She brushed away a crumb with a finger tipped in black nail polish and weighted with a heavy silver ring. Every finger on both hands bore at least one ring, most of them three or four. The woman apparently liked jewelry as much as she liked Goth makeup and the color black. "My fave. All right, then. Let's have it."

Lexi felt as though she'd fallen down the proverbial rabbit hole. "Have what?"

"Today, I'm representing the Wizard Council, darling. We work with T-FLAC's Internal Affairs division when it comes to the psi unit. Your report on Alexander Stone. Is he, or isn't he, a rogue operative?" Lark sipped her tea, waving the other hand in a circular "speak up" motion.

Lexi's mind went a mile a minute. She didn't doubt that Lark was who she said she was. But she found, despite her own pep talk, that she wasn't ready to report Alex's actions. Not yet. Not now.

"Untangle the emotion of it, lovey. Just tell me what you know. For example, why are you *here* when the rest of your team is at the Sydney Opera House, looking for the bad guys?"

"I don't have to call in until midnight." Lexi hated that she sounded as defensive as she felt. Not good. Relax. It's not as though the other woman could read minds . . . Her blood ran cold. Or could she?

The other woman tapped a short, black-lacquered fingernail against her cup. "What happened at the Opera House this morning?"

Shit shit shit. "I'm not sure."

"Yes, you are." The playful lady of the manor was gone. This woman, this *wizard,* wasn't dicking around. What did she know?

Lexi's palms felt damp. "I'm—Alex and Ruben Ginsberg got into a brawl backstage. I didn't see who started it. The end result was Stone stabbed Ginsberg."

"And killed him?"

Lexi bit her lip and nodded.

Lark's hair cascaded down her arm as she tilted her head. A flock of pink feathers floated in the air to drift to the floor. "You observed this?" She sipped her tea, watching Lexi over the gold rim of her cup.

Lexi felt sick to her stomach, remembering the two men circling each other backstage. Their faces contorted with anger, their Ka-Bar knives flashing as they feinted and parried. Why had Alex been so angry? She could have dealt with Ginsberg herself, he must've known that. "The fight? Yes." It had been brutal, and had terrified her. She'd known as soon as she'd come across the two men fighting that one of them would end up dead.

Lark put down her cup. "You'll file a written report, of course."

Lexi nodded. A lump in her throat made swallowing difficult. She felt the ridiculous, and nearly unfamiliar, urge to cry. Something she hadn't done since she was four and realized how damned useless it was. Keeping very still so that she didn't betray any of the turmoil she felt inside, she said quietly, "His actions must have been justified. He's not an impulsive or violent man."

"You know this about him, do you now?"

Lexi thought of the blood dripping down Alex's throat from Ginsberg's knife. The blood seeping into the fabric of his pants from the thigh wound. Even in such a short time he was bruised and battered. The fight had been brief and violent. "Yes. I *know* that about him. Whatever happened, I'm sure there was a valid reason for Stone's actions."

Pink feathers fluttered. "Hmm."

Lexi sipped the tea she didn't want to give her something to do.

It hadn't improved by getting cold. She put the cup down. "What's going to happen to him?"

Lark rose, the delicate layers and folds of her dress falling about her leather-clad ankles like rose petals. "Alex? This is a serious accusation, of course. We'll investigate it further. Ginsberg's body will be autopsied. Were there any other witnesses?"

"Y—No. Just me." She wasn't sure she'd recognize, or even *find* the two guys she'd seen briefly during the fight.

"Hmm." Lark murmured again, then disappeared.

Lexi stared at Lark's empty chair. "Hmm?! What the *hell* does *hmm* mean?"

"Fuck me," Daklin muttered after Kiersted repeated his story. They were meeting in the staff cafeteria of the theater where they'd had a quick lunch and discussed their options. "Impossible."

"No shit." Kiersted chugged his soda and lobbed the can across the room into the recycle bin. "First words out of my mouth when we materialized at the safe house."

Alex blew out a hard breath as he stood. "You're *sure*?"

"As death and taxes. Checked and *triple*-checked," Kiersted answered, as he, Lu, and Daklin rose as well. Lunch had been a quick sandwich and an unpleasant twist of a conversation.

Kiersted continued. "No mistaking it. Deader than a dodo. I teleported the body to HQ. Let *them* try to figure it out."

Alex started walking, and the men fell in with him. "Lexi didn't kill him. I was there for the end of it."

"*I* was there for the end of it, too," Kiersted reminded him as the doors swung closed behind them. "The dickhead was very much alive, although not kicking, at the time of teleport."

Ginsberg had been frozen, so, yeah, no kicking. And he hadn't goddamned stabbed *himself.* "I called in my report. They'll get back

when they know something." The whole fucking incident was illogical. Lexi out of control. Ginsberg dead. The vision. All of it
right in the fucking middle of an op.

If it wasn't so serious, he would have been amused. Because if
Lexi had been pissed at Ginsberg, it was nothing compared to how
pissed she must be right now cooling her jets at the safe house.

Alex pushed the thought of Lexi from his mind. She was at the
safe house because that's where he knew she was safest. And if that
made him sexist, he didn't give a flying fuck. He didn't ever, in this
lifetime, want to see her that badly hurt again. "Lu. Fill us in on the
school situation."

Alex was taking that extremely realistic visit/vision seriously.
Why he'd had the flash was still a mystery. But his gut said it was
important.

The other man took out a hand-drawn map of Sydney as they
walked. "You said the kids on the bus looked about ten or twelve,
right? So a primary school. That eliminates half the schools in the
area. The uniforms eliminated the government schools. These—
this one, this one, and these three are intercity schools. You said
suburban. This here might be the one—"

Alex tried to read the scrawl. "Jesus. Where'd you learn to write?
Give me some street names, let's see if I picked up any more than
images." Alex scanned the short list of schools and their addresses.
"That's it. Kilgetty Points Public School." He felt a rush of anticipation. "Daklin? Stay or go?"

Daklin met his gaze. "Go. Locals have this covered. My gut tells
me this isn't the target."

"What about Stone?" Lu asked casually. "She's got every right to
expect to be with us on this all the way."

Alex didn't needed reminding. "She was out of control."

Kiersted considered it for a moment. "An anomaly. Something
Ginsberg did might have aggravated her? Don't know. But she's a
member of the team, and as such, she belongs with us."

Alex wanted her with him. And the men were right. Lexi belonged with the group. "I'll go get her." He turned Lu's map right side up. "Meet you here in this park in ten. Stick together, and for God's sake—if anyone else suddenly starts behaving out of character, freeze and assess for possible instant teleportation to HQ."

There was a first time for everything. This was the first time Lexi had ever been invisible. It was pretty damned cool, really. Sure, she was still pissed off at Alex, but he got points for bringing her back in on the op. And double brownie points for letting her experience invisibility. She had a little vertigo from the teleport, but other than that she felt great. The five of them stood across the street from the single-story Kilgetty Points Public School building.

"Too quiet," Alex said softly into his lip mic and directly into her ear. He stood right beside her, and she felt the heat of his body against her bare arm. When he'd come to get her at the safe house he'd offered no explanation for his earlier behavior. He'd waited while she went to her room to get her backup Sig, offering no freaking explanation for not returning her Glock either. She wanted her weapon back. Both had been handcrafted especially for her.

She'd strapped her Ka-Bar into a shoulder harness, a small fighting knife to her ankle, holstered the Sig, and then gone back to give him a belligerent glare before he'd teleported them to join the team. The knife wounds he'd sustained in his altercation with Ginsberg were practically gone. Just a few thin red lines to indicate the other man had tried to cut his throat.

Alex could have died on that stage. Died and not known how she felt . . . *God, Alexis. Get a freaking grip. Working here!*

Lexi scanned the unnaturally quiet surroundings, opening all her senses. Pretty. Clean. The school was on one side of the street, the park surrounded by modest homes on the other. The lawns were all well manicured, flowerbeds well tended. She'd gone to a similar school, and lived in a similar neighborhood when she'd been eleven. Carson City, Nevada. Her parents had opened a T-shirt shop there.

The house had been a rental, and they'd only managed to pay the rent for five months before the shop went belly-up and they'd skipped town. But she'd enjoyed the community, and loved the teacher.

Forget the trip down memory lane, Stone. Look for clues. Anything. It was an advantage that they could see and not be seen. There was definitely something off here.

"Too quiet," he muttered again.

Alex was right. It *was* too quiet. The end-of-school bell had rung seconds after their arrival six point nine minutes before.

But no children burst through the double red front doors to fill the line of small school buses, or dashed out to catch their rides. On either side of the wide, tree-lined street, mothers and a few fathers waited in their air-conditioned vehicles for the kids to come out.

"No birds singing," Lexi observed. The silence was unnatural, eerie. The sun beat down from a cloudless blue sky, and the heat shimmered in waves on the street. A light breeze ruffled the tree-tops, but nothing else moved.

Someone honked their horn. It almost sounded like a bullhorn in a vacuum, it was so still.

Alex's voice rumbled again. "We're going in. Stay together at all times. On my coordinates, and my three. One—Shit. Open channel."

"Intel intercepted a 000 text message call, forwarded to the local PD by a Telstra Operator." Ellicott's businesslike voice sounded directly in Lexi's ear. "Tangos are holding children at the Kilgetty p—"

"We're outside," Alex informed her quietly.

"How—Never mind." The Control's voice evened out the slighted blip of surprise. "The text message was transmitted by Davi

Wislin, a thirteen-year-old student inside the building, and being held in the gymnasium with the rest of the hostages. According to school records, three hundred and eight students attended school today. Thirty-four teachers and assorted staff. They've never taken children hostage before this. But these are *definitely* our bar-coded tangos."

"Demands?" Alex asked.

Didn't matter, of course. Because no matter what the demands, they didn't really seem to want what they asked for. And like their Control, Lexi wanted to know just how Alex had known to come to an out-of-the-way suburban school, instead of concentrating on the Sydney Opera House. She wasn't a big believer in coincidence. And this was a stretch by any definition.

Dammit, Alex. What the hell are you up to?

"Eighty-seven jihadists are to be freed from the Lithgow maximum-security Correctional Centre, SuperMax wing. Eleven hours fifty-one minutes is our deadline."

"They won't wait that long."

"No," Ellicott told Alex, her voice crisp. "They won't."

"Are the jihadists even there?" Daklin wanted to know.

"Not anymore," Ellicott assured them. "How many people do you need to clear collateral?"

"Couple dozen smooth talkers. Make it fast," Alex snarled. The line went dead. He gave the team a few terse instructions, then started the countdown to shimmer inside the building.

Alex didn't know what the hell was going on, but he felt like Superman on steroids. All his senses were preternaturally sharp. He'd felt it to some extent outside, but the second they'd shimmered into the school building itself, his powers felt supersized. His vision alone was unbelievable. Walking down the wide corridors flanked by blue-painted lockers, he clearly saw a trail of ants three hundred feet away. Saw the ants *and* their antennae. Saw their *mandibles,* for Christ's sake. And he heard . . . he would have heard Lexi's breath as she walked beside him anyway, but now he could hear her bones and muscles shift as she walked. He heard Daklin and the others' hearts, beating at different rates. Heard his own steady beat, and the sibilant rush of his blood through his veins.

One minute he was walking with the others down the hall, the next he was inside the crowded gymnasium. The gymnasium did a slow spin on its axis, and Alex staggered to regain his equilibrium.

Just as he'd seen the street and the bus, he was right in the middle of the action. There, but not.

This time, despite the vertigo, and a disconcerting multiple viewpoint that made it hard to adjust his focus, he managed to use the tetrabyte image-capture implant to transmit images to HQ. He might not be able to bring everything clearly into focus, but the image-capture system was three hundred times faster than the human eye. The tangos, dressed in black, held their weapons in their left hands. Same guys. Same uniforms, same weapons, same damned bar codes on the left wrists.

School personnel stood in front of the kids, forming a human barricade. Not that it was going to do them a damned bit of good.

The collective roar caused by the *thump-thump-thump* of hundreds of rapid heartbeats echoed in Alex's ears, almost deafening him. The fear coming off the hostages was palpable, and he felt the tangos feeding off that negative energy.

As if he were inside their heads, Alex knew without a shadow of doubt that they had no intention of killing anyone. Not today. Today they were going to unleash the lethal coronavirus LZ17. Then let the hostages walk away.

No one would be aware that they'd been infected as they rapidly carried the deadly, highly contagious virus out into their community. Impossible to detect, it would be seven hours before anyone presented with the horrific symptoms and it would be too late to treat. Seven hours or less could mean several thousand deaths, multiplied with several more thousands that each of those people infected as children went to sports practice, families went out to dinner, bus drivers went to other schools and picked up more children in their infected buses, parents went to work or got on airplanes.

Literally within twenty-four hours, the entire continent, hell, possibly several, would be infected.

He touched his comm link. "Report," he said barely above a whisper. But he knew no one on his team would answer. He was talking to dead air.

Twelve

Alex was no longer walking with them. How Lexi knew, since they were all invisible, she wasn't sure. She just did. That Alex-dar thing again, she supposed. Dammit, where had he gone? Why had he gone? And why the hell hadn't he notified the rest of the team that he was taking a little freaking side trip?

Section five on Operation Protocol, subsection C on International Unfriendly Ops, paragraph four on Reporting Protocol clearly stated that team leaders were responsible to make their location known to team members at all times for reporting and organization of strategy during the execution of an operation.

If this wasn't a blatant breach of T-FLAC code, then she was a damn wizard.

Did the others know that he'd split? Torn, Lexi was painfully aware that if they *didn't,* and *she* didn't report it, she was an accessory after the fact. She hated being a snitch. *Hated* hated it. But the main reason she'd been assigned to his team in the first place was to watch him. Not easy when he was not only invisible, but AWOL as well.

She'd just been so happy, finally, to be on a field op. The idea of reporting his behavior hadn't bothered her in the least when she'd first been assigned. Okay, it had only bothered her a *little*. Now, it bothered her a great deal. She liked him as a person. She admired him as an operative. And God help her, she'd fallen more than halfway in love with the man without even realizing it.

She tried to reason with herself; he'd probably had a valid reason for taking a detour. But . . .

A team *leader*? Disappearing without notifying his team? It just wasn't done.

Damn you, Alex, where the hell are you? How long did she dare wait before alerting the others to his absence? A few minutes at most.

Silence echoed ominously in the hallway as the team, minus one, walked rapidly and quietly toward the double doors of the gymnasium straight ahead. The hallways smelled of sweat socks, chalk dust and bubblegum. It smelled, Lexi thought, like every school she'd attended over the years. Nice to know even halfway around the world, things hadn't changed much.

And on this team, like all of those schools, she was the new girl. Slightly out of sync with the rest of her peers. Just like now. Reporting Alex, when he might have a valid reason for leaving them, wouldn't endear her to the other members of the team.

I'm not here to make friends. I'm here to do my job. Yeah? Well then I shouldn't have had sex, no matter how spectacular, with the man I'm spying on, now should I?

Had Alex gone on to reconnoiter with the intention of reporting back? Had something gone wrong, preventing him from communicating?

The possibility bought him a two-minute reprieve.

Come on. Come on. Come on!

His instructions were clear. She and Daklin were to secure the perimeter, covering the others. He, Lu, and Kiersted would shimmer the hostages outside in batches of fifty, starting unobtrusively from the back. If these tangos were indeed like the ones in Taipei, London, and Russia, then one shot and they'd turn to dust. Creepy, but expedient.

Lexi's fingers tightened on the butt of her weapon. The SIG P220 Carry Elite was her backup weapon, but it came a close second to her Glock. She would've liked *seeing* the damn thing as well as feeling it. Invisibility hadn't been taught in any of her damned classes. Stealth, yes. Furtiveness, absolutely. Hell, *sneakiness* was practically a requirement. But while being cool, *invisibility* felt a little like cheating to her.

Had two minutes passed?

Hard to read a freaking *invisible* watch.

There was another set of double doors to the right, and twenty feet up ahead. When they reached those doors, she was going to alert the team that Alex wasn't with them.

Seventeen.

Fourteen.

Alex, get your butt back here!

Elev—

Fucking hell. Lexi? Alex's voice sounded inside her head.

She touched the comm link. "Where are you?"

"Who are you talking to?" Kiersted asked quietly in her ear.

"Al—" Had she imagined hearing Alex's voice? It had sounded so clear. "Just muttering to myself. Sorry." It was almost as if . . .

She took a deep breath and thought hard. *Alex?*

Lexi?!

Are you in my head? she asked incredulously, her footsteps slowing.

Apparently so. Have Kiersted teleport. Me. Your coordinates. ASAP!

For the first nanosecond Lexi was just relieved to hear the sound of his voice, even inside her head. Then she heard the tone. Not good. He was alive. And he was reporting in. But he sounded—*shaken.* Very un-Alex-like.

"Kiersted. Teleport Alex to our coordinates ASAP."

"Not until he sa—"

"Now!"

Several seconds passed with the open connection a sibilant sound in her ear. "No can do." Kiersted told her. Or told Alex. Was it possible the others had known he wasn't with them? Some sort of wizard nonverbal communication? No one seemed surprised that Alex needed to be teleported to their location.

Except her.

Wait a minute . . . No can do? Lexi's heart went into overdrive, and her steps slowed. *What? What? What?* What was *that* about? Kiersted couldn't bring Alex from wherever he was to where the rest of the team was? Why the hell not?

"Lu?" This time Alex's voice was in her ear, not in her head. He sounded calm. But almost too calm. Yet underlying that composure ran a thread of—God. *What?* Fear? Horror? Adrenaline surged through her system. She wanted Kiersted and Lu to hurry the hell up and get Alex back into the brightly lit hallway where she could see and touch him and assure herself that he was okay.

"Working on it, boss."

"If this doesn't fly, contact HQ," Alex told him tersely. "Whatever works. Do it *now,* God damn i—"

And he was back with them. His reentry right beside her, while invisible, wasn't exactly textbook perfect or silent. But Lexi shot out her free hand, wrapping her fingers around whatever part she could reach. It happened to be his rock-hard forearm. Even though she couldn't see him, he felt warm and solid, and *there.*

She squeezed her eyes shut, stunned to feel moisture on her lashes. How foolishly girly of her. Thank God she was invisible.

"In here." Alex pushed open the double door, which led into a cafeteria. Chairs had been placed upside down on tables, and a strong smell of disinfectant and pizza lingered in the air. "Keep up your shields, but we need face time."

They all materialized. It was extremely surreal. Lexi took a step away from Alex even though she wanted to curl around his body like an exotic dancer around her pole. She wanted to wrap him around her and cover herself in his heat. She wanted to run her hands over his body to make sure he was all right.

Instead, like the others, she lowered her weapon and waited for his explanation.

The color was leached out of his face, the skin over his cheekbones drawn tight. He ran a hand over pine-black eyes, then pinched the bridge of his nose. "In some inexplicable way, I'm connected to these tangos. I don't know how or why, or to what extent. But there's a connection that's fucking with my powers.

"That said, we have to get the hostages out of here ASAP. The streets have been cordoned off in a five mile radius. All the homes in the area have been evacuated, and hysterical family members are swarming the barricades out there. Not to mention the press, medevac choppers, and EMTs are out there in fucking droves. This situation has become a media circus and needs to be contained. *Fast.*"

"Five miles isn't going to be far enough if they detonate the LZ17," Daklin pointed out grimly.

"No shit. Here, look." Alex materialized a handheld device and stylus and sketched out with Xs where everyone was located. Lexi moved closer with the others.

"Three LZ17 canisters right here." Alex pointed to the left of the tangos' location. "First thing we do is get those teleported out of there. I tried, but they have a protection field so tight around them I couldn't even teleport the coronavirus out of the containers, and replace the liquid with water to avoid detection to buy us some time. Do one or the other. I don't care. But that shit has to be out of there before we go in guns blazing."

Lexi's heart raced. A few drops of LZ17 would be enough to infect everyone present. "Three canisters—whatever the size—seems like overkill. What are they planning to do? Take out Sydney in its entirety from here?"

"Good question," Alex said grimly. "Let's not have to find out."

Lexi read the strain on his face, and noticed the sheen of perspiration on his skin that shouldn't have been there. What had he seen inside that gymnasium that caused him to be—what? Scared? Nervous? Oh, God. *Guilty*?

Lexi didn't know. And while the operative spying for IA wanted to know, the *woman* in her wanted to fling her arms around him and assure him that everything was going to be all right.

Her hand "accidentally" brushed his as she tipped the screen he held. I'm here. *I'm with you, no matter what.* His skin was cold and a little clammy. Scared? Alex? No way. She dropped her hand, shoving it into the front pocket of her pants. Right now her job was to listen, and follow his instructions. Later . . .

"I don't have to remind you that the hostages for the most part are kids. Make every target count. And have eyes in the back of your heads in case one of these kids decides to play hero."

Alex tapped the screen, indicating the west side of the gymnasium. "Daklin, go round to this location. Come in from their flank. Counting down ninety seconds. Kiersted?" He nodded to the two men, and Daklin disappeared, teleported to his location by the wizard.

"Stone, with me. Lu, get that shit out of there by any means possible. Kiersted, start teleporting the hostages." He stabbed the stylus at his crude diagram. The data was being transmitted to HQ in Montana in real time, Lexi knew.

"Here, here, here, and here. The kids are in back, adults here, and here." His rapid-fire hail of orders paused and pale or not, he speared them with a glance. "Move fast, move efficiently. The tangos will notice, but we'll get everyone clear if we move. I want a handful of the bastards for identification and interrogation. Don't give a crap what condition they're in as long as we bag more than dust. Fifty-eight seconds and counting. *Go.*"

That left the two of them standing in the middle of the large cafeteria. Sunlight streamed through the bank of windows on her right, casting large white squares on the speckled linoleum floor. The faint *whop-whop-whop* of a chopper circling overhead mixed with the vibration of the idling engines of heavy vehicles in the distance.

The piercing scream of a distressed parent being forced to wait a long distance away from her endangered child cut through the general rumbles of conversation. Lexi could almost feel the waves of fear and panic pulsating off the crowds waiting outside. She blocked out everything but Alex. Damn, but he looked grim. Oh, man. His expression didn't bode well.

He was going to make her stay right there. Out of the line of fire. Out of the way of the bad guys. Dark green eyes searched her face as if looking for answers. The answer was: She was *not* sitting in here waiting for the men to kill off the bad guys! "Alex—"

He put up his hand to stop her. "Do me a favor. Please, Lexi." He briefly brushed her cheek with his fingertips before dropping his hand.

Please? She blinked. "Of course." Other than stand back while her team dealt with a situation she was trained for. Sure.

"If I act contrary to the way you'd expect me to behave— Terminate me."

"Alex, I've—" She literally did a double take, her protest dying. "What?!"

"Shoot to kill. Don't hesitate. Don't second-guess."

"I—"

"Your word." His eyes bored into her.

Lexi gave her word, and prayed as she'd never done in her life that she wouldn't have to keep it.

Alex was once again capable of teleporting both himself and others—at least for now. The second he and Lexi came through those double doors into the gym, he was aware Lu hadn't gotten the fucking lethal canisters out of there, and gave it another shot himself. Nada.

He knew Kiersted and Lu would continue trying, as would he. Knowing Daklin, he'd give *carrying* the containers out a shot if he saw magic didn't work. Whatever it took.

Were the damned things scheduled to detonate at a certain time? How *much* time did they have before they blew? Minutes? Seconds?

Since there'd be no indication the gas had been released it was impossible to know. Not until people presented with the horrific symptoms hours later, and it was too late to treat.

They'd know soon enough.

Returning to the gym brought back the splitting headache full strength. He did his best to block the pain. Making the most of his amplified powers, Alex shimmered eighty kids out of the gymnasium to safety.

Blocking out the sound of hundreds of terrified children screaming and crying, he and his team made damned sure the destruction of the tangos was swift and efficient. A delicate task because of the children involved, and the fact that bullets had a tendency to travel farther than their intended target. He didn't want any collateral damage today.

Invisible once more, Lexi and Daklin moved through the room behind the black-clad men, firing as they advanced. Kiersted and

Lu respectively maintained the two non-wizards' invisibility and protective shields. Alex didn't trust his own powers to keep her— *them* safe.

He charted their progress by the drifts of black dust left in their wake on the scuffed, bullet-ridden wood floor.

The terrorists seemed oblivious to their dwindling number. They remained oddly calm, almost impassive as they used the threat of their semiautomatics to hold their hostages in a tight knot in a corner at the far end of the room. Their movements were eerily choreographed as they moved as one, shifting from one foot to the other like a menacing black-clad boy band, all carrying MAC-10s left-handed.

Alex used the tetrabyte image-capture feature on the headset to transmit more images to HQ for rapid identification; more images of the bar codes on their forearms would net them more intel. More intel would lead to anticipating where these sons of bitches would go next.

There would be a next. There was always a next.

A dozen of their number turned away from the rest, in perfect precision, returning submachine fire in a barrage of bullets that destroyed the polished gymnasium floors and left gaping holes in the walls. The children's screams turned into shrieks of hysteria as they pressed closer to one another, closer to the floor. The flying bullets pinned them in place as effectively as prison bars.

The situation was controlled mayhem with frightened children trying to break free of the restricted corner, and their attending adults trying to stem their fear while dealing with their own. The problem was magnified because they couldn't see Alex and his team. All they saw were their menacing captors and bullets flying. And the tangos turning to dust.

There was no way to calm the fears of the hostages without revealing T-FLAC's presence and exact locations to the tangos. For now, the team stayed invisible.

As the three wizards worked, shimmering the hostages to safety, they, too, kept up a hail of bullets, keeping the tangos distracted and at bay.

The pain in Alex's head was almost unbearable, and his vision blurred and refocused with every throb. It was as if he were looking out of two different strength prescriptive lenses. Each eye was feeding his brain different images and there was a persistent, and annoying, buzz going on inside his skull. He closed his right eye. His point of view was twenty feet away from where he stood and he knew if he were visible he'd be looking right at himself. He shut his left and opened the right. Thank God that view seemed to be correct.

Materializing an eye patch to block his vision in the left eye didn't help the damned headache any, but at least he could freaking *see*. Alex used Temporal Acceleration to move through the room at lightning speed, picking off tangos, and teleporting as many people as he could snare at the same time.

It had probably seemed like hours to the hostages, but the entire op took less than two minutes start to finish. There were a few seconds when all the hostages were gone, leaving fifty or so tangos standing about with their dicks in their hands. But before any of his team could rush in to apprehend any of them, there was a flurry of black dust as the men disintegrated as one.

The instant they were gone, his headache disappeared. The knowledge that the two were connected made his heart race. Dread all but choked him.

"Shit."

Not one—*not one*—tango was left to question. How the hell did they move so fast? Faster than Temporal Acceleration. Almost faster than the eye could see. Who or what were they? And what did their collective disappearance mean? Had they all teleported out? Were they all dead? At the same freaking time? He had more damned questions than answers.

The three canisters sitting in the middle of the floor suddenly disappeared.

"Tell me that was us," he demanded into his lip mic.

"I live to serve," Kiersted responded. "Secured at HQ."

"Good man." Materializing, Alex looked around the empty gymnasium as he spoke into his comm link to notify the people outside. "All clear. No prisoners." Just small mounds of black dust to show they'd even been there. "Collateral damage?"

He listened to the report from the local T-FLAC personnel outside as his team materialized. Two nonfatal bullet wounds, scrapes and cuts. Mostly the three hundred plus hostages were being treated for emotional trauma. They'd be held in quarantine for twenty-four hours for testing for the virus, then released to their families.

It could've been a hell of a lot worse.

With a thought he magically inserted each pile of dust into individual, sealed baggies and teleported all of them to the lab in Montana. Someone better have some answers for him soon. Alex could practically hear the stopwatch ticking a fucking countdown in his brain. To what, he had no damned idea. But whatever it was wasn't waiting while they tried to figure it out. Enough people had died.

His team faced toward the center of the gym from their various positions in the large space, but Alex's attention was on Lexi. She glistened with sweat, her face streaked with dirt. She was the best thing he'd seen in—God. Ever. She appeared to be in one piece, her long legs eating up the distance between them, her eyes holding his as she got closer.

Are you okay?

Her eyes widened, clearly startled by his voice in her head again. *Yes. You?*

I'm good. Amazing. He'd *never* had a telepathic connection with another living soul besides his sister, Victoria, yet he heard Lexi's thoughts as if she were speaking out loud. When it had happened earlier he'd been startled as hell. With Lexi, it was a far more intimate process than it had been with Victoria. Victoria had learned to block his intrusion by the time they were eight. Lexi's mind was open and intriguingly complex.

Her lips tilted. *All you need is . . .* ". . . A parrot," she finished aloud. Her hair stuck to her damp face and neck and stood up in golden spikes where she'd obviously run her fingers through it. She looked sexy as hell. Focused. His heart did a somersault in his chest.

Daklin gave them both an odd look. "A parrot? What—oh. Yeah. What's with the patch?"

Alex imagined the patch gone. Checked his vision without it. Clear as crystal. "I'll explain later." *Right after I figure it out.* "Any injuries?"

"Negative." Kiersted holstered his weapons, looking around. He whistled.

The far wall where the students and teachers had been clustered was littered with kid paraphernalia; book bags, papers, gym equipment, etc. Alex did a sweep, shimmering everything outside to where authorities were now interviewing the hostages before sending them to quarantine. One of them used a bullhorn to reassure the families that their children were unharmed.

The press and people eagerly waiting for information would be soothed and given additional details by local T-FLAC personnel. Alex and his team were done here.

"Debriefing at the safe house in two minutes," he told them. "Stone. With me." The men shimmered, leaving them alone.

"Do you want me to—"

"No." He combed his fingers through her damp hair. Mental fireworks. A swirl of heat.

Lexi wrapped her arms about his waist, drawing him against her soft, lush body. She smelled of honey and hard physical labor, a little like gun oil, a lot like the woman he—A lot like Lexi. The scent of her, the taste of her turned Alex inside out, making his brain spin and his heart race.

Want me.

I do.

His pulse leapt as he bent his head and touched his mouth to hers. Lexi's tongue greeted him. He tasted her hunger and the smile curving her soft mouth, and welcomed the slick sweep of her tongue tangling with his.

A furnace of heat spiraled through him, making him wish they were anywhere but where they were.

Her hands fisted the back of his shirt as they kissed. She was panting slightly as their mouths broke apart. "We have to meet the others back at the safe house in—" She shot a glance at the large clock on the far wall. "One point seven minutes, but before we do—" She broke off as he nibbled the plump lobe of her ear. The rumble he made told her he was enjoying her shudder of pleasure.

"I want to t—" she tilted her head to give him better access to the curve of her jaw. "This physicality between us *has* to stop." She nipped at his lower lip as he trailed his lips across her cheek and back to her mouth.

"No, I mean it, Alex. First of all, Section whatever of whatever clearly states—whatever it states about fraternizing."

He made a noise that sounded like agreement as he continued his exploration of her neck.

"Second—Stop tha—Okay, just *one* more." She kissed him back hungrily, the fingers of one hand somehow entwined in his hair, her other hand, fingers spread, on the cheek of his ass. It was several seconds before she pulled away again. "I have to tell you something important." She placed her palm across his marauding mouth to prevent him swooping in for another drugging kiss. "Internal Affairs sent me to keep an eye on you," she finished quickly, waiting for his reaction, knowing it was going to hurt.

He kissed her salty palm. "Ah."

Her jaw dropped and she leaned away from him. "Ah? That's it?"

"Lexi. If it has to be anyone, I'm damned glad it's you."

That took her aback. Her eyes narrowed. "You are?"

"Hell, yes. I don't know what's been going on lately, but if I *am* going rogue, I trust you to be my moral compass, and to terminate me if necessary." He stroked a hand up her slender back, tugging her closer. "I asked you to do so earlier, and I meant it. I trust you to do the job."

"I—Wait a minute." She used both palms to shove at his chest. "What do you mean *if* you're going rogue? Don't you *know*?"

Thirteen

"No. I don't. And let's get back with the others. I have to fill them in on this, and I only want to say it once."

"Wait. I w—Honest to God," Lexi said crossly, grabbing his arm for balance as they materialized back at the safe house. She was almost used to this ridiculous mode of transportation. Almost. It wasn't even bad if one discounted the vertigo and slight nausea that traveling in utter defiance of the laws of physics caused. "I should shoot you for doing that without notice." Her stomach rolled.

"No friendly fire while I'm eating," Lu deadpanned, glancing up at their entry. He had the remnants of a large steak on the plate floating two feet off the floor in front of his chair. He materialized a bottle of ketchup and poured a dollop on top.

Lexi shuddered. "Sacrilege." Ketchup on a perfectly good steak?

Her stomach reacted to the sight and smell of food by growling loudly. She shrugged unapologetically as both men looked at her, brows raised.

"The coronavirus arrived safely at the lab," Daklin informed them as he passed through the room from the kitchen. He carried an oversized mug and a plate with several enormous sandwiches on it. The time of day didn't matter. Downtime, no matter how short, no matter when, was used for refueling, both food and sleep.

"Top priority," he continued, as he crossed the room to find a seat. "They're working round the clock to ID the manufacturer of the components now. Maybe they can get a hit on that while we're dicking around."

Lexi gazed longingly at his cup and plate.

"Lu's coffee's strong enough to strip paint, but it's hot." Daklin slouched in the chair Lark had perched on earlier, setting the mug on its wide arm. He rested the plate on his flat belly, and picked up one of his sandwiches. Lexi's stomach rumbled again.

"And they're sorting through baggies of evil tango dust as we speak." He took a bite, chewing methodically. Cold cuts, Lexi saw. Slabs of dark bread. Mustard. Like Daklin, she was on her own as far as food went. No magical room service for her. She was too tired to go and forage, but her salivary glands were urging her to get off her butt and go find something to eat.

Before Daklin finished the ham slices.

Across the room at the dining table, Kiersted typed on a holographic keyboard with one hand, and drank from his glass. Milk, Lexi noticed. Her stomach gurgled. Did she have time before the briefing to make herself something—

What kind of sandwich would you like? Alex's lips twitched slightly. Had she really been irritated with him and his magical self?

Grilled cheese. American. Two, on white. And Campbell's tomato soup. Are you going to make it for m—"Oh." *Six,* not two, hot, greasy, angle-cut sandwiches and a steaming blue mug, all on a large Spode plate, materialized in his hand. Lexi shot him a grateful smile as she took her meal from him.

"Thanks." Talk about fast food. Her mouth watered as she weaved her way between the furniture to the far end of the sofa.

"They've already identified some aspects of the dustlike substance," Kiersted tapped on a second screen, pulling up the report as Daklin inhaled his meal. "There's definitely human DNA in all of it. But these things don't appear to have blood per se. Powdered blood? Clear liquid, plasma? They should have a more extensive report back to us shortly.

"As for the coronavirus, it's a completely new strain of LZ17 but still has the same basic viral signature, it's just more virulent, lasting longer so that it can infect more people via casual contact. We compared the base viral signature against components gathered from various European locations. But there's no doubt that the viruses released in Africa, London, Moscow, and Taipei, and the one found here are all from the same manufacturer."

"What about the kids who sustained bullet wounds?" Alex asked, coming to sit on the arm of the sofa behind Lexi. He reached over her shoulder, snagged half a sandwich, and dipped it into her soup.

"One will be released later today," Lu told him. "Released into quarantine with the others, but out of ICU. The second kid's in surgery. Prognosis good."

"Anything else?" Alex asked. Lexi felt the heat of his body as he sat directly behind her.

"Not right now." Lu gestured to Alex with his fork. "Want to tell us what that was about earlier?"

Good question. Lexi leaned in a little as Alex's legs brushed against her arm when she shifted, reaching for another deliciously greasy triangle. Fortunately, stress had never affected her ability to eat. A good thing, because this whole business with Alex—all of it—was enough to turn a lesser woman off her feed.

How could she regret having sex with him? She couldn't. She didn't. The experience had profoundly shaken her.

Her feelings for this man went far beyond what she'd thought was a crush coupled with some serious hero worship. How could she have such strong feelings when she was halfway to reporting his actions to IA?

"As I told you, three weeks ago I started intermittently losing my powers," Alex told them. His voice, deep and steady, did something strange to Lexi's entire body. His voice seemed to stroke her skin almost physically. She vigorously wiped her hands on the paper towel he'd given her when he'd handed her the plate.

Do not fall in love with him.

She froze, paper towel in hand.

Oh, shit. Too late.

Lexi turned to see if he'd somehow read her mind again. It was one thing to take a meal order, and a whole other thing to telepathically hear her newest, most intimate freaking secret.

He didn't appear to have heard her girlish heart going pitter-patter. He just sat there, looking grim and focused. "Up until a few days ago I thought it might be some kind of cold or flu, but now I don't think so."

"What do you think it is?" Daklin asked, biting down on a pickle.

"Wish to hell I knew." Alex absently rested his hand on Lexi's shoulder, and the heat of his palm seemed like a brand burning through her clothing. "First, my powers. Then this thing with Lexi and Ruben Ginsberg at the Opera House—"

Lu glanced at Lexi. "You and Ginsberg got into a thing?"

Since Alex was the one laying things out on the table, Lexi felt a tremendous sense of relief that she wasn't the one who had to blow the whistle. "No. In f—"

"I believe some form of mind control was used on both of them," Alex said flatly. "Both behaved contrary to the way they normally conduct themselves. Yet there they were, middle of an op, with blood in their eyes and doing a damned fine job of attempting to kill each other."

Lexi spun around to stare up at Alex incredulously. The soup sloshed in the mug, and one of the sandwiches shot off the plate to land on the carpet at her feet. Her mouth was dry as she stared up at him, stunned that he'd tell a bald-faced lie to them, while she was right there to dispute it. Her personal feelings for him had nothing to do with the job she'd been sent to do.

"That is not what happened at all," Lexi said quietly, but implacably.

One brow went up. "Honey, you were so out of it, you don't remember clearly."

Oh, my God. Why was he making this up? Lexi's heart twisted painfully, then started a hard, uncomfortable beat in her chest. "That's not true, Alex."

"I'm afraid it is." When she shook her head, he indicated the others. "Ask them, they were there."

Lexi looked at each man in turn.

Lu shrugged. Kiersted nodded, and Daklin shot her a sympathetic look. "True. Stone placed a protective shield around you, and froze Ginsberg. I was there."

The room spun in a sickening swirl, and she squeezed her eyes shut, fighting for control. "I saw the fight." She opened her eyes and looked at the others. Why would they all lie to her? To protect Alex? "I *saw* it. Two guys watched practically the whole thing before they—"

"Who were these guys, Lexi?"

She shrugged. "I don't *know*. A couple of older members of the choir perhaps?"

"How old?"

"Seventeen? Eighteen? What does it matter?" She turned to the others. "Alex was in an insane fury—Ginsberg . . . I *saw* them." She remembered how scared she'd been that Ginsberg would hurt Alex, the two men had been insane with rage—She remembered the smell of blood and sweat on Alex—She remembered— Dammit, she remembered the fight. *All* of it.

Alex squeezed her shoulder. She froze under his touch. "I believe you," he told her quietly. "But what you think you observed didn't happen. I swear to you."

Lexi turned her head, her gaze going to his neck. The thin scar from Ginsberg's knife was still a faint white line at the base of his throat where a steady pulse now beat beneath his tanned skin. Wizards healed quickly. But Alex would always wear Ginsberg's scar.

"He cut you. Your throat, your arm, your thigh." There'd been a lot of blood. He'd clearly been in a great deal of pain—

"No. He stripped you of your LockOut then cut *you*. I took your wounds to keep you from bleeding out, and spare you the agony you would've felt when you came out of . . . whatever you were in."

Lexi licked her dry lips as her eyes locked with his. His green eyes bored into hers. *Believe me.*

She glared. *Get out of my damn head!*

Trust me.

Logic told her this was all bullshit. Her heart, dammit, believed him. Lexi dragged in a shuddering breath. "What's going on? Who's manipulating us like this?"

Kiersted leaned forward, his elbows on his knees. "You believe us, yes?"

"I don't know what I believe anymore," she said feeling icy cold and more confused than she'd ever been in her life. "I do know that both Stone and myself believe what we *think* we saw. Neither of us is lying. That means that one of us was made to *perceive* something that didn't happen. And yeah. I hear you guys when you tell me you also saw what you saw. But whoever is capable of doing this type of sophisticated mind control could just as easily do it to several people as to one. Right?"

"Stone has a point," Alex said behind her. He still had his hand on her shoulder, and she took comfort from his closeness. This was crazy. Way too freaking woo-woo for her liking.

"I saw those men, too. Twins, right?"

Lexi nodded. She had a vague recollection of two similar-looking guys just standing there.

"What connects the Sydney Opera House with a school?" Lu asked, sticking his feet, ankles crossed, up on the scarred coffee table.

"The same tango threat?" Daklin offered.

"There's that. I saw the school bus and the school when I was dealing with the fight backstage. Saw them as if I were standing on the curb in real time, watching."

Lexi placed the plate of food on the cushion beside her, her hunger gone. "A vision?" She picked up the jettisoned sandwich off the floor and tossed it onto the plate, then wiped her hands, the grease churning in her stomach.

"No, I was right there."

She frowned. "You mean you left the stage?"

"You were in two places at once," Daklin offered.

"Yeah. Same as when I was in the gym. That's why I conjured the eye patch. I saw fine from my right eye, but I was seeing someone else's view from my left."

"At the same time?" Lexi asked. The room was warm, but she had the urge to rub her arms to chase away the chill goosebumping her skin.

"Yeah."

God, she didn't want to ask. "Whose eyes were you seeing through, Alex? The tangos'?"

There was no hesitation, although his voice was grim. "Without a doubt."

Lexi's heart beat hard and fast. Worse and worse. IA's suspicions that he was turning rogue were correct. Did it matter that he seemed to have no control over it? "Is this one of your normal powers?" As if there was any damned thing normal about having powers in the first place!

"No."

If their roles were reversed, Lexi would be pacing. Alex however, remained where he was. Tension radiated off his large body in pulsing waves that she realized no one else saw or felt. Wow. Lucky her. His inner tension transmitted to her on a private wavelength; it made her heart race and her palms sweat.

Alex reached down and snagged one of the sandwiches Lexi no longer wanted to eat. "There's a visceral link between the tangos and myself. And whatever it is, we'd better figure it out fast. What do the bar codes tell us other than longitude and latitude of target cities? What do the other numbers represent?"

"Date of birth?" Lexi offered.

"Date of death?" Lu suggested, materializing a steaming mug of coffee in one hand, and an unlit cigarette in the other.

"Another location?" Daklin mused. "City of birth, perhaps?"

"Why would anyone care where they were born?" Lexi wanted to know. She shifted away from the heat of Alex's body, moving to the other end of the long sofa. Now she could try to read his face and perhaps his thoughts. Unfortunately, both were annoyingly inscrutable.

"What's unusual about these guys?" Alex wasn't asking, he was thinking out loud. "They're all left-handed. So, I might add, am I—"

"Seven to ten percent of the population are lefties, the one true minority," Lexi pointed out, horrified to hear her own voice sound a little combative, a little desperate. "Left-handedness is more common in males than females. And statistically, left-handed people are of higher intelligence. Not to mention that in comparison to the general population, being left-handed happens more frequently in twins. Don't you have a fraternal twin?"

Wiping his hands, Alex nodded. "My sister Tory. But she's not left-handed."

Something crossed his face, a cloud of thought that he quickly and expertly banished from his expression. Whatever thought had just occurred to him, he wasn't sharing, either verbally or mentally. And how freaking unfair was that? He could apparently communicate telepathically with her whenever he felt like it, but slam the door on her when he didn't want her to know what he was thinking?

She'd followed Alex Stone's career with T-FLAC for *years*. His record was exemplary. There'd never been even a hint of impropriety. Not a whiff of wrongdoing. He might not follow the rules to a T, but he had an admirable code of ethics that many less experienced operatives strove to emulate.

He was a hero, dammit.

Alex's gaze met hers. A private moment in the middle of the debriefing. Lexi's throat tightened.

"Those stats don't cover several *hundred* men," he said, breaking eye contact to encompass the rest of the team. "All in the same place. The odds of that are—Impossible."

"True. They also all look to be about the same age. Eighteen to twenty. They all have green eyes. They all—" she hesitated before stating the obvious elephant in the room. "They all look like you. Even the guy who attacked me in Rio was a younger you."

Kiersted shifted in his seat and his lips twitched. "I'm guessing that you didn't make enormous deposits in a sperm bank fifteen-plus years ago?"

"No. I d—" Alex's phone buzzed. "Stone. Yeah. Hang on." He put Ellicott on speaker.

"The lab results are in. I have the DNA results of your black dust." The Control's husky voice sounded grim. Lexi's heart ricocheted in her chest. "You want the bad news or the really bad news."

"Bad news first," Alex told her flatly.

"The results are conclusive. The DNA of our tangos indicates *identical* alleles. Not close. But *identical* in every way."

"Which means they're from a single source. Once we find it, we can eliminate it. So what's the really bad news?"

There was an unnaturally long pause. "These tangos aren't related to you, Stone. They *are* you."

The bottom dropped out of Lexi's stomach.

Lu whistled long and low.

"Holy-fucking-hell." Daklin sat forward. "They're clones."

"Well, that just puts a whole new spin on this dance, doesn't it?" Kiersted grumbled. "What now, Stone?"

Alex gritted his teeth, his jaw working furiously. *I'm a liability.* Lexi heard the unguarded thought. *I have to get to lockdown at HQ before I fuck anything up or get anyone killed.*

You aren't going to. We trust you. I trust you.

Alex swiveled, his green eyes meeting hers.

"Hello? Anybody home? We're in mid-debrief here." Daklin broke the moment.

Both Lexi and Alex turned to stare at the team.

"I think this gives me a pretty damn good reason to suspect that my powers flickering isn't just a phase I'm going through." Alex tossed the napkin onto their shared plate. "It's a direct connection to these clones."

Suddenly the greasy cheese in Lexi's stomach did a somersault backflip and stuck in her throat. She pushed away the plate and mug of congealing soup. "They may be genetically identical to you, but they're being controlled by something else."

"Yeah, did you see those guys move like the Borg on steroids or drone bees? I bet if I'd kicked one in the nuts they all would have gone down," Kiersted offered.

Lexi's head pounded. "Kiersted has a point. If we can find the trigger to control them, or find some weakness they all possess, then there's a chance at annihilating the entire infestation at once. Drones can't survive without their queen. They can't maintain their hive or feed themselves without her pheromone directives. What if these clones operate the same way?"

She glanced at Alex. "When you were out of it, having your vision, or connection or whatever it was, did you see a control? Do you have any idea who might be pulling their strings?"

Alex frowned. "Nada. All I could see was what they were seeing in their current position."

Lexi drummed her fingers on her thighs, her mind swirling, flipping through the vast files in her photographic memory marked miscellaneous.

"The only way we'll find out who's controlling these things is if I let them take—"

Furious, terrified, Lexi jettisoned off the sofa as if she'd been hit with a cattle prod. "*No*. Absolutely freaking *not*. You're not going to let them do a damned thing to you."

"If I'm bait, the rest of you will be able to keep track of where I go and who I'm with. We'll have access to whatever is controlling them, we can find it and target it."

"You want to let them, it, whatever it is, take you over? Use you? What if you can't get back, what if you become one of them? God, Alex. Think of the implications!"

"She's right. What if once you're under they can access everything you know about T-FLAC?" Daklin said.

Kiersted brushed a hand over the back of his neck. "Shit. Then they'd be able to yank our dicks in any direction they pleased while they just sat back and laughed."

"They'd be able to exercise control on any one of us," Lu muttered.

Alex spoke to the group, but it was Lexi he was looking at. "What if they already have?"

Fourteen

Wizard Council Chambers
Location: Unknown

Alex materialized—not in Montana, but twenty feet in front of a desk the size of a barn. Behind it, framed by plush velvet drapes, was a low, raised platform shrouded in darkness. Other than the dramatic addition of the dais, the Council Chambers looked like the offices of a prosperous law firm.

He looked around. He was alone. *Lexi*.

She'd been with him when he'd teleported from Sydney. Mentally he reached out for her. His heart knocked harder when he couldn't sense her anywhere close. Couldn't sense her at all.

He mentally reached out again, searching for any trace of her. *Lexi, where the hell are you?* There was nothing. No one knew where the Council Chambers sat. On a secret ley line, the location could, literally, be anywhere on the planet. Or beyond, for that matter. It was soundproof, bombproof, and magic-proof.

One came when ordered to do so. One left the same damned way. The slightly sweet smell of beeswax candles coupled with some sort of aromatic herb lightly perfumed the air, yet no candles burned. There was no need since the lighting in the room was bright enough to require freaking sunglasses.

He glanced around, when what he really wanted to do was find Lexi, then get back to his regularly scheduled program of reporting in, and finding out what the fuck was going on with the dust mite tangos. A visit to the Council Chambers was premature. He didn't have enough intel to share. When he did, he'd instigate a visit himself. Until then he had other things to do, other places to be.

Leaving him to cool his jets while he waited wasn't an effective form of intimidation. He'd spent months imprisoned in a five-by-eight cell on the island of Marezzo many years ago. Among other things, being caged had taught him how to bide his time. He had the fucking patience of a saint. He could stand here all damn day long if necessary. He hoped it wouldn't be necessary.

The plush, deep burgundy carpeting beat a vermin-infested floor, and unlike that tiny cell, the spacious room was easily a hundred feet long and thirty feet wide. Plenty of fresh air. No rodents. Much easier to hang here. Heavy leather furniture clustered in conversational groupings, luxurious claret-colored drapes broke up the long expanses of mahogany paneling. Alex bet there wasn't a single window in any of the twenty-foot-high walls. Three large, leather-covered wingback chairs stood a dozen feet in front of the antique rosewood desk.

"Stone." Duncan Edge materialized without fanfare. Behind him, on the curtain-draped dais, seven black-robed men and/or women also appeared, seated in a semicircle. All but hidden in their own personal shadows, their silhouettes were indistinguishable from their surroundings, their faces obscured by their cowls.

He'd known Duncan Edge for—Hell, he didn't remember how long. Eight, nine years? Known him as a fellow T-FLAC/psi operative. They'd shared a few beers and shot the breeze several times over the years. Duncan'd always been an affable guy, if a little intense. Dedicated came to mind. Word was he was excellent at his new post as Head of the Council.

The guy he remembered had little to do with the man wearing the ceremonial black-and-silver robes of the Head of Council standing straight and tall before him. There were few things that rattled Alex, but standing here in the large, light and shadows room, facing these men and women, facing *this* man, was suddenly one of them.

Seeing them all shrouded in darkness, while he was in a spotlight, was theatrical as hell. And as far as intimidation went, it worked.

Although he'd been brought here without notice, Alex sensed no danger with the arrival of the Council. The power pulsing in the room made the hair on his arms and the nape of his neck rise with static electricity, but there wasn't a direct threat. Still, his heart pounded in a fight-or-flight adrenaline rush.

Senses sharpened, he noticed a loose silver thread on Edge's sleeve, heard the soft, sibilant breathing of the silent motionless majority, felt the utter stillness in the room.

The collective strength of the Council was tempered with benevolence and profound wisdom. They were the good guys, he reminded himself. Still, he would've liked at least a few minutes' notice to collect his thoughts before he'd been summoned. Literally snatched out of thin air and delivered like a pizza without a fucking please, excuse me, or thank-you.

"Where's the woman I was with?" Alex demanded without preamble.

"Your Lifemate?" Edge's voice echoed slightly.

Romantic nonsense. There was no such thing. He almost said it out loud, but wasn't about to split hairs with the Head of Council. "Fellow operative, and a member of my team. Where is she?"

"Not here."

For fuck sake. *Clearly.* Squinting against the bright white light surrounding him, Alex took an aggressive step forward. "Don't dick with me, Edge. She's still my responsibility. Where is she?"

Duncan's eyes glittered beneath the cowl of his elaborately decorated black robe. Fire danced between his fingers. Like the council behind him he was cast in shadow.

He ignored the pyrotechnics. He hadn't been asked to sit. Fine with him. He didn't plan to linger. He had things to report and some tango ass to kick.

"She's safe, but if you want her here—" Edge's voice trailed off. The threat hovered, almost visible, in the charged air between them.

"HQ's good," Alex said between clenched teeth. Montana was a safe and healthy distance from the Council Chamber. They didn't need Lexi. What there was to know, he'd tell them. He didn't want her involved in any of this.

Fuck. Any of *him.*

The licks of flame traveled from Edge's hands up his arms and shoulders, eerily reflecting in his dark eyes and glinting orange in the metallic silver embroidery, turning his entire body to a living, breathing flame. "She'll be questioned, later, of course."

This *danse macabre* pissed Alex off. "*She* doesn't know a damned thing," he informed Edge, voice hard and cold. Hell, *he* didn't know enough yet. Not enough to share here and now. But here and now was where he was.

"We'll allow her to speak for herself."

Fuck this. Alex attempted to shimmer. Not a damn thing happened. His temper spiked. Caught between a rock and a goddamned hard place. "It'll be short," he said tightly, "and I'll be with her."

"You don't tell us how to do our jobs, Stone," one of the Council snapped as if he were a recalcitrant child. "It'll take as long as necessary."

"Miss Stone can be accompanied by a T-FLAC rep if she requires one," Edge added flatly. Despite the orange-and-blue flames leaping across the fabric of his robe, close to his face, it was still impossible for Alex to see—*read*—the other man's features.

"Let me make the position of the Council absolutely clear, Stone." Alex felt the cold fire of Edge's power on his skin. "You are involved in a grave matter, one that greatly concerns and affects *all* wizards. If not the entire human race."

One of the women seated in the darkness behind the Head of Council discreetly cleared her throat. Phlegm? Or a caution to Edge?

Jesus. He was paranoid. With cause. "Agreed. But it concerns *me* more." Concerned him and scared the bejesus out of him. He couldn't think of anywhere far enough away to stash Lexi until this was . . . Whatever the hell was about to happen. The fact that a matter handled by T-FLAC's psi unit was before the Wizard Council was alarming.

"It's bigger than you, Alex. A hell of a lot bigger." Edge threw back the cowl covering his head, and his chest lifted in a small breath. "You're a very small cog."

Yeah. Alex got that. He was expendable.

Duncan Edge walked around the desk and addressed the Council. The licks of flame that circled him subsided until there were just a few leaping about like playful orange curls against the dense black material surrounding Edge's powerful body. "Let's cut the formality. It has its place, but right now—*not*." Apparently receiving an affirmative, he held out his hand to Alex. "Good to see you. It's been awhile." They clasped hands. No power play, just a firm grip that made Alex feel considerably better than he had a few minutes before.

"This is grim shit, Alex, really grim. And I have to tell you not all members of the Council are in agreement on how to handle this extremely volatile situation. In the hope of getting a clearer picture, I've asked my brother Caleb to join us. He'll be here soon. Grab a seat."

He indicated one of the chairs, then returned to the other side of his large desk. Not a social call apparently, Alex thought wryly, as he took a seat and kept a neutral expression on his face.

Alex had never met the middle Edge brother, and he had no idea why he was doing so now.

"Tell us what you know about the Vitros," Edge's voice echoed slightly in the cavernous room.

Alex raised a brow. "Vitros?"

"The tangos leading you about by the . . . nose," Duncan Edge's voice was dry.

"I didn't know they had a name." In fact, Alex didn't like that they'd been *given* a name. He didn't believe in giving serial killers nicknames either. Too personal. Too fucking touchy-feely. Dig them out and blow the fuckers to hell. Done. No need for cute names.

I agree. "You've seen the DNA results?"

Edge was reading him clear as glass. Intrusive as hell, no matter how benign. Alex reminded himself to censor his thoughts. "I was en route to Montana when you—detoured me. Wanted to check the results myself before coming here." He'd decided to report to Ellicott directly and in person, then report to the Council. Edge apparently had other ideas on the order priority. Fair enough.

"This is a Council matter."

Alex kept silent.

"How severely are your powers impacted?"

That came as a surprise. "You know about my powers short-circuiting? How?" Must've been one of his team members, since he'd told all of them only a few hours ago. Or perhaps Mason Knight, whom he'd left messages for, but who had yet to return his calls. Jesus, where was he? Alex really wanted to run all of this by Knight before he opened a can of worms to anyone else. He hoped to hell the old guy was okay.

"None of your team alerted us," Edge said, reading his mind. Alex tried again to block him, but Edge was all-powerful here, and Alex's attempt to hold his intrusion at bay was laughable. "And we'd like to know the whereabouts of Dr. Knight as well."

Something in his chest did a double-clutch. "Why Knight?"

In the Council chambers, Duncan Edge was the five-hundred-pound gorilla.

The Head of Council's lips twitched at the gorilla reference, but he sobered immediately. "There were three sets of DNA."

That didn't answer the damned question of Knight, or who'd told the Council that his powers were flickering. Alex's heart lodged in his throat at the implication of the Council knowing about his loss of control. This was serious. Even more serious than he'd imagined. *"Three?"* Ellicott hadn't said a fucking word about there being three sets of DNA when she'd given him the bad news earlier.

Christ. Now what? Was this good news or bad news?

When Edge motioned, the draped sleeve of his black robe spread like the wing of a raven, the silver thread catching the light in almost liquid ripples.

"What the fuck?" Simon Blackthorne said indignantly, suddenly appearing to Alex's left.

A second later Lucas Fox stood to Alex's right. "Who the h— Oh, shit."

"Now that all three key players are here, the meeting can commence." A blurred holographic image suddenly shimmered over the polished surface of his desk and his older brother instantly ma-

terialized beside him. "Take a seat, Caleb. Yes," he said, obviously
answering a mental question from Caleb, "but hold that thought.
Be seated, gentlemen. We have a lot to discuss."

Lucas and Simon sat on either side of Alex, Caleb Edge
slouched in a chair a few feet away.

Duncan looked from Simon to Alex to Lucas. "Exactly how
long have you been aiding Vitros?"

The three men bristled. Even as Alex opened his mouth to rip
Edge a new one, Fox sat forward. "I don't even know what the hell
you're talking about, so how can I, or we be aiding them? Or it, or
whatever a Vitro is?" Lucas snapped.

"The three of you appear before the Council accused of *con-
spiracy* and *treason*," a man said from the darkness behind Edge.
"I suggest answering the questions in a respectful manner, Mr.
Fox."

"I think I speak for all of us when I say we don't know what a
Vitro *is*," Simon answered calmly. Alex tried in vain to pick up on
either Simon or Lucas's thoughts, to see if he could get any insight
on what they'd been up to. Going rogue wasn't even on the table
as far as he was concerned. These two men were brothers to him.
None of them would turn. Not now. Not ever. Were they holding
something back, though? Nothing came through.

The Council might be wise and just, but they also took a no-
prisoners approach to anything that threatened their rule of the
wizarding realm. If the Council's accusations were an indication,
they weren't just in deep shit, they were in hot-holy-hell deep shit.

"Heavy hand," a light female voice cautioned from the shadows.
Alex recognized Lark's light Scottish brogue. Great, the whole
fucking gang was here. His heart took up a harder beat, and he was
surprised to realize that his palms were a little damp.

"The DNA tests confirm there is a link between you and the
army of half-wizard clones appearing across the world." Another
man in the dark circle gave his two cents' worth. "Whatever it is

that you have done, we will know the truth. Let me repeat: What is your connection to Vitros?"

"Thank you, Jack," Edge said dryly. "I'm quite capable of conducting this interview without assistance."

Again from the dais came a distinctly female clearing of the throat and Alex shifted his glance from Duncan Edge to the cloaked figure behind him that had moved from the chair to stand just behind the Head of the Wizard Council.

"Excuse me, Duncan." Lark dropped her hood to her shoulders, her hair gleaming blue-black in the stark overhead lighting. Twinkling purple lights danced like tiny fireflies around her ears and wrists. "Perhaps they cannot answer us, because they are truly as in the dark about this threat as we are."

"What do you suggest?" Edge countered.

"How about—" Caleb muttered.

Duncan cut his brother off by raising his hand so Lark could finish. "Too many damned chiefs. One question at a time. Lark?"

"Beside the use of their DNA," she said quietly, the light catching both a nose ring and the sparkler in her dark eyebrow, "which may—*probably* was taken without their knowledge or consent, we have nothing to confirm their link to Vitros. I'm sure they realize the seriousness of this matter," Lark turned her gaze on Lucas, Simon, and Alex in turn, "and would be willing to do whatever is required to clear themselves of these charges."

"And if they instead succumb to it?" Edge challenged.

Jesus. We're sitting right goddamned *here,* Alex thought, as they talked about him rather than to him.

No hint of a smile curved Lark's purple lips. "Then we'll have to give them ample reason to ensure they don't."

Lexi had no freaking idea where Alex had disappeared to or why. Under normal circumstances she'd be annoyed that he hadn't in-

formed her before splitting. *Again.* But these weren't normal circumstances, she reminded herself.

Hundreds of his clones were running around terrorizing small
children, blowing things to hell and gone, and releasing a God-
awful—as Alex called it—frankenvirus to infect and kill hundreds
of thousands of people. The man had a lot on his plate. Excusing
himself was probably not on his to-do list.

But still . . . she'd thought they were at least past the need-to-
know basis and on a little more intimate terms.

She'd been stripped of her weapons en route. *All* of them. She'd
checked, then double-checked. Like she could miss the heft of her
Glock, for Pete's sake. That had pissed her off as well. What in the
hell did Alex think he was doing? It was bad enough to abandon
her in mid teleport, worse still to leave her unarmed, even if she
was at T-FLAC HQ. At least that's where she thought she was.

She sat on a hard bench upholstered in black leather in an empty
corridor. Waiting. For whom, or what, she had no idea. Alex hadn't
bothered to tell her that either when he'd grabbed her hand and
hocus-pocused them to HQ. At least she thought this was HQ, but
not a part she'd ever seen before. The hallway was two hundred
and eleven paces long.

The bare walls were painted a soft gray. The linoleum floor was
charcoal. No pictures on this floor, which was a little odd. As far as
she knew, every floor had stunning black-and-white photographs
in the hallways. And a lot more important than artwork—there
wasn't a door. *Anywhere.* Good damned thing she didn't have claus-
trophobia.

Alex? Lexi gave telepathy a shot.

She snorted. Honest to God, she couldn't believe she'd actually
tried, and *expected* a freaking answer. *Telepathy,* of all things. The
transference of thoughts or feelings between two or more subjects
through parapsychology. Somehow, since getting to know Stone,
she'd bought into all of his psi crap.

But was it crap? She'd seen and experienced things in the last few days that had no scientific explanation. No *Alexis Stone* explanation. She didn't like rhetorical questions. She hated illogic. She didn't believe in woo-woo. But she'd already been shoved down the rabbit hole and landed in Wonderland whether she liked it, whether she *believed* it, or not.

"Mind if I sit here?" A slight redhead, wearing shorts, a bright blue T-shirt, and kick-ass orange hiking boots indicated the end of Lexi's bench.

Lexi did a double take at her sudden, and unexpected, appearance. "Sure. Where'd you come from?" She hadn't been there a second before.

With a frown the redhead looked around. "Information dissemination department. Where are we?"

"*You* work for T-FLAC?" Lexi had a pretty good idea how the woman had ended up in this hallway so fast. The question was *why*.

"Couple of weeks." She offered a slim, ringless hand. Short, no-nonsense nails. Nice firm handshake. "Kess Goodall."

"Lexi Sto—Holy shit!"

"God. Sorry about that." A slender brunette with expensive golden highlights in her long hair removed one high-heel-shod foot from the instep of Lexi's boot, shooting her an apologetic smile. A slinky, strapless black T-shirt dress hugged her body and showed off her tanned, olive skin and ample bosom. She smelled like gardenias and looked like a million bucks. Lexi had an irrational and unwanted surge of relief that Alex wasn't there to see her.

The woman flicked her perfect hair over her bare shoulder and glanced up and down the empty corridor. "T-FLAC headquarters, I presume?"

"Magic carpet ride?" Lexi asked wryly. The psi department must save a ginormous amount on travel expenses.

The Jessica Alba look-alike smiled. "Yeah. You?"

Lexi pushed off the bench and stood. Expensive girl was tall, Lexi was taller. Lexi stuck out her hand and introduced herself. She turned to the redhead, who sat tailor-fashion on the bench, her back braced by the wall, her gray eyes heavy-lidded and sleepy. "And this is Cass . . . ?"

"*Kess,* actually. Kess Goodall." The redhead said around a yawn. "Sorry. I fell asleep watching a movie on TV and ended up here."

The brunette turned, and held out a hand to Kess. "Sydney McBride." Her hand was soft, her nails scarlet, her shake businesslike. And she wore a diamond the size of Mt. Rushmore on her ring finger. "Do these people know it's the middle of the night?"

"I doubt they care," Kess muttered, scratching what looked like an insect bite on her neck, and yawned again. "Why are we here, anyway?"

"I don't know," Lexi said grimly. She didn't like not knowing. It was her *job* to know things. Either this had something to do with the weird dust clones or IA was seriously pissed she'd missed her last report. "Let me guess. You both came into contact with a wizard recently."

Kess's eyes popped open from the doze she'd nearly dropped into and she jumped off the bench. "Yes. How do y—"

"This has something to do with Lucas's short-circuiting powers, doesn't it?" Going pale, Sydney frowned. "Where is he? I've been on tour and haven't seen him in weeks. Damn that man. If something's happened to him, I'll kill him myself."

Great.

"Lucas Fox—?" Lexi kept her on topic.

"Yes."

"Ah." Thoughts started tripping in her brain like the tumblers in a safe. Both women had T-FLAC psi in common. She'd been keeping her suspicions to herself, not wanting to freak out Alex until she was absolutely sure . . .

She looked at Kess. "Let me guess. Yours is Simon Blackthorne. And *his* powers have been screwed up as well." *Three* connections to Mason Knight. Lexi didn't believe in coincidences.

"Yes and yes." Kess dropped back to the bench, her eyes wide and worried. "What's happened?"

"Nothing. As far as I know." *Okay, Stone,* Lexi thought, trying *not* to jump to the same conclusions of death and mayhem as the other two women were doing, *get the hell back here and explain what's going on. To all three of us.* "But I bet my favorite Glock that this has something to do with Alex, Fox, and Blackthorne's faulty powers."

The redhead narrowed her eyes. "Alex?"

"Stone."

"Your husband?"

"No. No relation." Lexi left it at that.

Sydney tapped the toe of her pricey black sandal. "I'm not sticking around here waiting for . . . whoever to tell me what's going on," she told them. "The only person I want to see and talk to right now is Lucas."

"Ditto." Kess tucked her shirt into her jeans as she stood again. "Except with *Simon,* not Lucas." She turned to Lexi. "I haven't been here long enough to know my way around these damned labyrinths. You work here, right? Take us to someone who can tell us what the hell we're doing here. Or beam us back where we came from."

Take me to your leader, Lexi bit back a smile. *Now wouldn't that be nice? Nice, but impossible.* She might not know what floor they were on, but she knew what *division* of T-FLAC inhabited this area. The freaking psi unit, of course. "I'm not a wizard. But it wouldn't matter. If we were shimmered here, here is where they want us."

Sydney's chin went up, and she shot Lexi a haughty look. "And who are *they?*"

Lexi shrugged.

"There aren't any damned *doors!*" Kess suddenly noticed.

"Claustrophobic?" Lexi asked sympathetically, glancing at Sydney's back as she walked—stalked—determinedly down the blank corridor. *Lotsa luck, lady. Been there, done that, nothing to see.*

"Pissed off," Kess snapped. "Brace yourselves, I'm going to yell."

"It won't do yo—" She covered her ears as Kess let out a Tarzan-like yell. Like that was going to help. This time she did smile. "Feel better?"

"Not reall—"

A doorway silently opened in the wall in front of them. Kess looked at Lexi and cocked a brow. Lexi shook her head slightly.

"Sydney?" Lexi called softly, not shifting her attention away from the open portal. She had an un-warm and definitely anti-fuzzy feeling about this. Not exactly fear, but not optimistic either. The door might be open, but Lexi couldn't see anything beyond it. Nothing but misty white. For all she knew it was the end of the Earth and they were being asked to walk off the edge. In Wonderland, anything was possible.

Alex?! Where the hell are you?

Fifteen

"All right, Caleb," Duncan Edge told his brother. "The floor's yours."

"My brother asked me to TiVo time," Caleb said soberly as he rose to stand beside his brother's massive desk. He cast his hand over the shimmering hologram and it came sharply into focus. "Went back thirty-six years. Almost thirty-seven to be precise. To the moment of your conception."

"Oh, Jesus," Alex said with a grimace. "Don't show me my parents having sex, please. There are some images a guy shouldn't have in his brain."

Caleb shook his head. "That's what's interesting. Your parents *didn't* have sex to conceive you, Stone. Neither did the parents of Blackthorne or Fox."

"We were adopted?" Fox asked, surprised, but clearly not horrified by the notion. He shrugged. "So what?"

"No. Your mothers each gave birth. To you and your 'twin' sisters."

Alex frowned. "You lost me." Caleb manipulated the hologram to show a low-slung, white building surrounded by trees. "Okay. I'll bite."

"This was a clinic in Berkeley, California. Each of your mothers went to this particular clinic to find out if they were pregnant. They were. With your sisters. The clinic was legit. It was owned, however, by Dr. Mason Knight."

A buzz started in the back of Alex's brain. Whatever was coming next wasn't good.

"Our mothers were artificially inseminated?" Blackthorne said, clearly puzzled. "What are we missing?"

"When each of your mothers went to Knight's clinic, they were a month into their pregnancies with your birth sisters. They each carried a single child. Knight implanted in each of them a second embryo. *You.*"

Oh, Jesus. Alex's entire body went ice cold. "Show us how you put this together." God help him, he believed what Caleb Edge was telling them. He knew in his gut that this was fact. But he needed a few seconds to collect his thoughts. Fear, like a slimy black slice of evil, curdled in his belly.

Caleb showed them holographic images of Knight's progress with the fertilization process. Showed his failures, and showed his elation when each woman returned for their regular checkups.

Alex got a lump in his throat when Knight informed his young mother that her twins were in perfect health. The fucking sick son of a bitch.

His hands tightened into fists. Just wait until he got ahold of Knight. The black thoughts consumed Alex further as he sat there with the others watching the way Knight had manipulated their lives from the moment of conception.

Once his powers had begun to flicker, Mason had never returned his calls. Not for weeks. Unlike him. He always called back. He was interested in everything Alex and the others had done. Always had been. Until now. God . . .

"Christ. Look how *young* she was," Blackthorne said softly as a dark-haired woman entered the clinic. His mother.

Alex's heart pounded and his mouth went dry as he observed Fox's young mother sitting in an empty waiting room. The images flashed and flickered in fast-forward. Clearly these were different days, possibly different months, but it was apparent that the visits had been close together. His mom was next.

Seeing her beloved face, a lump formed in his throat. She was younger than he remembered her, but seeing her pretty face, her curly dark hair, and soft blue eyes caused a lump to form in his throat. He couldn't take his eyes off her. Wanted to reach out and touch her smooth skin, call her name. He could almost smell the floral fragrance of her perfume.

"Why them?" His voice sounded as raw as his emotions right then.

"Luck of the draw," Gabriel Edge told him. "Just luck of the draw. Knight had been trying for five years prior to this to inseminate unsuspecting women. He'd failed. None of those pregnancies reached full term."

The hologram now showed a much younger Mason Knight in a laboratory madly scribbling notes. Test tubes and petri dishes littered the counter space. The image of that much younger man also caused Alex to experience a sensation of nostalgia. This was the guy who'd helped him with his math homework, who'd given him an appreciation of black-and-white movies on their regular Friday movie night. He'd played baseball with him, Lucas, and Simon. Had encouraged and celebrated their hiring by T-FLAC—

"Did he have anything to do with all of us joining T-FLAC?"

"Without a doubt," Duncan Edge muttered, indicating his brother move on.

"I'm going to forewarn you guys—" Caleb glanced over at

them. "Knight was directly responsible for the deaths of your parents. None of their accidents were accidents. Their deaths were well planned and, no pun intended, carefully executed.

"I'm not sure this is helpful, but I have the entire thirty-six years of your lives in fast-forward for your viewing if you choose to do so. You can tell me later if you want a copy. For now, let's move on before my brother blows a blood vessel. Okay. These are Knight's notes. As you can see, in the same year he impregnated your mothers, there were seventeen other women he attempted to fertilize. None of them took."

Blackthorne looked grim. "Are you telling us that he's our natural father? Why didn't he tell us?"

What Knight had done, Alex thought, his temper rising in direct proportion to the hurt he didn't want to feel, was mentor. The son of a bitch watched them move from foster family to foster family, always there, always overseeing their education. Withholding the one thing they all wanted most—a family. "This is the tricky part," Duncan told them somberly. "Knight didn't use his sperm to fertilize the egg."

"Then whose?"

"Ah, shit!" Lucas Fox said with feeling. "I have a damned good idea. He was fucking-well pumping sperm from wizards at the medi-spa in Rio. There's our father. In a goddamned collective jar of slops." He rubbed a rough hand over his mouth in a gesture Alex could relate to.

"Tell them about the medi-spa, bro," Alex suggested, his own throat tight.

It took Lucas a couple of minutes to bring everyone up to speed as he told the Edges and the Council about several of his team being captured and unwillingly being sperm donors. Alex and Blackthorne both swore.

"The son of a bitch has been doing this for thirty-six years?" Alex demanded, horrified. "How many kids has he created?"

"He stopped in vitro fertilization after the three of you were born. He went bigger," Caleb told them. "Much bigger."

The hologram changed to the warehouse both Fox and Alex had visited in Brazil, then the warehouse in New Mexico. "Holy Mother of God. He didn't *steal* those babies," Simon breathed, appalled. "He's *manufacturing* them!" Duncan indicated the computer on Knight's desk. Alex recognized Mason's London home office. He, Lucas, and Simon had spent summer vacations there. Had played fort under that desk, and later had written their college applications there. On the credenza behind his desk was a familiar glass case.

World Series 1992. Minnesota Twins center fielder Kirby Puckett drilled an eleventh-inning, game-winning home run in the sixth game of the fall classic. It was one of baseball's most exciting moments. Alex had been there. He'd caught the ball, had it signed by Puckett, and given it to Knight for his sixty-second birthday.

He ran his fingers roughly through his hair trying to contain the pounding in his head that was threatening to explode out his eyes. His whole goddamn fucking life, all of it, had been a giant experiment to get Knight jacked off on some insane power trip. The hologram moved on. More notes on the computer, secret bundles of papers in the wall safe. A secret life as Knight visited warehouse after warehouse filled with babies. Every image, every new bit of information, hit his skin like a drop of acid, eating away his identity bit by bit. Mason was the glue that held him, Fox, and Blackthorne together. Mason was the poison that had tainted them all.

"Over a thousand children according to his records," Duncan informed them. "But wait—there's more."

"What?" Alex snarled, "A fucking Ginsu knife? I believe what I'm seeing and hearing. So can we cut to the chase here? What's the fucking bottom line?" He wasn't sure how much more of this he could take.

"Yeah," Blackthorne said flatly. "Give it to us straight, we already know this situation is FUBAR."

Listening to the Head of the Wizard Council, Alex kept his eyes glued to the fast moving hologram images and watched his entire life unravel.

Lark preceded three women into the room before disappearing into the shadows again. One of the women, wearing a cling-everywhere black dress, huffed as she looked around, missing the men seated way the hell and gone at the other end of the room.

"Very Gothic, wherever we are. Dammit, I was shimmered while in the middle of a very nice dinner with my publisher. I have *no* idea how I'm going to explain *that*. Why didn't she tell us what this is all about anyway?"

Alex only had eyes for Lexi. Dragging her into this was unacceptable on every level. Yes, she was a trained professional and could handle herself in any situation; as an operative he was perfectly aware of her abilities. As a man—

Fuck it. He wasn't afraid for her safety *here*. But God—He wanted Lexi as far away from this clusterfuck as he could get her, not drawn in further.

"Lark?" Lexi raised her voice, sounding impatient and worried. "Why are we here?"

"Over here," Alex raised his voice to be heard across the great expanse of the room.

All three women glanced around at the sound of his voice.

"Come on Duncan, Jesus, you know this is out of bounds," he said tightly, shooting a narrow-eyed glance between his friend and the woman he l—and his team member who was at that moment racing across the floor as if her ass was on fire. "She *shouldn't* be here. She's not part of this."

Slightly out of breath Lexi almost skidded to a stop beside him. Her chin was up. "Thank you. I can speak for myself," she told him mildly. She let her gaze run over Edge as if analyzing his physical composition for defects.

Having dispensed with the cowl, Duncan was bareheaded as he stood beneath normal wattage lighting. "Who are you," she addressed the Head of Council. "And what are we doing here?"

Not only could Edge be charming, and very likeable, he was a decent-looking guy, and his mantle of authority might easily turn a woman's head. Not, apparently, Lexi Stone's. She was glaring at him as if Edge were a personal affront and Alex l—admired her for it.

"Duncan Edge, Miss Stone. Head of the Council, and we have a problem. A big damned problem that I hope you ladies can help us with."

Lexi cast Alex a worried look. "Of course." *Are you in trouble? Is there anything I shouldn't say?*

"You can say anything, none of the guys is in trouble," Duncan answered Lexi's thought, which made her eyes go wide and startled. "And we'd appreciate your being perfectly open with us."

Edge materialized more chairs to the left of Fox. "Please be seated, ladies."

"I'll be happy to." Lexi didn't sound in the least bit happy, Alex noted. "As soon as I rearrange the furniture." She grabbed the arm with both hands, putting her back into dragging the heavy wingback toward Alex's chair. For the first time in hours, hell, *days,* he wanted to laugh.

Shaking his head slightly, Edge let out a small sigh, then shimmered the chairs, rearranging them in pairs, side by side.

"Thank you." Lexi sat down and immediately reached for Alex's hand, pulling it into her lap and twining her fingers with his. The fact that she'd forgotten herself, allowing a PDA, showed Alex how rattled Lexi was. Tension radiated palpably off her and her palm was

a little sweaty. His intrepid, fear-nothing Lexi? Nervous? Yeah. Un-
derstandable under the circumstances.

"I'm going to have Alex recap what we know as fact so far. After
that I'd like to hear what you ladies have to contribute, if anything.
Since we've got a cast of thousands participating here, it might be
best if we go around the room when Alex is done, and see if and
what any of you might have to add. One at a time," he said dryly,
clearly realizing that with this many people vested in the proceed-
ings things weren't going to go one at a time. "Alex?"

Alex made it short and sweet. Inseminated. Donor unknown.
Parents purposely killed. Manufactured children. He kept his tone
cool and his emotions under wraps. He didn't know how to begin
to describe his inner turmoil over this whole mess. Betrayal. Anger.
Disappointment. Fear.

The first three he could shove into some secret dark place to examine later. The fear was a whole new ball game, and one he'd
never experienced before, but it was damn close to the burning
pain he'd taken for Lexi after Ginsberg had carved her up.

Lexi's fingers squeezed his in a death grip, even as her eyes darted
from one face to another. Lucas took up the story and told them
what had been discovered in the warehouses.

He didn't want Lexi anywhere near Knight. *Where can I take her?*
Alex's thoughts raced. Somewhere secluded. Somewhere she
wouldn't be found until he came to bring her back . . .

Sobering thought, because God damn it, there was a very real
possibility that he wouldn't be alive *to* retrieve her.

"Let's start with facts, go to suppositions, and finish with theo-
ries," Edge told the ladies when Lucas was done. With a slight
movement of his hand, Edge once again rearranged the seating.
This time, they were moved into a tight circle around a circular
cherrywood table. Which left the council on the outskirts still
emersed in shadow. The close proximity made conversation easier,

and brought him from behind the massive desk. He also dimmed the interrogation lights.

"Now, does anyone have anything new they can add? The more we know, the better we'll be able to deal with Knight. Who'd like to get the ball rolling?"

"I will," Lexi told him, her tone grim. "Mind if I walk while I talk?" She released Alex's hand and stood. "Easier for me to think that way."

Without waiting for Edge's consent, Lexi began pacing. Due to the excellent acoustics, her voice carried easily in the vast room as she walked away. "Intellectually I understand that Knight produced three children with in vitro fertilization. But for one thing, it's statistically impossible for them all to left-handed and green-eyed."

That hadn't occurred to him because he'd considered those small details immaterial. Fascinated, Alex watched Lexi power on her brain, pulling connected facts out of the corners of her mind, things she'd read and stored, but possibly not connected before.

God, he admired her mind almost as much as he lusted after her. Who knew the brain was an erogenous zone? Didn't hurt that she was also funny and sexy and had a body that made him salivate.

"I don't understand the purpose of the babies." Lexi stared at a gilt-framed landscape on the far wall, clearly deep in thought. "So I can't address that." She turned, striding back, long legs encased in dark pants, boots thudding on the plush carpet underfoot. She looked like a warrior princess with her black clothing, empty holster, and shaggy blond hair.

She circled a decorative table on her return trip. "But I believe the liquid obtained from dissolving wizards and the bodies of organ donors is being used in some grotesque way to manufacture the clones. Much like embryos in advanced in vitro cloning."

"And your educated guess as to why Stone, Blackthorne, and

Fox have been used as models for these embryos? They're called Vitros, by the way."

"I don't make *educated* guesses," Lexi told him shortly. "I like facts, backed up by statistics and freaking pie charts."

"What exactly is Mason Knight *doing*?" The woman beside Lucas Fox asked tartly as she crossed long, tan legs and used a slender hand to twist the ring on her left hand in a nervous gesture. Lucas reached out and took her hand in his. She shot him a grateful smile.

"He's breeding superwizards," Blackthorne told her grimly.

"That's who—*what* the babies are? Manufactured wizards?" Kess Goodall asked, clearly repulsed and appalled by the notion; her pale skin went a little whiter.

"We're still not certain how the babies fit into all this." Edge leaned back in his chair, steepling his hands. "One more detail we've been able to piece together from images taken at each of the bomb sites, is the totality of the information on the bar code tattoos on their left wrists."

"Other than longitude and latitude?" Lexi asked, returning to the group and squeezing between her chair and Alex's to sit down again.

"Date of death," Alex told her.

She turned to look at him, her brow furrowed. "They know when they're going to die? More to the point, they're programmed to die?"

"They have an expiration date. When it's time, they disintegrate."

"Or when one is shot," Fox pointed out dryly.

Lexi glanced around at the group. "Has anyone noticed their age? How can they all be—what? Twenty or thereabouts?"

"They're not," Alex said flatly. "As far as we can ascertain, they're all twelve months old."

Her eyes grew wide. "They grew from birth to adulthood in one *year*?"

"Apparently."

"Accelerated growth creates premature aging," Sydney murmured, picking up her water glass but not drinking.

"Bingo," Fox said flatly.

"What on earth is their purpose?" Kess asked. "Terrorists for hire?"

Simon nodded. "You can say that. Nothing can stop them. A bullet gets one, there are thousands just like it right behind him. It's a tango army, armed and souped up with wizard powers."

"God," Lexi breathed, clearly horrified.

"Helps those who help themselves," Edge finished, Sahara-dry. "We have to find *where* these Vitros are being manufactured, *how* they're manufactured, and how to annihilate them on an epic scale. And we have to do it *now*."

"Agreed." Lexi speared Edge with a glance. "Why have Alex's powers been short circuiting?"

"And Lucas's?" Sydney added.

Kess chimed in. "And Simon's?"

"There's no need to t—" Tell the women this part, Alex wanted to say. But Edge shook his head.

"We believe they're operating on a collective mind set. That all of these Vitros, like drones, are becoming a single entity. Many bodies, one brain. One control."

"What are you saying?" Sydney said, her voice raw with fear.

"He's saying," Lexi told her flatly, "That all three of our guys are being sucked into some sort of communal paranormal mind control that's going to take them—Alex, Lucas, and Simon—away from *us,* and force them all to do the freaking bidding of that damned megalomaniac, Mason Knight. They'll end up being exactly the people they're here to eliminate. Our guys will be *terrorists*." Lexi took a deep breath.

"That these three men right here are the originals for the Vitros. Isn't that what we're dancing around here?"

"Thus far it's only supposition," Edge informed her without inflection.

"No. It's more than that." Lexi shifted to sit on the edge of her chair and braced her arms on the table. "We have to find Knight, and we have to figure out how to take him down. Take down the head, down comes the monster."

That was his Lexi. Straight to the point and already figuring the angles. Alex felt a surge of pride coupled with his fear for her safety.

"What does this bastard *look* like?" Kess demanded. "I want to recognize him when I see him."

"You'll *never* meet the son of a bitch," Blackthorne told her unequivocally. "You're never going to be anywhere *near* him."

She laid a pale hand on his arm, her orange boots scuffing at the floor. "Fine. But just in case shit happens and I *do*—I think we all need to know what this monster looks like."

Caleb conjured a holograph of Knight in the center of the table. "This was taken a month ago. He hasn't been seen since."

Sydney rose, flattening her palms on the table as she studied the image. "I saw this guy."

"Where?" Fox demanded, touching the small of her back in a protective way that spoke volumes about their relationship.

Without looking away from the image, Sydney answered absently. "At Novos Começos Medi-Spa."

"Did he talk to you?"

She shook her head. "No. I was in the medical building, and was going to try sneaking upstairs to the third floor to see if I could discover anything. But there were armed guys guarding the elevators. This guy—Knight—was talking to them. Clearly he knew them. In fact—he looked to be in charge. They let him go up."

While the exchange of seemingly random bits of intel was vital if they hoped to apprehend Knight and destroy his "Vitros," Alex's druthers was being out there, beating the bushes, rather than sitting here—wherever here was—*talking* about it.

"One question we *haven't* covered is why these guys have been having power outages," Lexi observed.

Alex locked eyes with Duncan. *Need to know.*

Edge shook his head so slightly no one else would see it. *They're invested in this. The women* do *need to know.*

Hell.

"We believe we're being assimilated into the collective of the Vitros," Alex told her with grim reluctance. "Knight's plan is that everything we are, everything we know, will be absorbed by these—Vitros."

"That includes all our inside knowledge and training from T-FLAC," Lucas added.

"And our powers," Simon concluded.

"And *what,*" Lexi demanded fiercely, "does he plan on doing with what's left?"

That was the million-dollar question.

Sixteen

"That went well," Lexi said dryly, getting to her feet with the others as Edge teleported the hell out of Dodge. She sucked in a breath and muttered a curse as, a second later, she found herself standing weak-kneed in an opulent, unfamiliar, bedroom.

The crackle of the fire blazing in the stone hearth sounded so . . . normal. The flames on the tall, lightly tuberose-scented white tapers flickered with the air current stirred up by their entrance.

Staggering, Lexi used both hands to grab Alex's arm for balance. "Don't you people ever give a freaking heads-up?"

Sliding an arm around her waist to keep her steady, he glanced around. "Definitely not HQ." His tone was martini dry.

"Not unless your pal Lark has secretly gotten a sideline decorating, no." Lexi tipped her head back to study the twenty-foot-high, elaborately carved wood ceiling. Definitely *not* Montana. The room was dominated by a massive four-poster bed draped in bronze silk and heavy autumnal-colored tapestry fabric. The carpet underfoot was a deep chocolate color, the walls lined with the same dull-sheened silk as the bed hangings. Very plush. Very fancy. Not her style, which tended to run to serviceable neutrals, but pretty damn cool nevertheless.

It was the kind of place that looked as if it should have portraits of stern-faced ancestors in odd outfits lining the walls. Fortunately, instead there were beautiful landscapes in huge gilt frames. Definitely better than staring eyes.

She felt the chill of the outside air even through the leaded windows directly behind her, but the room was toasty warm and very romantic for two counterterrorist operatives.

"Nice, in a Barbara Cartland-meets-Mary Queen of Scots kind of way." She tried to gauge Alex's response to the undoubtedly romantic setting.

Of course, Alex being Alex, he was a master at hiding what he was thinking; his face revealed nothing. A great trait for an operative, and Lexi had been trying to emulate it since the op started. But it was damn hard to keep a poker face around wizards, where strange goings-on were a matter of course. She was just fortunate she didn't walk around with her mouth hanging open in horror/awe/shock 24/7.

She glanced out of the window at the brilliant moonlit snow-scaped garden below the rough stone walls. Apparently they were in a castle. *Somewhere.* She didn't even bother to try to figure that one out. It had been a hell of a night. Lexi's heart ached for Alex. What could she do? What could she say?

Nothing.

This was something Alex—and the others—had to wrap their brains around themselves.

The meeting had been intense.

The new intel terrifying.

He needed to unwind, to forget, if only for a short time, the implication of everything he'd learned tonight.

She *hated* that. Hated that she couldn't just damn well step in and fix this for him. She'd spent years fixing things minor and major for her feckless parents. Here was someone worth putting on her armor and going into battle for. Unfortunately she knew that not only was this not her fight, it was something she *couldn't* fix.

Turning, she shot him what she hoped was a naughty look. "I think it's against the rules for us to share a bed." The truth was, even though she'd had a couple of lovers in the past, she'd never instigated their lovemaking. She'd never flirted, hell, she didn't even know *how* to flirt.

But God, she loved this man.

Alex's eyes gleamed intensely as he walked her backward, crowding her against the window, his body tense, his green eyes glittering in the moonlight.

She could feel the aftermath of his adrenaline high; it surged through him still. Sliding his fingers between hers, he brought both hands up to his mouth. "We're going to share more than a bed." He kissed her fingers, his breath warm against the back of her hands. Her heart started to race in anticipation as he drew her hands up to shoulder level, pressing their clasped fingers against the chill of the leaded window.

A few kisses would be great. Alex was a superlative kisser . . . Lexi let her lashes flutter to her cheeks as his lips grazed her jaw. Kisses were good. She turned her head to give him access to her neck. Smart move because the sensation of his damp mouth against her throat shot down to all her girl parts and made them sit up and take notice.

Naked, she thought dreamily as he trailed kisses along her collarbone. Hmm. Skin to skin. Sleeping in his arms spoon-fashion. Bliss. The problem was her sleepy blood was starting to wake up.

Not enough to insert tab A into slot B, but horizontal, and spoon-ing. *There* was a plan.

"There's a bed not twenty feet aw—"

"Too far."

Shimmering would take all of a second and they'd be on a warm horizontal surface. "Hocus—"

"Concentrating on the *pocus* here."

Lexi huffed out a laugh. "That was terrible."

He released her hands and she used one to cradle his head as he kissed her again, sliding her other hand to the small of his back. His body was a furnace against hers. The juxtaposition of his resilient heat against the unyielding cold of the glass at her back made Lexi shudder.

Wrapping her arms around his neck, she lifted up onto her toes and captured his mouth with hers. Without hesitation he kissed her back. A kiss so deep, so carnal, she forgot how to breathe. She traced the tender bottom curve of his lip. His strong white teeth nipped at her finger, and just a rim of green showed around his black pupils as his gaze held hers.

After minutes—or was it days—he broke away, only to nibble a path of need from her ear to her mouth. "I'm not good with words."

He didn't need words. The way his gaze held hers, the intensity of his kisses, told her enough. Enough for now. "I'm okay with that. I prefer a man who's good with his hands." And other mov-ing body parts.

She tasted his desire on her tongue, his hunger in the fierce grip of his fingers on her bottom as he urged her closer.

For a woman who three minutes before had only wanted to go to sleep, she was already wet and burning up. Her skin was on fire. Her lips pulsed. She couldn't seem to get close enough. She *had* to feel his bare skin and slid her palm under the back of his shirt. Her fingers encountered hot, satin-smooth skin—until she moved

higher. The hypertrophic scars from his time spent caged and tor-
tured on Marezzo years ago were a stark reminder of what this
man had already been through. His marauding mouth stilled.
"Don't—"

"Shh." Lexi knew her light caress wasn't hurting him. The nerve
endings in her lips tingled, and transmitted a signal to her vital or-
gans. But this was about him . . . As she smoothed her fingers across
the lines of scar tissue indicating how frequently he'd been
whipped, she wished she could take this away for him too, then
realized how incredibly foolish she was being. Lord, Alex would
laugh if he knew how desperate she was to protect him. Keep him
safe, to see him . . . *happy*.

Not your job, sweetheart.

Hell. Of course he knew. He could read her mind. *Lofty goal,
huh?*

Can take care of myself.

I know.

Right now how about we make each other happy?

I lo—"Like—I like the way you think—ah—right there," she
managed to praise as he gently sucked on the spot under her ear.
The spot that made her knees go weak, and her insides sing. The
sensation was compounded as he cupped her breast through her
shirt and bra, to find her nipple hard and aching. He measured her
breasts, weighing each one in his cupped hand and then tormented
her by skimming each nipple with his thumb.

Her back arched as she leaned forward. She wanted to remember these moments together. She wanted to imprint him into her
DNA. She wanted to mark him with her scent, so that no matter
what, he would never forget her.

Her lips found the pulse pounding at the base of his neck. Hers
throbbed even faster. Her hands skimmed down his biceps and she
looked up at him with her heart in her eyes.

His thumb roughly stroked across the hard peak, causing Lexi to

hum low in her throat and rise up on her toes the necessary inches
to get their pelvises aligned.

He raised his head slightly. Inches away, his eyes appeared so
green, so translucent in the snow's reflection that Lexi imagined
herself underwater. Which explained why she couldn't catch her
breath.

He gently brushed aside a lock of hair that had fallen into her
eyes. "Lex . . ."

He didn't finish, but hearing her name on his lips, hearing the
desperation in his voice, made her feel almost freaking invincible.
Lexi's heart pounded in response to his touch and she smiled up at
him. This is what he needed, what they both needed—mindless
physical release.

"I thought we were supposed to be relaxing?"

"I promise, we'll be extremely relaxed when we're done." He
touched her cheek. Softly. Reverently. His touch shimmied to her
toes. She shifted restlessly, her breasts aching for the feel of his
hands on her bare skin.

His fingers glided up her cheek and combed through her hair.
He cradled her head in his large palm, then drew her toward him,
inch by slow inch. Cool air bathed her naked back. He lowered his
head, and she touched his face with just the tips of her fingers. His
jaw felt rough as his mouth crushed down on hers, and she tasted
anger mixed with the fear. She understood it, savored it, because it
matched her own.

She met his almost violent demand. Her teeth raked his lip. His
scraped her tongue. She heard a low, fierce growl and realized it
had come from her.

His erection pressed against the juncture of her thighs, a-l-m-o-
s-t where she wanted him.

One large hand shifted from her behind to her breast. Her nipples ached. She pressed her chest against his, trapping his hand.
Making the pressure harder. Unbearable.

He nudged her back a little, just enough. His fingers found her nipple through her shirt. He squeezed to just this side of pain, then captured her cry against his neck. Lexi panted. She pulled his T-shirt up to his shoulders. He did the rest, magically making it disappear.

Magic was excellent. "My turn?" she asked hopefully, trying to get his belt undone.

"Uh-uh. I'm going to peel you out of these clothes the old-fashioned way." Sneaking his cool hand up under the front of her T-shirt he spread his palm across the swell of her breasts, then ran the back of his fingers inside the lace edge of her bra, *almost* touching her nipple. "I love touching your breasts. Firm and soft and the perfect size for my hands." Lexi wiggled to get closer.

He kissed her again, his tongue scorching, insatiable, driving her own need higher. Higher. Lexi kissed him back with hot, sweet abandon, a low hum in the back of her throat. Nothing held back, no artifice. Her tongue active, insistent, ravenous, a blatant simulation of the more intimate act. Frantic hands brailled his naked back and shoulders, crushing his hand between their bodies.

Oh. So much for the old-fashioned way. There went her T-shirt and pants. "Boots?"

He lifted her easily. *Look Ma, no hands,* then hooked her leg over his arm. "Just a suggestion," she murmured dryly when he ignored her. Lexi wrapped her legs around his waist. Crossing her feet in the small of his back she slid her arms around his neck, gripping his hair.

He braced her back against the chill of the window as he lowered his head to rake his teeth across her nipple. Her back arched as he stroked a line of fire down her throat, across her chest, and paused at the juncture of her thighs. She loved the feel of those callused hands on her skin. Wherever he touched, flames licked and spread. Her hand clenched in his hair as he sucked the hard peak of her nipple into the hot cavern of his mouth. His teeth lightly scored her areola and her breath strangled in the back of her throat.

Her stomach contracted as his fingers found her slick folds beneath the panties she still wore. Oh, God. So not fair.

"Panties. Off."

He chuckled. "That doesn't work."

"I know," she could barely talk. "It was a prompt." To show him that turnabout was fair play, she dipped two fingers into the waistband of his jeans. He dragged in a breath, and they slipped down farther, her fingertips brushing his sex. Their hands, trapped between their bodies, bumped. "Wanna play chicken?" she taunted, pushing her hand farther until her fingers brushed against his satiny length.

He slid another finger deep inside her. She whimpered, her body bucking at his touch. The scent of her own arousal made her hotter. And him harder.

"I can't get enough of you," his voice was raw as he tasted a damp path across her breast to give the other one equal attention. "I want to taste every part of you, hell I want to devour you, consume you—"

"Let's stick to taste. No devouring. We're in a spooky castle, God only knows where."

Alex chuckled against her neck, and he took a playful nip. That stung a little, and shot her heart rate up several delicious notches.

"Are there by any—chance—" she attempted to speak in full sentences when there was barely enough air in her lungs to say a word. "Wizard *vampires?*"

He lifted his head and grinned. "Probably."

That gave her pause. "Really?" Only half the word was pushed out because she was so close to orgasm she could barely suck in enough air.

He shook his head. "I have no idea." His hands moved over her body, demanding, seeking, pressing. Frantic, bruising caresses—and

hers were no less gentle. He filled her world with his taste, with the
Alex smell of him, with the rough texture of the hair narrowing
down from his chest to his groin, to the tensile strength of his muscles.

"Get rid of your pants!"

"Yes, ma'am."

Oh, she *loved* magic. "Now my panties. Come *on,* Alex. Really,
make it—" He sprang free, pulsing, ready. *There.* "Oh, God," she
dropped her forehead to his chest. "Thank you." Her hand found
him like a heat-seeking missile. Her fingers curled against his hot
flesh. His eyes closed and his stomach muscles clenched as she
stroked and teased with just the right pressure to make him even
harder. His stomach muscles tightened convulsively.

"Enough . . ." he sucked in air as her fingertip found the head of
his sex, rubbed at the bead of moisture there. "Enough talking."

"I was done chatting *hours* ago."

He knew where she was most responsive, where she was the
most sensitive, and brought her close to the brink as he played his
fingers over her, in her, until she begged for release. "Please, Alex—"
she panted, incapable of drawing a full breath. "I'd—really like—to
say—I don't want to rush you. But could you *please*—hurry—"

He slipped into her wet heat, entering her on one long, deep,
gut-wrenching thrust. "Oh God. Alex!" Her curves complemented his hollows. Her softness his hardness. Pelvises locked together as they surged. And ebbed. The window behind her rattled.
She didn't give a damn if they went sailing into the night.

"You feel so good, so good." Her breasts slid against his chest.
Too sensitive. Too exquisite a sensation. She cried out softly, burying her face against his arched throat. She kissed the hard thudding
beat of his heart. Praying for more, satisfied with less. Her eyes lost
focus, her breath caught, and her internal muscles clenched around
him like a fist. Digging her heels into his taut flanks, Lexi knew that
every thrust reaffirmed life. With every pump of his hips, every flex

of his muscles, every thrust, he was rejoicing in being alive. Being together.

"That's it," he said gutturally, through clenched teeth, as he thrust powerfully again. "Take. More. Take it all."

She watched him as she climbed, closer and closer until she just couldn't focus on his features anymore. Her breath tore on a strangled sob as she peaked. With an inarticulate cry, Alex joined her release.

After several minutes where the only sounds in the room were their ragged breathing and the snap, crackle, pop of the fire, Lexi managed to lift her head from his shoulder. "My assets are freezing."

He lifted her away from the window, running his hands down her back, taking the chill away with each stroke. "Better?"

She nodded, too filled with emotion to talk. With apparent reluctance he helped her lower her legs to the floor. Lexi slid her arms around his waist and stood on her toes. "Take me to bed." Her voice was soft. She loved him so much her chest ached with the sheer size of her emotion.

"Take me to bed and make love to me again until I can't think straight."

"You mean like this?"

Cool sheets beneath her, hot Alex on top. Perfect.

Lexi wound her arms around his neck. "Yes," she murmured against his throat. "*Exactly* like this."

This time they made love slowly. They were both physically and mentally exhausted. Wrung out.

He pulled the cool silk sheet over her shoulders, tucking Lexi against his side.

"Know when I first saw you?" He trailed his fingertips up and down her back.

"Sure." The moment had changed her life forever. "Your Chilean op four years ago."

"No. Beijing. Two months before that."

"No. I distinctly remember doing your research for the Chile op. You wanted intel on *Movimiento de la Izquierda Revoluciónaria,* remember?"

"I was walking down the corridor on my way to Accounting, when I heard a woman laughing. It sounded . . . Man, I can't tell you what your laugh sounded like to me right then. Free. Pure. Uninhibited." He brushed a kiss to her forehead. "Joy."

"Joy?"

"Everything you are was in your laugh that day. Everything. It was like standing outside on a cold day and looking through a window at a fire. So near, and yet so far. I wanted your heat. Your . . . joy."

Lexi sang very softly. "You are my sunshine, my only sunshine. You make me happy—"

Alex chuckled and for a moment Lexi understood what he meant by joy. Pressed against his side, she drifted in a rosy postcoital glow. *This* was the kind of magic she understood. Alex had left no part of her body untouched, unloved. Whether he felt as she did was still a mystery to her. Loving Alex was too frail and new an emotion to take out of the secret recesses of her own heart and share. But for now, Lexi was too happy, too replete, to try to decipher the workings of this particular male mind.

Cradling the back of her head, Alex lazily combed his fingers through her damp hair. In turn she stroked her foot up his hairy calf. "I'm sorry about Knight," Lexi told him softly. "But I stand by what I told Edge—who by the way might be kind of good-looking and the most powerful wizard in the world, galaxy, whatever, but he's ruthless and only a little charming. Still, I'm glad he's on your side.

"I suspected Mason was behind the dust bunny tangos before I went into that room. A logical process of elimination and taking into account all the facts, Mason is the *only* person who connects all of you, she said."

"I had the same gut feeling a few days ago. So did the others. Damn. I hate that he's the one . . . Fucking *hate* it."

"You trusted him, loved him, and he betrayed you."

"Pisses me off."

"Look, let's not talk about this anymore tonight. You need to sleep so you're sharp and at your best tomorrow."

He lifted her chin on two fingers, the wicked glint in his eye making Lexi's heart do a samba beat in her chest. "Operatives don't need much sleep. Didn't you train for it?"

"I excelled at it," she said primly.

He smiled, brushing her hair out of her eyes. "Of course you did."

"There might be more. I mean different ones that aren't copies of you three."

"No. Just us lucky ones."

"You'll find and destroy him. *And* those Vitros of his."

"I wish to God killing him was the answer. But until we uncover what his master plan is, until we know the *how, where,* and *why* of these Vitros, even if we find him, we can't *kill* him."

"The odds of the three of you, with your combined powers, focused on one man gives you a seventeen percent edge over Knight and his Vitros."

"Seventeen percent, huh? We're meeting the others in a few hours. Close your eyes and get some sleep. We have a busy time ahead of us."

"You're taking me with you?"

He hesitated a second. "Any reason I shouldn't?"

"No—no reason. I want to be with you when you capture this guy."

"Scratch that." His chest rose and fell beneath her splayed hand as he blew out a harsh breath. "I lied."

"About what?"

His eyes turned hard. Glittering chips of green glacial ice. "Taking you with me. Lexi, I can't think of you as an operative when I'm lying here naked with you. Do you get that? I can be dispassionate, and expect you to be the same. Mason Knight has turned into someone, some *thing,* I don't know. He's going to be unpredictable. Dangerously unpredictable. He's a very powerful wizard. And I need to use every ounce of concentration to best him."

"I totally understand. But I know you. Better than anyone else. Fox and Blackthorne know you as friends. I know you as your lover. I can anticipate your wants and needs. It's a different kind of knowing. I'd know the nuances if those things take over your mind again." She brushed her fingers through the dark hair at his temple. "Better, we can apparently perform telepathy. *That* skill, that *connection,* might save your life.

"I won't get in your way. And God only knows, I won't do a damn thing to stop you. He has to be stopped. Stopped cold. And soon. Do you have any idea where he might have gone to ground?"

"Blackthorne has been to every location Mason might be. It's as though he never existed. No papers, no personal effects. Nothing. And yeah, before you ask—our forensic SCI teams are all over each one of the locations. If there's anything to find, they'll find it."

Lexi wasn't sure if she'd managed to persuade him to take her with him. All she knew was that she had to be there. Had to be with him for the confrontation. She didn't know why, other than she didn't want to see the man she loved hurt—either physically or emotionally. No, this drive went deeper than that.

Whatever it was, Lexi wasn't going to ignore it.

For several minutes they lay silently, their hands stroking each almost absently. After a while Lexi said softly, "I'm sorry about your parents."

"Yeah. Me, too." His fingers stilled in her hair.

"They died in a plane crash, right?" Hardly loverlike conversation, but she wanted to give Alex anything—*everything* he needed right now. She could only imagine what he must be feeling after the blow of Knight's betrayal. She couldn't fix his past, but she could be here for him, and try to ease his hurt in the here and now.

"Yeah." He went back to stroking her hair. Lexi loved his gentle touch and brushed a whisper soft kiss to his shoulder. "Tory and I were six. Our father was a stuntman. Good at what he did. He specialized in aerial maneuvers and was in high demand. That particular movie shoot was in Spain. Apparently it was his day off and he took my mother out in one of the planes used in the movie. The single-engine, propeller-driven Yakovlev Yak-52 crashed in an alfalfa field. And all these years I thought it was an accident."

His eyes were closed, spiky black lashes masking the pain in his beautiful green eyes. Lexi's heart ached for him. Lines of strain bracketed his mouth, and his skin looked tightly stretched over his bones. She laid her open hand on his cheek.

She attempted to block her thoughts, hoping she was successful, but knowing. *I love you Alex. I'll always love you. No matter how you feel. No matter what happens.*

He took her hand and placed a kiss in her palm without opening his eyes. Had he heard her? She'd never been touchy-feely before. She hadn't been brought up that way. She was uncomfortable with public displays of affection—hell, she was a little uncomfortable with *any* displays of affection. "Investigated, I'm sure?" She pitched her voice low as his breathing became slower and more even.

Sleep my love. I'll take the first watch. She didn't give a Continental hoot *where* they were. Nothing and nobody was getting anywhere near Alex until he was good and ready to confront them. In the meantime, Lexi planned to guard him. With her life if necessary.

"The Spanish equivalent of our National Transportation Safety Board did a thorough investigation." He yawned, the arms supporting her head tightened a little, and he tugged her the last eighth of an inch closer until their hearts seemed to be beating in syncopation.

"I've read the report a dozen times, there was *nothing* suspicious about it. A private investigation company, hired by the film company, also did a meticulous examination at the crash site. No foul play suspected."

"And yet—"

"Yeah—and yet. Lexi?"

On the precipice of sleep, she murmured, "Hmm?"

"Don't."

Seventeen

Alex left Lexi sleeping in the giant bed. Fuck. He had a bad feeling about Knight's plans for his Vitros, hell, for all of them. A gut-deep premonition seemed to have taken residence beside his heart. Ticking away the seconds to detonation. His detonation. Halfway to the door, he turned back.

One more look. One more—

Standing beside the bed, he allowed himself to take his fill of this woman who'd turned his life upside down in another way. For such a fierce warrior, she looked shockingly small tucked between the rumpled silk sheets, her kiss-reddened mouth soft and lax, her serene features nothing like the animated woman she was when she was awake.

She was spectacular both ways.

Very gently he brushed a strand of sunny hair off her eyelashes, allowing his finger to trail briefly across the silky skin of her warm cheek. A strange ache permeated his chest. *Lexi.*

He wanted to grab her, hold onto her warm supple body, feel the beat of her heart, see those soft gray eyes light up when she looked at him. It was good to want things, he thought, curling his fingers into his palms to prevent himself from being a selfish prick.

Soundlessly he turned, striding back to the arched bedroom door. Thing had been locked last night. Better damned well not be locked this morning.

Lexi was going to be pissed he'd gone on without her. Pissed and hurt, he knew, Couldn't be helped. He wanted—hell—needed to talk to Lucas and Simon. If the damned door was still locked— The elaborate iron handle turned easily this time. Nice, really frigging nice to lock up a guest.

Place was a castle. Enormous. Corridors and staircases every which where with no rhyme or reason. He figured he'd wander around until he found someone who could tell him where he was and where he was supposed to go. Because while this entire Vitro-Cyborg, mind-meld shit affected pretty much the entire god-damned planet, it was the three of them who were the last defense before the shit hit the fan.

Three men against whatever the fuck Mason had up his sleeve.

He didn't have to look far for roadside assistance. Lark waited for him in the wide-paneled corridor as he closed the colossal oak door quietly behind him. "Sleep all right, did you?" She tilted her head, her curling black hair falling across a skin-tight, bright red T-shirt that she'd paired with a black leather miniskirt and knee-high red-and-black leather boots. Across her chest, spelled out in two-inch-high, black-sequined letters was what he imagined was her mantra: *I tried being good but I got bored.*

She bit into her glossy red bottom lip as her kohl-lined eyes dissected him as if checking to see to the second how much sleep he'd actually managed.

Probably thirty minutes. Maybe less.

While Lexi had kept guard over him, he'd been aware of her every breath, her every light touch as *he'd* watched over *her.* Hell, be real. He hadn't wanted to waste what could possibly be their last few hours together. Idiot.

"No. I see you didn't," Lark said regretfully. "I'm sorry for that. But hopefully this will be over sooner than later."

"Yeah. Hopeful—" He squinted against bright sunlight streaming through wide windows as suddenly they stood in a sunny kitchen. A large wood, stone, black iron kitchen with a fireplace big enough to roast a cow in. Ah. Just as he'd suspected, Gabriel Edge's castle on the plains of Montana. Nice to know where the fuck he was.

Lucas and Simon sat at the table, nursing mugs of coffee. Jesus, it was good to see them. Good to be together again. Good, God help him, to know he wasn't alone in this. "Morning, fellow Borgs."

"What's a Borg?" Lark asked following him, her high-heeled boots clicking on the tiled floor.

"It's a reference to the television show *Star Trek.*" Duncan, wearing jeans and a thick cream sweater, indicated the half-empty pot set in a fancy Italian coffeemaker.

"We have new intel," he announced, pushing away from the counter to join the others at the table. "Want the good news or the bad news first?"

"Christ. I thought we got a pretty large dose of bad news last night." Lucas reached for the pot Alex had brought to the table with him. "What the hell. Go ahead and hit us with the bad first."

"I don't know how to tell you guys this, other than flat-out. None of you are full wizards."

Simon paused, his mug halfway to his mouth. He put it down on the scarred kitchen table very carefully. "You're kidding, right?"

Impossible. Alex knew he and his friends were full wizards. They couldn't have gotten into T-FLAC/psi if they weren't. "We were tested."

"We don't have Half Trace," Lucas, who could pick out a Half from a mile away—literally—pointed out.

"You're not Halfs either," Duncan said grimly. "Each of you is technically a *third*. For all these years, Knight has been able to manipulate your powers, and your Trace signals, to indicate that you're fulls."

Alex couldn't wrap his brain around the concept of not being who he believed he was. The last shred of his identity turned to confetti. Thirty-six years of lies. And if he wasn't a wizard, then what the fuck was he? Just a manufactured freak?

Sunlight bounced off the snowy grounds outside the thick castle walls, flooding the warm, homey kitchen with light. His vision dimmed and everything looked bleak and gray.

This was inconceivable. Impossible.

Fucking bullshit to the tenth power. "No mistake?" he demanded, mouth dry. He tried making sense of this latest blow. Duncan Edge shook his head.

From Lucas's shell-shocked expression he was thinking the same thoughts as Alex. *"Why?"*

"Genetically?" Duncan shrugged. "We don't know the logic. But it's indisputable. Look guys, everyone we have has been pulled off other ops to aid us in solving this one. T-FLAC/psi and regular operatives. From the damned accounting departments to the janitorial staff."

Lark, who was sitting up on the counter nearby, leaned forward, her sequins and various piercings sparkling in the sunlight. It was disconcerting looking at a woman who didn't behave, or think, the way she appeared. It might have to do with her age. He supposed a five-hundred-and-thirty-two-year-old could dress, and speak, any way she pleased. What the hell did he know. At least she knew who and what she was. He wasn't even a goddamn wizard anymore.

"Everyone is working around the clock to give you boyos as much information as possible before you confront Dr. Knight." Empathy lit her dark eyes. "You're not alone."

Alex glanced at each of his friends.

Yeah. They *were* alone. Very much so.

Because Mason Knight had manufactured them, then seen to their training, developed their powers as if they were full wizards, and now planned to assimilate them into the collective brain of his damned Vitros.

"Right," Simon responded skeptically. "What's our next step?"

"I have the relevant captured images of the left arm of seventy-three Vitros," Lexi said quietly from the doorway. Far from looking sleepy, she was wide awake, wired, and on point. All before he'd had his first cup of coffee of the day. She was wearing her black cargo pants, combat boots, and a fuzzy, pale pink sweater. Presumably borrowed from one of the resident, but unseen, Edge wives.

She looked smoking hot. A fact he wasn't about to share with her. He didn't want her here. But Lord, he was happy to see her beautiful, determined face. Another hour's reprieve? He'd take it.

"I've separated them into two piles." She acknowledged the other men in the room with a nod, but kept talking, gathering steam as she got closer. "Partials. Which, while those can give us a better understanding of locations, et cetera, aren't going to give us the full picture."

She got to the table. "Like these will." She splayed a stack of eight-and-a-half-by-eleven images on the table and kicked a chair free of the table with her foot. The images, an enlargement of the forearm of one of the Vitros, exposed the complete line of the bar code. The date and location of the picture ran across the bottom.

"Out of those seventy-three, we have sixty-two complete bar codes." She sat down beside Alex, sliding his untouched mug a little closer to her. Picking it up in both hands she took a sip. "We're going to triangulate Knight's location from what we have."

"Makes sense—thanks," said Duncan as he provided everyone with a computer, already humming, a holographic keyboard, and filled the empty pot with steaming, fragrant coffee.

Without hesitation, Lexi's fingers flew across her keyboard, fascinating Alex in spite of his own need to concentrate on gathering any pertinent data himself.

"You guys don't need to figure out locations," she told them absently, completely focused on her monitor where numbers scrolled. "I'm on it."

He'd observed her doing just this on more than one occasion before he'd materialized in her office and made himself known. She clearly had an affinity for finding pertinent facts. Fast.

Her pale nape looked vulnerable as she bent over the keyboard. Alex wanted to shift so he could press his mouth there. She had a little spot just behind her ear—"You're not looking at the pictures," he murmured, fascinated by the smooth line of her neck, and the silky hair at her nape.

"Photographic memory. Remember? HQ supplied the coordinates of every major city. I'm cross-matching those with the bar codes on the Vitros . . ."

"While Lexi does what she does best, let's recap what we know. The bombing and release of LZ17 was part of Knight's show-and-tell." Alex pulled his attention away from Lexi's neck.

"Yeah," Lucas inserted. "In each instance the highest bidder gets to choose the city of detonation—just a small taste of what using LZ17 can do. Clearly graduated annihilation; the explosions have been getting a little bigger each time."

"And presumably the money increased exponentially," Simon offered. "But that's not Mason, is it?"

All three men looked at each other.

Alex shook his head. "He wouldn't care about the money. That would just be a means of keeping score. He craves power." The memory snuck in delivering a sucker punch to the gut. *You boys have such fascinating jobs, there with T-FLAC. I'd be honored to do consulting work for such a fine organization. Hey, Alex-boy. I'd really like to get in on the ground floor on that Afghani op you mentioned. Can you say a word?*

And because he loved the man, he'd been blind enough to gladly oblige.

Simon rested his elbows on the table. "He's renting out these Vitros as a sustainable resource. I'm thinking he's giving various terrorist groups a sample of what an army like this can do. They wouldn't need a bomb delivery system. The Vitro is *it.*"

"Not in the school in Sydney," Alex pointed out. "There they had the LZ17 canisters."

"In the hope the media would get a good shot and publish it for bigger fear factor?" Lucas suggested skeptically.

"I don't know. Maybe."

Fingers still flying, Lexi cleared her throat. "He's been amassing viable Vitros for at least the past five years. I'm finding reports of unexplained black dust residue after terrorist attacks across the world. Hang on . . ."

"I thought you were getting us the coordinates of future locations?" Alex retrieved his coffee and drank.

"That's working in the background. This is interesting—They apparently need heat to germinate or whatever they do. That explains Rio, and also New Mexico. Of course there are plenty of hot spots in the world. I'll run a probability study . . ."

"I'd like to hear *your* experiences with these power shortages." Looking at the guys, Alex slung a casual arm across the back of Lexi's chair. There wasn't an atom in his body that felt casual about the conversation or the situation. The galling truth was he needed the physical connection with Lexi. Needed, like an addict needed his next fix. "I've gotta tell you guys I was kinda embarrassed by it."

"Were you?" Lucas gave Alex a knowing smile. "What's the bet that deep down we were all freaking shit-scared we were losing our powers? I know I was."

"Yeah," Alex leaned back in his chair. In his peripheral vision he could watch Lexi. "I know I was. Christ, do you realize if we hadn't been such idiots, we would have known about this *weeks* ago?"

"Hey," Simon filled his mug. "I tried calling you guys when I was in Mallaruza. You never returned my calls."

"Now isn't that fucking odd?" Lucas said flatly. "I called and left messages for both of you as well."

Alex frowned. "Ditto."

Lexi glanced up. "None of you got those messages? Are you saying someone inside T-FLAC sabotaged you?"

Alex looked from Lucas to Simon. "Thinking what I'm thinking?"

"Why don't you share with the class," Duncan suggested coolly.

"One of Knight's powers is the ability to suggest the Death Urge."

Duncan cursed.

Lexi looked up with a slight frown. "What does that mean? None of you died. You just didn't get your voice mail."

"Eliminating communication is child's play for someone like Knight. No, what we're talking about is his ability to make you believe you're all alone in the middle of your own worst nightmare. It translates to the situation at the Sydney Opera House with you and Ginsberg. All those feelings you experienced were an example of Knight's manipulation."

"That and I wanted to commit *suicide* in Russia," Lexi told him tightly. "I had an insane, overwhelming desire to jump off a fifteen-story building! The son of a bitch. He's been watching us the whole time. Watching us and manipulating—*all* of us."

The three of them would deal with Knight. But just the idea that he'd already been in Lexi's mind, not once but *twice,* scared the shit out of Alex. How in the hell could he protect her from that?

She got up. Alex knew she needed to pace to think things through. Instead of walking, she gripped the back of her chair, her knuckles white. "If he has this power, has he been able to transfer it to the Vitros?"

"I'd say—yes." Alex started typing. "I'm getting a full list of Knight's powers. Major and minor. Let's see what his damned army of Vitros has to offer us."

"You three need to list all of your powers, minor and major, too," Lexi told them. "He has powers. You have more."

"He's a strong and powerful wizard, Lexi." Duncan's expression was grim. "And he's had three times as long to accumulate and fine-tune what he has. He'll make a formidable opponent."

"Against Alex, Lucas, and Simon? Against the entire Wizard Council?" She was indignant.

"Screen nine," Alex told them. Everyone clicked over from their own project to the scrolling list of Knight's powers.

"Shit."

"Fuck."

"*Damn.*"

While Lexi knew all three of the men wanted go out there and find Knight, Duncan Edge had kept a cool head, and his will prevailed. There was no point going off half-cocked when they had no definitive destination, and before they came up with a viable plan.

She figured that all wizards had similar powers, in similar strengths. But apparently that wasn't the case. Knight's powers and magical skills put the powers of his three protégés in the shade. And these were only the skills they knew about from firsthand experience, and from documentation.

They were going to have to play this faster and much, *much* smarter than the man who'd taught them everything they knew. Tall order. "Of course," Lexi had pointed out five cups of coffee earlier, "he *didn't* teach you guys *everything* you know. You collectively have more than forty years of T-FLAC experience. Life experiences that you might have told him about, but he didn't experience with you. So he doesn't know every trick up your collective sleeves, does he?"

While Fox, Blackthorne, and Alex hadn't been exactly jazzed by that observation, it had given Lexi something positive and concrete to focus on.

Kess had come down a couple of hours before. She'd lingered looking over Simon's shoulder as he inputted information and then left to go to work. Her job at HQ was too new for her to take any time off, although Lexi could tell she was reluctant to leave Blackthorne. Even for a few hours.

Blackthorne walked her out into the entry hall to say good-bye before teleporting her to work. That means of transpo had allowed Kess an extra cup of coffee and thirty minutes to loiter. She was smart and intuitive, and Lexi, who'd never really had girlfriends because of all the middle-of-the-night moves, thought it would've been nice to have her with them.

Their good-bye had taken upward of eleven minutes, and Blackthorne looked a little shell-shocked when he returned to the war room—*kitchen.*

Seeing Kess and Blackthorne together had given Lexi a little ache of jealousy in her chest, which she quickly tamped down. Clearly they were in love, just as Fox and Sydney McBride were. The two men looked at their women as though they'd hung the moon.

Far from giving her loverlike looks, Alex was always shoving her hair off her face and scowling at her. So she needed a haircut, so what? she thought belligerently. He paid attention in bed. But that was . . . sex.

Has this got anything to do with the problem at hand, she demanded of herself, blocking her thoughts from Alex—and Duncan Edge—as best she could. *Absolutely not. Then focus, Stone. Concentrate on what can help. The rest is immaterial.*

The ache in her chest felt pretty damned lethal, but that wasn't based on logic. There was no proof that a broken heart could kill. It just felt that way.

"Okay?" Alex asked softly, as people shifted in their seats, or got up to stretch. Conversations would break out as one or the other brought up a point for debate or analysis.

Lexi didn't glance up. "Hunky-dory."

Fox's fiancé, Sydney, wandered downstairs in the late morning, then went off with the creaky and charming MacBain to the "sunroom" for tea. Sounded boring as hell to Lexi, who'd rather be in the middle of this strategic meeting than just about anywhere else.

Don't? What had Alex meant? Don't stay awake guarding him? Not likely. Don't love him. That's what he'd meant. Don't love me. Why? Because he didn't return the feelings? Wasn't going to make a damn bit of difference in the intensity of *her* feelings. It sucked that he didn't reciprocate, but either way she wasn't going to stop loving him. She couldn't stop. Simple as that.

"Hell, look at this."

Alex's exclamation made her jump. "Page?" Lexi asked. The little screens flickered as the new pages became an additional popup window on their monitors.

"Three-sixty-four."

"Jesus," Fox said softly as his eyes scanned the pages slowly scrolling in front of all of them. "This is proof that he's amassing an army for hire." His voice shifted into an annoying imitation of an announcer in an infomercial. "Got an enemy? A head of state? An annoying neighboring country? For a fee, I'll take care of them for you. No need to deplete your own resources. My tangos are a renewable resource, and have infinite applications."

"Well, isn't that just fucking green of him," Blackthorne muttered.

"Look at the intel two paragraphs down," Alex told the others. "Not just money changing hands. Favors, like a fucking mafia. The

son of a bitch is asking that as a show of good faith the buyer take
out someone else's enemy. You want to take out the government of
Uzbekistan? I'll send in my Vitros, in exchange you take out one of
China's enemies."

"That doesn't tell us *where* they are," Blackthorne snarled,
scrolling through the intel Alex had up. "Where are you, suckers?
Where is he keeping you? Where is he manufacturing you?"

"They're human," Lexi said quietly. "*Almost* human, anyway.
Page two-sixty-eight. Look at their makeup in this lab report. All
intel suggests that he's worked on making these clones—*Vitros*—as
human as possible. My educated guess is that he's tried and failed,
tried and failed. I showed you that report of terrorist activities over
the years with the black dust residue, so we know he screwed up—
a lot.

"Now we have warehouses of infants." Lexi got up to pace
around the large kitchen. It was getting dark outside and someone
had come in and unobtrusively turned on the lights. She smelled
something savory cooking, and heard the sound of female voices
from another room.

"We also have enormous tanks holding thousands of gallons of
liquid human remains. We have wizards—and Halfs—donating
sperm. Let's say he did some sperm-washing and has now come up
with the Vitros, his version of a mean-tempered pit bull. Is it possible that all the wizard . . . remains used to feed—God that's disgusting—feed these Vitros as they grow, is it possible that they also
got those donors' powers? Is it possible for Knight to have given
some of his powers to the Vitros, do you think?"

"First of all," Alex stood to stretch his legs after sitting so long.
"These aren't well-trained pit bulls. Vitros are ice-cold killing machines. Second, if Knight could transfer his powers or those of the
donor wizards, they'd be more powerful. But they're fairly easy to
kill. Yeah, they're trained. As well trained as we are to a certain extent. But basically they're expendable drones."

"But they *don't* have Knight's powers. That's the good news, by the way," Duncan added.

"Now you tell us?" Fox muttered.

"Seemed rather anticlimactic after the bad news," Duncan answered.

"But that's good, isn't it?" Lexi perked up. "They don't have Knight's entire range of superpowers. That's actually excellent— What? Why do you all have that same weird expression?"

"Because," Alex told her grimly, "that's something Knight *can't* do for whatever reason. Something he's clearly tried and failed to do over the last thirty-plus years, otherwise he wouldn't need anyone else to make this work. Knight *can't* transfer his powers to the Vitros. But *we* apparently *can*. *That's* why our powers have been flickering."

Fox took a deep breath, held it, let it out. "Knight *has* a power source—"

He looked at Blackthorne.

Blackthorne looked at Lexi. "We're the goddamn batteries for his little army. We're being fucking absorbed into the collective."

"What?! Wait. Are you telling me that the son of a bitch set up your deaths thirty-six years ago?" Lexi demanded, incensed. "His insane master plan all along was that eventually your minds, powers, and skills would be absorbed by the collective? That the stronger the *Vitros* become, the weaker the three of you will become, until you're completely absorbed and *die*?"

Alex looked at his friends, turned to hold Lexi's gaze. "That pretty much sums things up in a nutshell. If we're *lucky,* we'll die. The alternative is he'll control us as easily as he does our clones. Bottom line? We're to be 'one' with the collective. We'll become Vitro power chow."

Eighteen

"We're missing something," Lexi muttered, her entire focus on her monitor. "*I'm* missing something." *What?* The fact that the kitchen was filled with people—walking around, talking on their phones, opening and closing the refrigerator, eating, drinking, didn't impact her concentration one iota. Being this close to Alex sent her mind spiraling, and she had to constantly pull it back into focus.

"Come on come on come on. Where are you? *What* are you?" Somewhere in this mass of numbers and charts and statistics and accumulated intel was the missing key. All she had to do was *find* it.

"Lexi," Alex squeezed her shoulder. "We can't make whole cloth of this many bits and pieces. Not without hundreds of hours of using what we have to find him. We don't have hundreds of hours to spare."

"No, we don't. But this is just one giant dot-to-dot. And I was always good at those." She shifted the bar code location to the side, and brought up temperatures. Longitude and latitude. The ages of the Vitros. The ages of Alex, Blackthorne and Fox . . . The DNA reports. Just bits of information. Nothing connected the dots. Yet.

"Okay. Let's see if we can pinpoint a location as a start," Duncan Edge suggested. He was a lot less intimidating out of his official robe and wearing jeans and a sweater.

Great suggestion. Manageable, and instant gratification. "Good plan." Lexi let out a tight breath. This was her job. She was supposed to be able to take countless pieces of unconnected data and form some sort of cohesive—*something*. But first things first.

"Most of the world's deserts are clustered between five to thirty degrees north and south of the equator, in the subtropical zones. That covers a considerable number of miles to search. A lot of miles, and—I think you're right—not a lot of time. Here's where you guys need to look first." She enlarged the data to fill their monitors. "Page nine-eighty-one."

Alex looked at hers over her shoulder. "Death Valley in Nevada, and while whoever is there might as well hit the area around Avondale, Arizona, as well."

She added a graphic, because it helped make things more visual and dimensional. "El Azizia, Libya. Situated right here." She added another little flashing beacon graphic to the northern part of the African continent as well. "And the Tirat Tavi area in Israel. Statistically these are the three most likely places he's breeding the Vitros."

"Good job," Alex said, then quietly repeated what she'd said into his sat phone, presumably reporting in to Ellicott. For once Lexi was almost—*almost* unaware of him.

What am I missing? It's here. Somewhere. If I just knew where to look . . . Ack! This incomplete data was as maddening as unraveling the mystery was fascinating.

"We have the three most logical locations." Alex brushed the back of her neck, making her shiver, as he removed his hand from her shoulder. "We'll divide and conquer. Split up, each take a psi team—we'll find him."

"Uh-huh," she muttered absently, her fingers flying across the keyboard. If she moved this intel over here, then added this to that, and carried these stats forward to go with the reports on the latest Vitro events and cross-referenced the data on their expiration— Damn. It still wasn't enough. They might know statistically where Knight would likely be, but they had no way of knowing when he'd hit. One little puzzle piece was missing.

Her computer dinged. Excellent. New data. "Shit!"

Edge, who'd come up beside Alex, moved to stand behind her chair. "What do you have?"

"Check this out." Heart pounding with excitement, Lexi's fingers flew across the holographic keyboard.

"Ah—what do the numbers represent?" Blackthorne asked apologetically.

Odd, because to Lexi it was perfectly obvious. "These are all the dates of applicable terror incidents that took place over the last five years. Some of these places and dates are confirmed Knight hits. There are a handful that I can't confirm or substantiate, but I believe due to witness reports that these are his as well. Hang on— let me put them in order as if they *were* actually confirmed . . . There."

She scowled at the screen. For a second there she'd been sure this was going to answer at least some of their questions. "Hang on, let me make a graph so—"

"We don't need a graph," Edge said politely. "Just tell us."

"The graph is easier to read—No? Okay. This is completely illogical. There's no rhyme or reason to what's going on—Let me
take this one out. And these three . . . Now let's see." She shook her
head and manipulated more dates. "It doesn't make any kind of
logical sense—I don"t see a damn pattern of—Wait—" She turned
to meet Alex's eyes.

"If I'm interpreting this mess correctly—and I believe I am—
According to these numbers, the big bang is in seven hours."

Before he left for Libya, Alex had a private meeting with Blackthorne and Fox in Gabriel Edge's impressive library. Yeah, this had
become everybody's business, but theirs were the lives, souls, whatever the hell they were on the line.

It wasn't Lexi's "big bang" he and the guys were worried about.
There were so many T-FLAC and T-FLAC/psi operatives on it
that it would be a miracle if Knight managed to start so much as a
campfire, let alone blow up a country. They hoped.

It was that, the prelude to the big bang event would be the *as-
similation* of the three of them. Since they had no idea how that
worked, or when or how it would happen, they all agreed that
they had to get their affairs in order.

They had to take into account that the world would be saved.
They would not.

Suddenly wills had to be changed, provisions made, financials
set. Being wizards helped, but the arrangements still took thirty-
two minutes of precious time.

"One more thing," Lucas said after the legal guys shimmered out
of the room, and just before they returned to the ever-growing
collection of assorted specialists in the other room.

"What?" Blackthorne indicated that Fox, closest to the door,
open the damn thing, they'd wasted enough time. "Our dicks fall
off to give us a warning?"

"Sydney amps my power when we're together. More so when we physically touch. Either of you experience something like it with your ladies?"

"No," Blackthorne answered flatly. "Open the door. Let's get this show on the road."

"How does it manifest itself?" Alex asked. The way he felt when he was around Lexi amped . . . something. He didn't think it was his powers, however.

Fox described what happened when he and Sydney touched. Alex felt a ridiculous surge of envy. It sounded cool. He wanted that—hell, he wanted everything—with Lexi. "Nope. Not that way for us." He shot a glance at Blackthorne. "You?"

"Unfortunately not."

"Then we're not all the same, are we?" Fox said quietly.

"Or having the women amp our powers hasn't started for us yet," Alex offered.

Fox put his fingers on the ornate door handle. "Or maybe you two don't have the *right* women?"

"No," Alex told him coolly. "Not the case."

"Same here," Blackthorne said firmly as he tossed something into the air.

Before he could catch it, Alex beat him to it with a lightning-fast reflex. Opening his hand Alex saw the glint of the golden circle and the sparkle of the diamond. "What the hell are you doing with this?"

Blackthorne snatched the ring out of Alex's open palm. "I'm making things right with Kess before I go. You might want to think about doing the same with Lexi."

"It's not like that."

Blackthorne and Fox both laughed. "Deny it all you want, bro. You've fallen for her," Fox said, slapping Alex on the back.

"If she's the right one, then what does a ring matter," he retorted.

"Well, replied Fox, if they are the right ones, then we have to presume that like Sydney and me, the pair of you could potentially have your powers amped by Lexi and Kess. It might make the difference between 1—"

"Immaterial," Alex cut him off, reaching over to pull the handle since Fox seemed to be on a mental field trip. "Fucking power surge or not, I don't give a damn that she's a trained operative. She's trained for everything but dying a slow and painful death. I'm not taking Lexi anywhere *near* Mason."

Blackthorne nodded, his expression grim. "Now *there's* something we all agree on."

Lexi and the other women were sitting on the lower steps of the enormous sweeping staircase outside the library when the three men came out.

"Here's something that not only all of *us* agree on," Sydney said mildly, getting to her feet. "But *Duncan* agrees with us. We go where you go."

"No!" Alex, Lucas, and Simon said simultaneously.

"You're taking a full team," Lexi said reasonably, also standing. Adrenaline pumped through her system, making everything appear bigger and brighter. She wanted to leap from the third step and fling herself into Alex's arms. He looked grim and unyielding. In the thirty-some minutes the guys had been doing whatever it was they'd been doing in their host's library, she'd retrieved her weapons and listened to Edge's logic about why the three women should join the teams. "*I'm* a member of your team."

Alex gave Lexi a cold look that could slice steel. "No."

Kess opened her mouth. Simon swept her with a glacial green glance. "*You're* not an *operative*. You work in the damned information dissemination department."

"And you don't work for T-FLAC at all," Fox concluded, glaring at Sydney.

She walked down the stairs to stand toe-to-toe with him on the stone floor. Like Lexi and Kess she was dressed in black cargo pants, a black long-sleeved shirt, boots, and underneath—LockOut. The only difference between Sydney's outfit and the other two women was that she'd pinned a small yellow flower she'd found—somewhere—to her lapel. "I'm a temp. Deal with it."

Lexi bit back a smile. A *temp*?

"Jesus." Lucas looked at Sydney with horror. "You're *armed*."

"My brothers—"

"Taught you to frickin' shoot *tin cans* in the backyard!"

Sydney turned to Lexi and Kess. "Years and years at the shooting range. Own a gun. *Extremely* proficient."

Lexi bit her lip so she didn't laugh, giving Sydney a thumbs-up. It was no laughing matter. Not even close. But Duncan Edge wanted them to go, and go they would. Lexi kept to herself that she thought the beautiful Sydney and perky Kess weren't in any way qualified to go on an op. She'd been trained for this. And she was going. Come hell or high water. Or Alex.

"What are you thinking?" Simon Blackthorne glared at Kess. "Are you a souped-up marksman with years of experience I don't know anything about?"

Her chin tilted pugnaciously. "I know which end of a gun bullets come out of," she answered grimly. "I know how to pull the trigger, and Lexi showed me how to install a clip."

"Hell."

"Shit."

"Damn."

"Is that a yes?" Lexi asked.

"*No!*" The three men shouted in unison.

El Azizia, Libya
32° 31' 48" N, 13° 0' 36" E
T minus 6.5 hours

"—than ninety percent of the country is desert or semidesert," Lexi told the men, running a bottle of tepid water across her cheek, as they drove through shifting sands. "Water here is a *big* problem. Twenty-eight percent of the population doesn't even have access to safe drinking water. Can you imagine that in this day and age?"

The rhetorical question was met with a few grunts and a "huh?"

Lexi was part of the twelve-man team. Eleven men, one small, gray-eyed, bull-headed female. Alex was glass-chewing-head-exploding-*furious* with both Duncan Edge and the Council for even *suggesting* that Lexi and the other two women be allowed anywhere near Mason Knight.

Fox, just as pissed, had reluctantly taken Sydney and his team to Death Valley. Blackthorne, Kess, and his team headed for Israel. Alex took El Azizia, Libya. Even in the winter it was hot. But tolerably so. The fact that he was hot under the collar was not due to the thermometer nor mitigated by full-body LockOut.

He'd stuck Lexi in the middle seat of the twenty-something-year-old passenger van. The middle of the fucking middle seats. Surrounded by hundreds of pounds of wizards in full-body Lock-Out, and as much wizard power as they'd been able to muster. The only way he and the others had relented, and that had taken precious time arguing at full voice, was if the Council put protective spells on the three women, gave them some powers of their own, and ensured—fucking-well *guaranteed*—that *no matter what*—they would be protected at all costs.

It still wasn't enough. Not for Alex, not for Lucas or Simon.

"The Phoenicians were the first to establish trading posts in Libya," Lexi informed the hot, sweaty, spoiling-for-a-fight wizards trapped in the fast-moving vehicle with her. "When the merchants of Tyre—that's present-day Lebanon—developed commercial relations with the Berber tribes and made treaties with them to ensure t—"

Her voice was like nails tapping through his skull. Each word a reminder she was here instead of someplace safe. And it was fucking killing him. "Stone? Give it a rest. We'd like to hear ourselves think," Alex said from the seat behind her.

"The radio doesn't work," she pointed out reasonably. They'd been driving for forty minutes. She'd been talking for at least thirty-nine of them.

"Got a damn iPod?"

She shrugged. "Not on me."

"Then *sing.*"

Several guys cleared their throats. One was stupid enough to laugh.

"I don't know how to sing."

"Perfect. Then just be quiet. Problem solved."

Lucas had shared his Trace Teleport ability with both himself and Simon. Edge had amped their powers. Alex cast the Trace out as far as he could. Half-wizards here and there. Going about their businesses as they'd done in this area for hundreds of years. Merchants, not tangos. Not Vitros. Not goddamned Mason Knight.

"I don't suppose anyone wants to hear how the Greeks conquered Eastern Libya when, according to tradition, emigrants from the island of Thera were commanded by the oracle at Delphi to find a less crowded place to live in North Africa. They founded the city of Cyrene in 630 B—"

Cranston, sitting next to Alex, burst out laughing, a couple of the other guys muffled their amusement. Alex grabbed the back of Lexi's neck and gave it a warning sqeeze.

"Just saying—" *Sorry. I can't help myself. I'm so freaking scared I can't shut up.*

He knew she was, which was why, against every instinct, he hadn't teleported her back to Eldridge Castle for safekeeping where she'd be even more afraid. Becaue Lexi, being the woman she was, wasn't in the least bit afraid for her own safety. She thought she was there to protect *him*. Her bravery, her single-mindedness, her sheer *guts,* humbled him.

Wanna come back here with me?

From this close he could feel the relief roll off of her. *Please.*

At this point why the hell did he care if his men knew he and Lexi were— Whatever they thought was immaterial. He didn't fucking care. All he wanted was Lexi. Lexi close. Lexi happy. Lexi safe. "Cranston? Switch seats with Stone. I think I have some duct tape in my pack."

T minus 4 hours

They stopped for gas. Everyone got out to stretch their legs or hit the head. "He's not here, is he?" Lexi asked Alex quietly. In a small square of shade, they leaned against the wall of a market while Williams filled the tank. "Thanks." She took the soda bottle he opened and handed her. She drank deeply. It was some kind of orange drink, and warm, but at least it was thirst quenching.

"I'm sorry we weren't the ones to find him."

His throat moved as he chugged his own drink. His skin gleamed with sweat, his damp hair clung to his face and neck. He looked hot and sexy. If one didn't know him as well as Lexi did, one would miss that he was pale under his tan, that his respiration was a little too shallow, and that his mouth was tense.

"Lucas and Simon didn't have any better luck than we did."

"I'm sorry," Lexi repeated. It was her fault for sending all these people on wild goose chases all over the world when the clock was ticking.

"Gotta play the hand you've got."

She turned her body toward him so that none of the others could see what she was saying. "Are you feeling okay?"

His hesitation was infinitesimal, but Lexi saw it. "I feel—Hell, Lexi. I don't know . . . Pulled? Drawn?"

"He's calling to you?"

"God. I wish it were that simple. Something's happening, I know. It's *what* that I don't. Whatever it is is getting stronger and stronger. And I'm feeling weaker and weaker, like I'm a goddamn energy drink and somebody's stuck a straw in me and is slowly sucking everything out."

"Take the power the Council gave me," she said urgently. "Do it. I don't know how to use it anyway."

He shook his head. "Four hours. Where the fuck *is* he?"

Lexi screwed her face up in concentration. There had to be something. Something that wasn't in the data. Something personal that was a key to all of this, because for Knight this was all about him. "Did he have a favorite place that he took you guys when you visited?"

"His London house, usually. That's not warm enough to hatch these damned Vitros."

Lexi tapped her mouth. "Anywhere he liked to go on vacation? A weekend retreat? A *book* he shared with you?" She was reaching, but they only had a handful of hours left. "Anything could be significant. How about a—"

Alex swept her up in his arms and gave her a quick, delicious kiss on the mouth. Lexi drank it in like the sand beneath her feet absorbed water, unfortunately it was over too quickly. "You're brilliant," he said, smiling as he put her down and touched the connection on his ear that linked him via sat phone with Lucas and Simon.

"I know where he is," he told everyone involved in the hunt. "Hang on—Lexi can give you the latitude and longitude."

"I can?" she mouthed.

"Morocco. Casablanca, to be precise."

Nineteen

"How did you figure *this* out?" Duncan Edge gave Alex a concerned look that Alex chose to ignore.

At least a hundred wizards crowded in a parking lot a mile from a warehouse on the outskirts of the city. As did Alex, Simon, Lucas, their teams, *and* the Council.

Edge and his Council had come on a freaking *field trip*.

Alex swallowed intense nausea. While his senses swam a little, his vision was preternaturally sharp. He'd had to ask Duncan to conjure high-tint sunglasses to cut the agonizing brightness of the sun.

Lucas and Simon had requested the same. They both looked as bad as Alex felt.

A buzz of a million bees made thought and hearing damned difficult. He forced himself to take small sips of air, and tried to concentrate. It wasn't easy. This was taking brain fog to a whole new level. He heard *everybody's* thoughts in a low, indecipherable, incredibly irritating, *burble*.

He and Lexi half stood, half sat, braced against the front of a derelict 1940s Ford pickup truck. No paint, no engine. No back half. The metal was hot through his clothing. Hot through LockOut. Shouldn't have felt *anything* through the LockOut, but he felt it all. The heat, the softness of Lexi's skin where she was tucked against his side. The silk of her hair where her head rested under his chin.

If someone had asked Alex to push away and stand on his own he wasn't sure he could do it. Lexi had both arms wrapped around his waist. Neither of them gave a damn who saw them.

He was glad for her support. Both physically and emotionally. He didn't want her there. God, he really didn't want her within a million miles of Knight. But the fact that she was here now touched him deeply.

"What?" He remembered Edge had asked him something. "Oh, yeah. He likes the old black-and-white movies." He had to breathe through his mouth. He didn't remember feeling this weak in his life, and that included being starved and beaten for weeks on end in Italy all those years ago, or the first time he'd had malaria. Or—hell, a host of other job-related crap that had knocked him on his ass over the years.

This was worse. Much worse. Somehow on those occasions he'd known he was going to make it. By sheer guts and determination he'd never lost sight of the prize.

Now . . . He swallowed hard to prevent heaving. He put up a hand to indicate it was talk and puke, or shut the hell up.

"Casablanca was his—Jesus. Be right back." Lucas peeled away from the group and ran behind the clothing store in the middle of the weed-infested lot where they'd gathered.

Not only could Alex hear him puking, he heard his heartbeat separated from everyone else's. He heard Lexi's eyelashes brush her bangs, and a mouse scurrying in the grass three hundred feet away. He could even hear the scratching of a beetle on the fence across the street.

They'd lost twenty excellent psi operatives in the last ten minutes. The do not disturb was that strong. The men had been the first wave to attempt to enter the warehouse. Edge had insisted, no, *ordered,* the three of them to stand well back.

The men had literally bounced—hell, they'd been flung back so hard and so fast they'd landed with every bone in their bodies shattered, their flesh and bones pulverized as though they'd been tenderized like raw steak thrown out of a cannon. "Friday nights," Blackthorne's skin was ashen, but he valiantly tried to complete the thought Alex had started and Lucas had picked up. Simon's sweaty face was ashen, his breathing labored. "Movie night. Christ, I . . . *Casablanca* was Knight's favorite."

Kess slid her arm around his waist, almost holding him up. "You need to lie down, dammit, Simon!"

"Later."

Lucas returned, clearly weak. Sydney made a grab for him as his knees buckled. With her arms wrapped tightly around his waist, she glared at Edge. "*Do* something, dammit!"

"Cone of privacy," Edge said. "More," he instructed the Council when he didn't believe it was strong enough. Nice to fucking note that the Head of Council didn't ask the three of them to put in their two cents' worth of powers right then. Did they even have any?

"Everyone knows what's happening here," Alex pointed out when the noise level lessened to just those in his head.

"This they don't need to hear. Here are the cold hard facts,"

Edge told them. "In less than an hour if our suspicions are sound, you'll all be assimilated into this insane experiment of Dr. Knight's. We can't allow that to happen." His eyes lit on each man in turn. "You understand that, right? It *cannot* be allowed to happen. If these Vitros absorb your powers, there'll be nothing to stop them. Collectively they'll be stronger than anyone we have."

His dark blue eyes looked black; his expression was as grim as Alex had ever seen it. "The three of you have to make a choice."

"*What* choice?" Lexi demanded, tightening her arms around Alex, her body all but surrounding his, and as tall as she was, he still outweighed her by fifty pounds.

His warrior. "Don't worr—"

She turned on him like a viper. "Don't you dare tell me not to *worry*. I'm *way* freaking beyond being worried." She glared at Edge. "What choice do they have to make?"

"They have to *die,*" Sydney said flatly. The jaunty little yellow flower she'd stuck in her buttonhole was wilted, and Alex heard the petal that fell onto her shirt. "Isn't that right, Lucas? You guys have to *die* so you can't be assimilated."

Kess stood up straighter, her red hair like fire in the sunlight. "*That's* not a fucking choice. I am not letting *Simon* die."

"There's another way." Lexi's jaw was rigid, her entire body pulsing with fear. Alex smelled the perspiration on her skin, heard the frantic beat of her heart. "Take *away* their powers," she told Edge. "Take them away *now*. Knight won't want to assimilate them if they have no powers, right?" She looked from Edge and the Council behind him to Alex and back again. "Right? Just take away their powers, for God's sake."

"You must all agree to do the same thing," Edge said somberly. He glanced at his watch. "If Lexi's estimate of the time left is correct, you have fourteen minutes. If she's off—"

"This is not their decision to make." A tall, beak-faced member of the Council interrupted as he stepped forward in a swirl of black robe, his cowl pushed to his shoulders. Jack Anderson was even more by-the-book than Lexi. "There's no time to waste. We've indulged them too long as it is. I vote that they be terminated immediately. Dr. Knight is powerful enough to reinstate their powers if they're temporarily removed. And any wizard would rather perish than lose his powers for all time. All in favor of death?"

"Aye."

"Aye."

"Nay."

"Aye."

"Nay."

"A—"

A sickening swirl of white alerted Lexi as they teleported. Blindly she reached out for Alex, then almost wept with relief when her fingers encountered his bare arm. She gripped it with one hand, and reached for her weapon with the other. No weapon. Crap.

She wobbled as they materialized. Thank God no nausea this time. She was becoming an old hand.

She blinked the surroundings into focus.

Oh, crap. Nausea would have been the *least* of her problems.

The interior of the warehouse was brightly lit, almost clinically so. Large black boxes, like upright coffins or mainframe computers, marched in straight rows as far as the eye could see in every direction. Wrist-thick electrical cords—*umbilical* cords?—snaked up to the ceiling.

Against the south wall stood five enormous Type 304, stainless steel storage tanks. The rumble of heavy machinery pulsed through the muggy air and vibrated beneath her boots. A trickle of perspiration ran down her temple. The place was like a sauna.

She turned to Alex. First, he appeared transfixed by the magnitude of the—whatever the boxes were. Second, and more important, he was *naked*.

"Ah, my boys. Thank you for following the bread crumbs. This is exactly where and when I wanted you all here. Perfect timing."

Mason Knight.

He referred to his "boys," but as far as Lexi could tell, only she, Alex, and Knight were present.

"The women have nothing to do with this," Alex told Dr. Knight. "Get rid of them and we'll talk."

"You always did think you could talk your way out of a fix, didn't you, Alex? Tenacious. Amphibious. Your ability to null psionic fields. Ah, let's not forget your skill at Temporal Acceleration."

He had a genial, avuncular smile. Lexi loathed him on sight. "And Lucas. There you are. Your contribution is just as important. Trace perception, ubiquitous vision, and Empathic Perception, a skill that will enhance what I've already taught my Vitros. Ah, a fanciful name, and one the three of you had every right to coin. I like it.

"And Simon. Your contribution will be your skill at Remote Viewing, and the ability to duplicate yourself as a hologram—My God. Your collective powers will be invaluable."

"How can you do this to them?" Lexi cried, enraged. "They thought of you as their friend. A father figure—"

"Don't engage him, for God's sake." *I don't want him to take any more notice of you than he has to.*

Rather me than you. What are we going to do?

Working on it.

"Ah. Alex, she's lovely. And delightfully spirited. She'll do well."

In spite of the sweltering wet heat, Lexi went cold. "Do w—"

"Do well at *what,* Mason?"

"It's been quite inconvenient and complicated obtaining the fluids of suitable wizards and Halfs, my boy. Due to your diligence, and that of Lucas and Simon, you've gifted me with three lovely, healthy young women as breeding stock."

Bile rose in the back of Lexi's throat.

"Unacceptable."

Yeah. That, she thought, tamping down unproductive terror and a good dose of hysteria. Neither of which was going to solve the problem of besting Knight and getting Alex as far away from him as humanly possible. Emotions had no place in any of this. She had to keep a cool, *logical* head.

Knight laughed with genuine amusement. "You think not?"

"Teleport Lexi outside, and we can talk about this project of yours."

"I'd like to give you a little tour before we begin. An *overview,* if you will."

"Screw you, you sick fuck! Not until Lexi leav—Aargh!" With a cry of agony, Alex dropped to his knees, his face contorted as he doubled over. Whatever Knight was doing to him, Alex's body shook. The muscles in his back and arms bulged and contorted as he fought the pain.

"Stop it!" Lexi dropped to her knees beside Alex. She couldn't help him to his feet because his entire body was wracked and contorted by the agony Knight was inflicting on him. She spread her fingers on his sweat-drenched back. *I'm here. I'm not going to leave you. Ride the pain.* His skin felt like ice despite being washed in sweat. She lifted her head, furious because her eyes swam with tears. "Dammit, stop it, you're killing him!"

"Don't be tiresome, gentlemen," Knight muttered as though Lexi hadn't yelled at him like a madwoman. "No talking. Come along, ladies, the boys can catch up when they decide to behave themselves."

Alex shot to his feet as though he were a puppet on a string. His sudden movement knocked her on her ass, and she shot him a terrified look as she scrambled to her feet. He seemed oblivious. Oh God, oh God.

"Come along, girls. Let's start here," Knight suggested, leading Lexi between the tall boxes. She turned her head, reluctant to leave Alex, and dreading following Knight. Divide and conquer?

Alex's arms hung to his sides, his chest heaved with every breath as though he were under unbearable torment. He seemed to be almost in a trance. Lexi's heart was beating so hard she was afraid she was literally going to have a heart attack right there. No heart attack, don't be dramatic, she told herself fiercely. *Forget everything but staying cool and calm and using your God-given smarts.*

"Alexis? Come along, my dear. I think you'll quite enjoy this."

As much as she didn't want to leave Alex's side, she considered the possibility that if she went with Knight, Alex might figure out a way to break free. But—Lord. Was he changing into one of these . . . *machines* right before her very eyes? She didn't know what to do . . .

"The Alex version 2002," Knight paused. "A *very* good year, and one I like to call the beginning. The Lucas model peaked in 2004, the Simon model later that same year. As with anything, practice made perfect. And here they are." He opened his arms expansively. "My creations. Like the three boys, *creations.*"

Alex? Snap the hell out of it. We have to get out of here.

No response. Sweat oiled his body, his eyes were glazed and unfocused. The muscles across his chest looked carved from stone. This was bad. Really, really bad.

She had to follow Knight as he strolled between the black glass-fronted boxes, display cases, whatever the hell they were.

"Of course this started almost forty years ago," Knight said amicably as they walked. "But I'm sure you don't want me going *that* far back."

Alex. Talk to me.

Knight kept talking, and Lexi dared to take her attention away from Alex for a second to see what Knight was showing her.

The Vitros.

Naked, blank-eyed duplicates of a twenty-year-old Alex.

Alex times a thousand.

Their glass-fronted containers went on to what looked like infinity. Lexi couldn't breathe.

"How—" Her mouth was so dry she could barely push the words out.

"How do I do it?" Knight asked, clearly pleased with the question. "Oh, now that I've almost perfected their production, I do it very well indeed, my dear." He laughed at his own little joke. "Very well indeed." His American accent had a slight British undertone, Lexi presumed from living there for many years. His *teeth* had been done in England. They were too big, and too white under a sinister black mustache and surrounded by a gray beard that matched his hair.

He looked exactly what he was. The villain.

Forget the man's teeth, Stone. Think.

"The infants are created in a test tube," he told her with not a little pride. "The gestation period for my Vitros is twelve months. Birth to death. One year. That was part of their wrist marking, of course. Longitude and latitude of where they were hatched, then their expiration date one year later."

She was going to keep the son of a bitch talking until she could figure out how to get Alex and herself out of here. Or die trying. "Where are the babies?"

"Ah, the maternal instinct. Yes, let me show you the fourteen-day-olds. You boys wait here. This way," he said to Lexi.

There were no *boys*. There was Alex. Alone. Where were the others? Lexi had no idea. And she couldn't worry about them. If she didn't keep on task, and think fast and smart, Alex would be lost to her forever.

And she'd be a broodmare for Vitros. Bile rose up the back of her throat as they turned down a corridor made up of staring Vitros. The completely nude drones were in various stages of development. In one long row of gestation cases, they looked about six, another early teen, in another their late teens. Tubes and electrical cables ran in and out of their bodies while the bank of various colored lights behind them flashed and flickered, indicating . . . something.

They emerged from between the tall boxes to an open area. Thousands of square feet filled with the same isolettes she'd observed in New Mexico. This time they were occupied by what looked like newborns. Her heart twisted. Hal . . .

Every infant was the same length and weight. None of them moved about like normal babies. They stared at her blankly, with identical green eyes in identical little faces. Babies. But not.

Wires, bundled neatly, hung from a dropped ceiling, attached to each—not child, Lexi thought, repulsed. Each clone.

"The twenty-nine-day-olds are automatically transferred by this conveyer to the larger incubators. Ah, there's a batch being moved now. Would you like to watch the transfer?"

No. It was the very last thing she wanted to do. She followed him anyway. Lexi was ready to kill this monster with her bare hands. If she had the physical strength to do it, she would. Every step of the way she'd looked for something—anything—she could possibly use as a weapon.

"Sure." *Any time you want to freaking chime in, Stone, feel free.*

Nothing from Alex. *Lucas? Simon? Anybody?!*

Knight talked as though everyone was together. But there was no indication that Simon and Lucas were anywhere near. She and Alex were it. And Alex . . .

She was it.

Beyond the thousand isolettes, smaller open bassinets took up a quarter of the vast warehouse. There was no such nicety as a blanket, or anything else soft one expected around an infant. *Not babies,* she told herself. *These are not human babies. Get that out of your head.*

These Vitros were bigger than the "newborns." They had the same blank stare, the same rigid limbs. Yet their eyes tracked her movement, and their small lungs rose and fell.

God, it's hot in here. Hot and close, and terrifying.

Right. It is. Now get over that and figure out what you're going to do to get out of here.

It helped—*slightly*—knowing Edge and the Council and a hundred powerful wizards were practically outside the door trying to do exactly what she was trying to do. Save Alex and the others.

The sound of moving machinery snagged her attention, and she watched transfixed as large, rubber-tipped tongs passed over each bassinet. A slight creak as the metal opened, and they dipped inside, picking up each clone by the head. *Not babies. Not babies. Oh, God. Not babies.* The tiny naked forms rose in synchronized batches to the continuous belt crisscrossing the ceiling like laundry on a moving clothesline.

This is a replica of Alex.

God, I can't think like that.

Not. Babies. Clones. Not Alex. Clones.

There's a special place in hell for you, you sick bastard. "Then what happens?"

"Then they're inserted into these development tanks. Watch."

She could tell he was very pleased with himself. Lexi's fingers flexed at her sides. Sweat glued her hair to her face and neck. She shoved her bangs out of her eyes. If she could find something to use as a weapon. Something heavy. Something hard. Something sharp . . . Anything could be made into a weapon.

Knight was a powerful wizard. But he was also an old man. His steps faltered slightly as he walked as if his joints and bones ached.

"This stage always gives me a thrill," he said with a little smile.

With small, repetitive clicks, the glass doors on the large boxes opened. A baby clone was released inside. Arm and leg bands snapped around their limbs holding them upright, tubes snaked around their small pale bodies and were then inserted. Presumably delivering nutrients.

The doors closed. Click-click times a thousand.

Lexi did a quick scan of her surroundings and saw she was still alone. Her tongue stuck to the roof of her mouth. "How long?"

"Until they resemble a twenty-year-old? All told, twenty-two days. Then they're ready to go to work."

"Interesting. But hardly genius."

Mason turned to her, his pale blue eyes glittering and hard, and a little bit crazy. "You think not?"

"Anybody can biologically produce a child. It takes more than that to be a parent." And given her own experience, and that of her baby brother, she should know.

He was, of course, delusional. How could that help them?

"Ah yes, parenting. I think I did a splendid job mentoring the boys, didn't I? Encouraging their latent talents to develop without getting in their way."

He hadn't had a loving relationship with the three young boys he'd mentored. At least *he* hadn't loved *them.* It was the boys who'd worshipped Knight . . . Lexi started systematically filing all the information she had on Mason Knight in her brain, just as she'd do a research project on her computer in Montana.

There was something—something she'd seen or heard that was going to trip up this bastard and be his downfall. She just had to access the information.

Fast.

Twenty

A swirl of white indicated Alex was teleporting.

No.

Being teleported.

Against his will was a given.

Lexiiii?! he yelled into the ether.

Would his being ripped from her side save her? Or would his removal expose her to more of Knight's evil machinations? He fought the temporal power pulling at him.

Knight.

His efforts were puny against the force. Wherever he was being taken was completely out of his control.

Lexiiii?!

She was a smart and resourceful woman, an operative in her own right. But he knew that wasn't going to be enough to best Knight with his formidable powers and the wiles of a soulless predator. He'd never felt more helpless, more powerless in his life.

He materialized on a dark street.

Christ. What now?

The pain Knight had inflicted, while no longer debilitating, still echoed like a shadow along his nerve endings and deep in his muscle fiber.

It took longer than normal to orient himself. He ran a finger under the tight shirt collar binding his neck as he took in the tall poles with their flickering gaslights, the cobbled street, and the out-of-context but strangely familiar surrounding buildings. "Shit."

"Damn."

"Fuck."

"Excellent," Alex said dryly. "The gang's all here." The only thing that would have pleased him more was seeing Lexi. On a beach somewhere. Far the hell away from wherever the fuck *here* was.

Blackthorne glanced up and down the empty street. "Where the hell are we?"

Alex pointed to the arched sign on the building across the street. Rick's Café Américain. "Nineteen-forty-two."

Fox did a classic double take. "You are shitting me."

"Welcome to Casablanca." A cold wind blew the hem of Alex's long woolen coat around his booted calves. "Apparently we're the bad guys." They all wore full Nazi dress uniforms. Sans weapons, of course.

Nazis. He got the drone parallel.

The heavily studded double doors of the café swung open against the stucco walls with a slam as loud as a double rifle shot. The sound of piano music, glasses clinking, and people laughing spilled onto the previously silent street.

Blackthorne raised a brow.

"Lexi better not be inside," Alex snarled. "I'll rip his balls out through his fucking nose."

Fox started walking. "Let's get this fiasco over with."

"Got a plan?" Alex inquired politely as they crossed the street.

"Working on it."

"Yeah. Me, too."

"As Heinrich Heine said, 'Thought precedes action as lightning does thunder.'" Alex quoted softly as the three men strode into the cool dimness of the bar, their booted steps loud on the tile floor. Whitewashed walls, arches, and mood lighting filled the café. A low cloud of smoke, cigarette and cigar, hung over the empty tables and moved slowly with the help of the lazily spinning fans on the ceiling. The place shimmered and rippled with expectation.

A quick visual scan showed Alex that neither Lexi nor the other two women were there. Whatever was going to happen was between the three of them and Knight. Just the four of them. Till the end.

Alex focused on his mentor.

He sat with his back to the door. The piano music, glasses, and voices were nothing but sound effects. Like canned laughter in a television sitcom. Knight was the only patron of Rick's, although Alex was certain he would have preferred a studio audience. The noises of the bar were as jarring as being in this perfectly re-created movie setting.

He rose now at their entry, suave, and in his mind, no doubt, debonair, dressed in black dress pants and a well-cut white tuxedo jacket, crisp, pleated-front shirt, and bow tie—all circa the '40s.

His hair was slicked back and he held a short Waterford crystal glass in one well-manicured hand as he rose to greet them. Alex knew the amber liquid was a 1926, sixty-year-old Macallan's revolutionary Fine and Rare, single-malt Scotch whiskey. Knight had drunk the same appallingly expensive Scotch as long as Alex had known him.

Knight smiled. The sight made Alex's gut twist. This was the man who'd taught him to ride a bicycle. The man who'd commiserated when he'd smoked his first and last cigarette. The man who'd mixed him a Bloody Mary the first time he'd gotten drunk. The memories came crowding in. Alex did everything in his power to push them the hell out. Knight was activating old memories, polishing and enhancing them to a fine fucking shine to blind him to the reality of the *now.*

"I came to Casablanca for the waters."

"The waters?" Alex said his line. "What waters? We're in the desert."

"I was misinformed." Knight grinned.

They'd done this so many times—all of them quoting lines while watching the movie—that they could all play all the parts. Knight was always Rick.

"Mace, you can't go through with this insanity," Alex said as reasonably as he could, trying to appeal to the man he'd once believed he knew, not this crazy megalomaniac. "You must stop."

"You boys disappoint me," Knight said as if he hadn't spoken. "I thought you would have figured things out long before now."

Beside him Fox flexed his fingers hard enough for his knuckles to crack. "We're here now, asshole."

Knight gave him an expressionless glance. Lucas yelled in agony. Alex knew exactly how the searing white-hot pain, and the sensation that one's spinal cord was being yanked out his neck felt. Lucas fell to his knees, doubled over in agony.

When he could breathe again, he returned Knight's glare. "What the fuck purpose did that serve? You like inflicting pain just for goddamned *sport?*"

Don't engage him. Alex helped him to his feet.

Don't engage him? Lucas mentally snarled. *The fucker's about to suck us dry. What do you suggest?*

Mason had never been able to hear their silent communication.

A definite asset now. They needed every advantage right now. "This is overly dramatic, Knight," Alex told him, no longer pretending affability. He was done with that shit. "Even for you." The setting was a holographic image, the edges were just a little out of focus. To maintain an image of this complexity took an enormous amount of skill and power.

How would that knowledge benefit the three of them? How long could Knight maintain the illusion? What powers were unavailable while he kept up this Casablanca facsimile?

"Where are the women?" Blackthorne demanded through his teeth.

"Getting acquainted with the facility." Knight took a sip of his Scotch, rolling the smoky liquid around in his mouth before answering. "My hologram is about to show Miss Stone her worst nightmares made real in our production lab, while Miss Goodall is given a public relations nightmare to deal with and Miss McBride must convince some law enforcement authority she's not lying in hopes of saving you.

"By the way, thank you for giving me such wonderful access into their individual psyches. It makes controlling them so much easier while I deal with you."

Fox launched himself at Knight only to bounce off the field around him like a Super Ball off a concrete floor.

Knight tsked. "So irrational. Did you really think I'd bring you here simply to give you an opportunity to work against me? I had somehow hoped that my efforts would continue to improve after the initial creation. As I said, a disappointment. Fortunately I have a way you boys can make it up to me."

"Not a fucking chance," Alex told him. Shifting slightly, he reached out to rest his hand on a chair back. Holograms made shit weapons. There was nothing there. But when he moved, his booted foot bumped an object he *couldn't* see. He shifted forward and came in front of whatever it was, then brailled upward behind the protection of his body and the all-encompassing greatcoat. Something flat. Coolly metallic. This section felt like glass? Yeah. Glass and metal. He rested his palm on the flat surface and felt a small electrical vibration.

Knight continued as if he hadn't heard Alex's outburst. "My army is ready, boys. With the—what do you like to call them? *Vitros?*" He smiled, toothy and white beneath his mustache. "Oh, I do like that name. With my *Vitros'* chemical and biological makeup, and your powers, I'm about to launch a super-wizard army that will be invincible. Everything that you are, everything you've learned to enhance your powers will go into the collective. I will be the brain, you and your fellow Vitros will be the brawn."

"You want them? Why don't we just *give* you our damned powers?" Blackthorne suggested. "Take the damn things. None of us give a shit. Just let us walk away."

Alex presumed Blackthorne had a solution as to how the hell an army of drones with *their* combined powers could be vanquished.

"Ah . . ." Knight pretended to consider the suggestion. "No."

"We have no say in the matter?" Fox demanded. "After knowing us for thirty-six fucking years this is your way of repaying our love and trust? Do you feel absolutely nothing?"

Knight smiled again. A pleased, triumphant show of teeth with not an iota of remorse evident. "Ah . . . What can I say? No. The three of you were nothing more to me than a means to an end. This end."

Of course. Not that it should have surprised Alex, but it still felt like a full-on punch to the face when he heard it out loud. Love. What a joke. Love and family were the two things none of them had been allowed to have. All part of Knight's plan. The bastard's voice chilled Alex to the marrow.

"I allowed you to have thirty-six years to hone your powers and develop certain skills I deemed necessary for my army. You have all exceeded those expectations. I brought you into the world, and it's my prerogative to take you out of it. Rest assured, gentlemen, your legacy will live on for all time."

"And how exactly are you going to transfer our powers to your robots?" Blackthorne demanded as he too realized the props in the room weren't there. *I think we're still in the warehouse,* he told Lucas and Simon.

Yeah. That was Fox. *Standing on a bundle of electrical wires.*

"Nutrients are fed to the Vitros by a complex liquid compound. I believe you discovered several of my tanks in Rio, dear boy. A messy business, really. Messy and time-consuming."

Alex shut off the mental communication for a second as the reality slapped him upside the head. His body went ice cold. The twenty-thousand-gallon repurposed wine storage tanks. "Knight, for Christ's—"

"With the assistance of your three lady friends," Knight continued, enjoying his moment. "Using a new technique I've spent a decade perfecting, I've been able to shorten gestation in the human female to twenty-two days instead of nine months."

"This has nothing to do with the women," Alex snarled, pushing back his fear for Lexi. He reached out with his thoughts. *Fox, can you access your amped-up powers if Sydney's still in this building?*

Yeah. If *that's where we are.*

Blackthorne butted in. *I might be able to as well. Something clicked when I proposed to Kess. It's like some switch got hit. Let me see what I can do.*

Knight threw back the last half-inch of Scotch in his glass, savored the taste on his tongue, then swallowed. "By my estimates," he mused, "that would give me approximately sixteen Vitros, per woman, per year. Forty-eight viable, healthy Halfs with full wizard strength, thanks to the superjuice they'll be fed."

Alex ground his teeth together. He'd be double damned before Knight used Lexi for anything. Both Fox and Blackthorne seemed to be weathering this experience with Mason better than he was.

Neither was still dressed in their Nazi attire. What had changed in them that hadn't for him?

Blackthorne's hand, behind his back, was exploring their real environment, just as Lucas and Alex were doing. All Alex could do was keep Knight talking. "That's—"

"I know," Knight's glass appeared full once more. "Brilliant! Given that I have the capability to clone a thousand Vitros a day with the current method. I'll have *three thousand* stronger, more powerful Vitros than even I thought possible. Incredible."

"And what are you going to do with this invincible army?" Alex asked. The longer Knight bragged, the longer they had to figure out how to break the bastard's hold on them. Longer to figure out why *he* wasn't experiencing amped-up powers when he was around Lexi.

They were definitely still in the warehouse. He stood beside a row of the cases Knight was growing his clones in, their cylindrical glass smooth and round beneath his fingers even though on the surface it looked like stuccoed stone.

"Vitros for hire, of course. I've already given the world's underworld leaders a few tasty samples of what my private army is capable of. Offers are flooding in."

Knight placed his empty glass down on a nearby table with a small clink. "That's enough chitchat boys. Time to fulfill your collective—" He laughed. "Yes. Your *collective* destinies."

Before he could fight it, Alex suddenly found himself plunged into pitch darkness of thousands of gallons of a viscous, blood-temperature liquid. The sound of tons of metal sliding over him as the lid slid shut echoed in his brain like a death knell.

Lexi tore her gaze away from the macabre nursery. For a moment she thought it was a trick of the light, or perhaps a problem with being transported too many times in too short a period. But it looked like, for just a mere second, as if Knight had flickered.

Hologram? That was one of the powers Blackthorne had. Did Knight have it too? A surge of hope hit her blood. He was playing them, isolating them like prisoners in a detention camp to keep them from communicating with one another.

Screw that. He didn't know that the ladies had been gifted with temporary powers by Duncan and the Council to deal with this crisis.

Lexi edged away from Dr. Knight, retreating to an area near the large computer banks, hoping the mechanical hum would block out the sound of her breathing. She reached out telepathically to Sydney and Kess. *Hey. Where are you?*

Kess answered first. *I'm in some office waiting to talk to the president of the United States. T-FLAC has stepped across some government biological experiment that Knight was heading up. This is a fucking nightmare and we're suspected of espionage and threatening homeland security!*

It's a trick. He's manipulating your mind.

If he is, it's working on all the cops in the area too, Sydney chimed in. *I escaped, but nobody will believe me. They're giving me the runaround and running a background check, calling the local mental hospitals. How the hell do we get out of this?*

Focus. I need you both to teleport to me.

I don't know if I can. The fear came through loud and clear in Kess's thoughts.

Don't think about it. Just do it.

Kess shimmered in first, followed shortly by Sydney.

"Damn. It worked!" Kess grinned. "Now what?"

"Now we kick some ass and find our guys."

Twenty-one

"Kess, keep an eye on Dr. Knight," Lexi instructed. They stood between two rows of Vitros. Lexi chose to turn her back on the row of glass-fronted boxes containing almost fully developed Vitros. Even though the row she and the other woman stood in were Simon Vitros, it was still creepy having so many unanimated green eyes boring a hole into her back. She'd rather stare at the back of the boxes on the other side, with their electrical cords, and blinking status panels of red, white, and green lights.

"Let us know if he stops talking or notices we're not hanging on his every word," Lexi instructed Kess.

Kess nodded, then walked quietly back the way they'd come. She turned, her brand new engagement ring winking on her finger as she gave them a thumbs-up.

Knight's hologram was still yakking away. Good. That bought them a little time.

She turned to Sydney, who was staring at a Vitro as if trying to read his mind. The thing didn't *have* a mind. Which made it that much creepier. Would she know if Alex had already been absorbed? Would her heart know? Would she look into one of the young Alex Vitros and see him inside those green eyes, looking back at her, like she did with the Simon Vitros?

She shuddered. Do not *think* like that. Think like a damned operative. That's what I am. That's what I'm trained to be. An operative. "Okay," she said snagging Sydney's attention. "First thi—" A loud, metallic clang, like something large and heavy closing, echoed and re-echoed through the warehouse. Startled, the two women's gazes clashed.

Lexi spread her hands in a what-the-hell-was-that gesture. Sydney shrugged.

"We need to get outfitted, LockOut, et cetera," she told Sydney urgently; the incredibly loud noise, coupled with the almost preternaturally machine-humming-quiet of the warehouse made her nerves stretch like rubber bands about to snap. The soft, sibilant drone of Knight's voice, and the slightly uneven gait of his footsteps as the hologram hobbled just like the real thing did, was far off as he continued walking and talking, unaware that he was conversing with no one. Or maybe he didn't care?

Whatever had caused that loud clang was probably not good. Lexi couldn't begin to imagine where Alex and the others were. But she trusted that Alex was doing everything in his power to stop Knight. She'd like to believe he was also doing everything in his power to get back to her. But that was thinking like a woman, not an operative. And right now she was an operative first and foremost.

Alex would be working on stopping Knight. That's all that would be, should be, on his mind right now.

Alex, where are you? She hated, hated, freaking *hated,* that she couldn't sense him anywhere. What was the point of having a telepathic connection if they couldn't communicate?

If the man with her and the other women was a hologram of Knight, then the real Knight must be with Alex, Lucas, and Simon. Lexi could practically hear a freaking countdown clock ticking off the seconds in her head. Knight had manipulated them into coming. There was no reason for him to delay. Unless he has something worse planned.

He wanted Alex's powers, and he'd take them. However one wizard took another's power—he'd do it.

Was it over? She couldn't believe she wouldn't know. She had to believe that Alex was okay. Had to believe it. Because she couldn't imagine life without him. Even if he didn't feel what she felt, at least she wanted to know that he was somewhere. Anywhere. Alive and well. Thinking about her. Hell, as *miserable* without her as she was without him.

Lexi had calculated the odds of survival here today. Any odds were good odds. Any chance of stopping Knight and this crazy clone scheme was worth all the personal risk.

But the odds were not in the good guys' favor.

If Duncan Edge and his Council, and all the wizards outside in the parking lot couldn't break into the warehouse with all their powers, and all their might, what hope did six of them have of bringing down such a powerful wizard?

Reality check. They couldn't.

Alex, she knew without a scintilla of doubt, would not stop until he'd destroyed Knight and every last one of his Vitros. He'd die trying.

Lexi knew she could do no less.

There had to be some reason that Knight had needed her and the other two women to come inside when the most powerful wizards in the world had been locked out.

And she was damned if that reason was his intention to use her as a walking uterus.

Her temples pounded as she concentrated. What had Edge told her when he'd given her powers? *Don't try too hard. Think it. Expect it, and it'll happen.*

Boy, talk about taking a nosedive into an alternate universe. No black. No white. No *rules.* Just touchy-feely hocus-pocus. "Okay," she said under her breath. "Here goes nothing." She thought about LockOut, hard body armor, boots, headsets, and lip mics.

"Holy shit," Sydney whispered, her eyes round with amazement as all three of them were suddenly dressed in combat gear from head to toe.

From her post at the other end of the aisle, Kess spun around, her face white. Even Lexi was impressed. She indicated she'd been the one to suddenly clothe them all in combat gear. Kess gave a holy-cow-color-me-impressed nod, then turned back to watch the hologram expound the virtues of terrorists hiring clones instead of soldiers.

Since tangos and clones were all expendable to Knight, Lexi figured one put money in his pockets, the other didn't. It was a matter of commerce.

Knight's voice faded, almost inaudible as he moved away from them. The machine's low hum and slowly blinking lights caused Lexi's nerves to stretch even further.

"Now for weapons." She thought of her lovely custom-made Glock left at Edridge Castle. And her Sig, while she was at it. And a couple more loaded weapons. And her Ka-Bar. And the hunting knife. And . . . Oh, yeah. This worked! The weapons appeared around her feet. Pop. Pop. Pop. Woohoo!

She thought and expected a few extra goodies. C4, timers, charges, the works to blow this place sky-high.

Ta-da. Man, was this a cool skill, or what?!

She'd never cast aspersions on the benefits of wizard powers again.

"*Now* we're talking," Sydney said softly and with great relish, as she pulled a Glock from its holster and checked the clip. She held out her hand, paused, then looked pleased when a rubber band appeared in her palm. Satisfied with her accomplishment, she gathered her hair into an untidy ponytail.

Lexi checked that both her Glock and the Sig were loaded. They were. Good. Next she picked up the Ka-Bar and stuck it in the leg holster, then inserted the small fighting knife in the upside-down holster strapped to her left shoulder.

"Damn, that's impressive," Sydney said, admiring her arsenal. "Do I get a knife?"

Lexi gave her a considering look. Sydney had stuck a freaking *flower* in her lapel to go on an op. She looked like she'd be pissed if she broke a nail. But even in the short time Lexi had known her, she knew Sydney's girly looks were deceiving. The woman had brass. Lexi liked her.

Still—"A knife is up close and personal. And messy. Up to you."

Sydney shuddered. "Um . . . no. Backspace and delete that question. This gun will do me." She looked at the rest of the weapons laid out on the floor at their feet. "Maybe I'll take this little gun, too." Picking up a Ruger .22, she stuck it in an ankle holster, her streaky ponytail bobbing as she stood upright. "Ready?"

Lexi nodded. "Kess?" she called softly.

The redhead came back, and whispered. "He's about four hundred yards away. Doesn't look as though he's missed us."

"Let's keep it that way," Lexi told them, her heart thumping and adrenaline starting to surge through her system again. "I'll take out the central computer. Kess come with me. Sydney can set the—"

"Do you know anything about setting explosives?" Kess asked Sydney, who shook her head. "Okay. I watched them do some demolitions in Mallaruza. I'm not an expert by any stretch of the imagination, but I know which end to light."

"Kess, we'll join you over there as soon as chaos ensues. I hope

to hell turning everything off is enough. We want him so busy trying to get the computers and electricity back on, that he doesn't
notice us blowing this place to hell."

Kess fingered the butt of her Glock. "What if Knight is on Mars
or somewhere and doesn't even know his precious clones are
being vaporized?"

"Then we consider half the job done, and go after his ass afterward." Sydney bent over and picked up a small hunting knife and
shoved it into the thigh holster. "I might get over my aversion to
up close and personal."

"I wish we had a few hand grenades," Kess said as wistfully as if she
were thinking about craving an iced latte. "I throw like an outfielder."

"Think it. Expect it." Lexi quoted Duncan Edge.

"Do you think it'll wo—Holy shit!" Kess said, cradling an arm-
ful of grenades.

"I'll take a few of those." Sydney plucked several off the pile in
Kess's arms, and tucked them in her tac belt, and one in the free leg
holster.

Lexi shook her head, amused. "I'll relieve you of a few as well.
Okay. Everybody ready? Kess, set your charges, then report in."
Lexi nodded and Kess picked up the canvas tote filled with C4.
"Synchronize watches. Six minutes?"

"Five." Kess countered. "We can't afford to wait."

"Okay. T minus five minutes. *Go.*"

05:00:00

Alex plummeted head over heels through the tepid liquid in the
tank, hitting bottom with the force of his entry. He opened his
eyes. Pitch black.

Kicking off the steel base automatically, he swam as fast as he could to the surface, recognizing the deep mechanical growl of the lid-lifting arm followed by the definitive clank of the two-ton lid coming down over the four-thousand-gallon tank.

His window of opportunity slamming closed. Fuck it.

The sound vibrated like a gong through the liquid, hurting his eardrums and causing his body to vibrate painfully with it.

He jackknifed down. Not water. Too thick. Acidic. Poison. Dragging it through his gills burned like a bitch. Still, it contained enough saline that he could breathe. No matter how painful.

Wasn't gonna last long in this. And that was a fact. Already felt like a severe sunburn as the top layer of his skin started to peel in the acid. He tried to calculate how much time he had. Before his gills collapsed. Before his flesh was eaten by the acid.

Optimistically?

Five minutes.

His heartbeats sounded unnaturally loud in his ears as he swam as far as he could to the right, arms extended to feel the depth and breadth of his prison. If Lexi was right about these being repurposed wine storage tanks, and he'd bet his last cent she was, then there should be a side entering, sixteen-by-twenty-inch inside closing manway and two-inch outlet clamp connection.

If he couldn't escape from the top, he had to find that manway, and break out from the bottom.

Lucas and Simon's powers seemed to be stronger than his for some reason. With any luck they were dealing with Knight while he breathed his last fucking breath.

Lexi.

His fingers felt the side of the tank for the outlet clamp. He'd left her well provided for. A will. A freaking piece of paper. Official words. But not the words he needed to say to her. The words he wanted to say to her . . .

God, it *burned.* Fire through his gills, liquid flames scoring his flesh. Alex felt the acid eating away at the molecules of his skin. He was slowly dissolving like the Wicked Witch in *The Wizard of Oz*. I'm meeeelting . . .

Something backhanded him. Jesus . . .

He grabbed at the wrist in front of his, yanked it up and over. Fuck you! The body went over his head, drifting toward the bottom. Alex went after him/it. Grabbed something. Hair. Yanked. Went for the throat.

St—. C—t. Br—the! Fox sounded frantic.

Someone grabbed blindly at his leg. *Where?* Blackthorne's thought was weak.

Okay. Not vanquishing Mason. But here.

Here in a fucking tank of acid that no amount of drown-proofing training would save them from.

Just stay focused on holding your breath. I'm going to see what I can do to get us out of this tin can.

Grabbing Simon by the hair, and Lucas under his chin, Alex kicked upward, dragging their asses through the liquid as fast as he could swim.

And as fast as he could swim, he knew it wasn't going to be fast enough.

04:54:18

Sydney and Lexi ran between the rows of upright Vitro containers. The space was barely wide enough to walk, let alone run flat out. Worse, since they couldn't see over the top of them, there was no way of knowing if someone was keeping track of their progress.

Vitros watched them pass with blank-eyed stares. These looked to be preteens, the next batch toddlers. It didn't matter that Lexi had looked at identical age-grouped Vitros hundreds and hundreds of times as she ran, they still freaking creeped her out.

Keep your eyes on the prize, Lexi told herself as they came to an intersection in the closely spaced rows. She took a left, Sydney on her heels.

The prize was a bank of mainframe computers looking almost identical to the row upon row upon row of Vitro cases. Lexi pointed, and together she and Sydney hauled ass toward the complex computer mainframe. Her hair clung damply to her cheeks and neck as she ran. Her lungs had to work twice as hard in the thick, muggy air. Beside her she could hear Sydney having the same problem sucking oxygen into her heaving lungs.

Moving fast, Lexi yanked out a couple of screwdrivers from her tac belt as she ran.

The mainframe was bigger than she'd first thought. Twelve feet wide by eight feet high, enclosed in an unpainted louvered metal grid. She imagined the doors gone. Nothing happened. She started working on unscrewing the faceplate, still trying to use her unfamiliar powers. Still nothing. They couldn't wait.

After a brief hesitation, Sydney figured out what was where on the unfamiliar tac belt at her waist, and held a Phillips screwdriver in her hand. She didn't waste time, merely started unscrewing.

Lexi started unscrewing as well. Magic wasn't working, but a good old-fashioned screwdriver would do the trick. "As soon as we're in, unplug, untwist, un whatever. *Go.*"

04:50:08

Alex breached the surface, holding Simon's and Lucas's heads above the surface. A bubble of air remained in the few inches between the solid metal lid and the viscous surface of the liquid. *This is as good as it gets for air, guys. Suck it in.* Not exactly a healthy breath because what little air there was was filled with acidic vapor. But right now it was better than nothing.

The men gagged and choked as they struggled to remain on the surface and not sink like rocks. There was no purchase, they had to keep moving, and every movement was agonizing as the acid ate at their flesh.

Eyes and skin burning like a son of a bitch, Alex knew there was only a small window that he could get them all out of there, four minutes tops. *Gotta find the outlet manway. Hang on. Right back.*

Jackknifing, he arrowed down to the bottom through sheer agony. He had to find a set of thumb-sized lugs, unscrew them, and remove the plate. In the dark.

Four minutes and counting.

04:32:02

"Kess? How's it going?" Lexi whispered into the lip mic as she wiped sweat out of her eyes with a quick swipe on her shoulder. She pulled out the last twist of a screw by hand, adding it to the handful already in her tac belt.

"Five more charges and we're good to go," Kess said softly. "You guys?"

"Good." Lexi inserted the head of the screwdriver into the next screw. "No sign of Knight?"

"Negative."

"South wall in four." That would give them mere seconds to find a way out and they all knew it.

"Got it." Kess went silent.

"I think there's one more; yeah. There," Sydney whispered, pointing at the last screw holding the faceplate on. Her flushed face dripped perspiration, her perky ponytail had gone limp.

"Got it." Lexi stood on her toes to reach it, then backed up, hands outstretched to catch the cover as it fell forward. It was heavy, but between them she and Sydney managed to lift it so it didn't drag on the cement floor and make a hell of a noise.

The inside was a mass of neatly bundled cords and wires accompanied by flashing lights. "*Un*—Everything."

Any other time Lexi would have been fascinated to learn how this puppy worked, how much data it could store, how it regulated the Vitro tanks.

Sydney reached in with both hands and started yanking out the heart of Knight's Vitros, fistfuls of cables at a time.

Lexi quickly and efficiently started unscrewing the hundreds of cable connectors as fast as she could go.

The tone of the electrical hum of the thousands of Vitro cases changed slightly. "Faster!"

04:32:00

The pain had progressed from agony to the so-fucking-agonizing-he-couldn't-feel-it-anymore-stage. Alex found he barely had the use of his fingers. Must be swollen. Fuck, for all he knew they'd fallen off minutes ago and he just didn't know it.

Lugs. Where the fucking goddamn hell were the *lugs*?

There—

He swept the area with both hands. *Yes!*

He started twisting the giant screw, top right.

Slow. Too freaking slow.

They were going to die like this. Because if he knew Lexi, and Alex was pretty damn sure he'd never known anyone better, she would be working on a plan to blow this facility sky-high the first chance she got.

And he'd never get to tell her. Tell her what? She already knew he admired and liked her. Respected her. Needed to be near her like he needed his next breath.

But it was more than that. He lov—he wanted. No, he loved her.

The sudden jarring bump of a body against his back startled him. What the—*Blackthorne. Fox. Answer me, dammit!*

Nothing.

He dragged Blackthorne back up to the air, up to where they might have a fucking chance.

Coughing. Spluttering. A ragged drag of tainted air, then down again.

03:59:07

Sweaty and slick, Lexi's fingers slipped on a connector, as she worked against the clock.

"Please God the guys aren't in the building." Sydney whispered like a prayer, her voice thick with fear and jerky with the speed in which she was pulling at anything that could be pulled.

Lexi didn't answer. They both knew the guys were in the building. Where else would Knight want them?

02:45:56

Blackthorne? Can you hologram outside this tank?

Yeah, trying. Kess's close, I can feel it. If I can get Nomis to her, I can get her to spring the release cover. On it.

If Kess was close so was Lexi. While Blackthorne sent out Nomis, Alex put every ounce of energy he had left into loosening the bolts holding the plate onto the lower section of the tank. Once open the liquid would be released and they'd go through with it. If he could get the last of the four lugs unscrewed. It resisted his every effort.

Worse, he was getting weaker and weaker.

Lexi.

Alex! her voice abruptly sounded inside his head, startling him. *Thank God you're a—Where are you?*

Alex wasn't a praying man, but the sound of Lexi's voice in his head made him send up a prayer of gratitude. *She's alive. Thank you. In the warehouse. Tank of some kind.*

There are a dozen tanks.

Blackthorne's sending his hologram to show the way. And Lexi?

Yeah?

I lov—I need you . . .

02:58:26

"They're in one of the tanks," Lexi told Sydney, her fingers automatically twisting, twisting, yanking while her heart filled with joy and anticipation. He was alive. In good enough shape to communicate. Alive. Where there was life there was hope.

The hot lights overhead flickered. Then an entire bank went dark.

"You go. I'll finish here."

"Are you—"

"Go. I've got this."

Lexi ran.

02:44:08

Well? Did it work? Alex battled the last fucking lug with every last ounce of his strength.

Think so. Blackthorne's thoughts wavered and faded.

A triple knock on the outside of the tank. Nomis.

Christ—Blackthorne wasn't cursing. A silent prayer answered.

Nomis or not, Alex was determined to get this damned screw

undone. If the hologram didn't return in time, if . . . *Lucas, when did your powers start amping up around Sydney?* He was just making convo, just trying to keep them all alive, and alert.

Moment I slid the rock on her hand to fool the Halfs into believing I was her boyfriend.

Me too. Blackthorne's thoughts were muddy and weak. Bastard was giving it his best shot, though.

Ring, huh? Alex braced one foot on the side of the tank and tried brute force. The lug stayed put.

Maybe that was it. Maybe the reason why Knight's powers weren't impacting Blackthorne and Fox the same way was because they'd found something Knight couldn't control. They'd found love. The one thing Knight couldn't manufacture.

Yeah. Why? Fox asked. *Thinking of proposing?*

Neither the fucking time nor the place. But it was worth a shot. *Seeing as how we might dissolve before that happens, I was thinking sooner might be better.*

Lexi?

Coming as fast as I can. Charges are set to go off in three. We've got to hurry this along.

Lexi?

What?!?

Lexi, will you marry me?

Are you sure now's the right time? I mean, is this some weird kind of wizard thing, because last time I checked, weren't you supposed to ask that kind of thing in person?

Lexi. Shut up and listen. I'm hoping you make it in time. But I don't know if you can. We're in some kind of toxic soup that's already dissolving us. Can you just give me an answer?

You're in what?

He sighed and pushed every ounce of will he had left into the thought. *I love you, woman. Will you marry me?*

Nothing.

Jesus, Lexi, answer me.

02:50:53

Lexi ran flat out. Blackthorne's hologram flickered as it dashed between the reflective surfaces of the Vitro cases making it seem like he was double and sometimes triple at once. Right on her heels were Kess and Sydney.

The machinery was powering down rapidly, and the overhead lights were going dark one bank at a time. The red-and-green lights inside the Vitros' cases flickered, but didn't go out.

Shit. Of course. There was a damned backup generator somewhere.

"This way." The hologram, which looked *exactly* like Simon Blackthorne, dodged left, stopping at one of the enormous shiny steel storage tanks. The thing was three stories high and a hundred feet across.

Sydney looked up at the pressure-cooker-like metal cover over the top of the colossal tank. "The power's shutting down. How the hell are we going to get them out?"

Lexi glanced at the timer strapped to her wrist. Less than three minutes until that was a moot point. She scrambled up the stairs that circled up along the edge of the tank, following its curve toward the top.

Halfway up, her body slammed up against an immovable object. Knight appeared six steps above her, a shield firmly in place blocking her access to the control panel farther up the stairs on the landing behind him.

"And just where do you think you're going, my dear?"

"Get the fuck out of my way."

"Tsk, tsk. Such language. You need a lesson in manners."

He moved a finger, just a subtle movement. Pain radiated down her right arm, immobilizing her gun hand.

From behind her Sydney shoved forward. Gun pointed directly at Knight's forehead. Knight raised an eyebrow. The shield dissolved and the barrel of the Glock began to melt like a candle in the heat of the sun. With a yell of pain, Sydney dropped the super-heated weapon.

He can't see me. Stay right where you are, I think I can get him. Kess's thought echoed in Lexi's mind. As the pain in her gun arm receded she realized Kess was going to do what Sydney had tried and failed to do. Shoot him.

Don't. Won't work, she telegraphed. *Soon as he sees you there, he'll stop you. Can you reach the knife in my ankle holster?*

She felt the brush of Kess's fingers against her ankle, then the cool hilt of the knife, placed with surgical precision, in the palm she had extended behind her.

Lexi staked her knife throwing skills over a civilians shooting skills. She'd come second in knife throwing class at the academy. She hoped to hell that humiliating fact wasn't going to bite them all in the ass right now.

For a second everything seemed to go in slow motion as she sized up the distance between herself and Knight, then brought her hand up and over in a perfect throw. The blade created a blurred, gleaming arc as it went hilt over blade.

A second later it stuck, hilt deep, in Knight's throat. With a look of shock he toppled forward, eyes wide. His mouth moved but only gargled sounds emerged.

The three women shifted out of the way of his tumbling body as he bounced noisily down the metal stairs.

Unconscious, or dead, Knight landed in a crumpled heap at the hologram's feet.

"Instructions," Blackthorne's look-alike asked with a smile.

"Yeah. Stick him in an empty Vitro case and lock it," Lexi instructed, taking the stairs two at a time, the other women on her heels.

02:41:54

Answer?

Can it wait? Lexi, Sydney, and Kess were trying to figure out what was what on the control panel. She pointed out the obvious. None of the lights were on. The power to the tank was cut. *Trying to get you guys out first—Good God, Alex!* A diamond ring suddenly appeared on Lexi's left hand.

Say yes, dammit!

Yes, dammit!

Suddenly the guys were *there*. Naked. Glistening, their skin raw and angry-looking, but alive. Sprawled out on the small metal landing at the women's feet.

Lexi dropped to her knees, but Alex held up a hand. "Second, sweetheart." He dragged in a breath, then magically appeared, dressed and clean. He stood, holding out his hand to her. Lexi let him pull her to her feet.

"Knight?" Fox, also clean and dressed in LockOut, asked Sydney, who was tucked against his side like a Siamese twin.

"In one of the Vitro tanks."

Blackthorne wrapped his arm around Kess. "Time?"

He meant, Lexi knew, time to detonation. "Two. Forty-one."

Twenty-two

01:10:03

Nomis had stuffed Knight in one of the cases close to the tank. The arm and wrist bands were snapped nice and tight. Knight hung limply from his restraints.

"Dead?" Alex took in at a glance Knight's battered face and profusely bleeding neck wound. "Your handiwork?" he asked Lexi, who was standing beside him.

"Kess."

"That's my girl." Blackthorne gave Kess a squeeze. She grinned.

Knight opened his eyes to a slit, due to the rapidly swelling area across his nose and forehead. Even behind an inch of plate glass his expression was murderous. "Get me out." His words were inaudible through the glass, but his fury was easy to read as he twisted his wrist restraints hard enough to leach the blood from his hands.

Alex was aware of Lexi moving away from the group, but his entire focus was on Knight. The son of a bitch was healing rapidly. He, Fox, Blackthorne, and Nomis used every ounce of their considerable combined powers to hold Knight exactly where he was. But the wizard was gathering strength, amping up his powers to—

Alex blinked. What the fuck?

Knight's eyes widened, and he pounded on the glass with his fists. The gray in his hair reverted to black. His face became clean-shaven. He was becoming younger. Younger. Younger. Younger. He was a youth. A teenager. A young boy. His eyes indicated he knew exactly what was happening and was powerless to stop it.

Alex flicked a glance at Lexi, who was controlling Knight's speedy age reversal with a small handheld device. She looked fierce as she turned the dial counterclockwise.

"Shit."

"Damn."

"Fuck."

Recognition leaked out of the child's eyes as Knight became a toddler. His flattened hands pressed beseechingly against the glass.

Not a chance in hell, you sick fuck. Alex smiled a feral smile.

"Keep going!" Sydney told Lexi with relish.

"Make him an oil slick!" Kess ordered.

Lexi kept turning the dial as Knight reverse-aged until he was a small baby—then . . . nothing.

At the bottom of the case was a smear of moisture, nothing more.

Lexi glanced over at them. "*Sperm* good enough?"

Alex grinned as he reached over and grabbed her hand. "Thirty-eight seconds, people." He shot a last glance at the remnants of Knight. Lexi obliterated even that.

"Go. Go. Go!"

T-FLAC HQ
Montana

To expedite matters, everyone gave their debriefing verbally, in separate rooms. The Council sat in to save time and the duplication of efforts.

As far as Lexi's first debriefing went—it was hellishly long. She had a thousand questions for Alex, and only a handful of them had to do with their shared experience in Morocco.

The incredible explosion of Knight's warehouse and all the bells and whistles inside would be the benchmark for every other explosion she was yet to see.

The wizards outside the warehouse had instantly thrown a cone over the explosion, keeping every scrap of debris from being jettisoned far and wide. Even what was left, Lexi was informed, was then obliterated so that no trace, not an atom of Knight's lifework, was recoverable. By anyone.

Kess had done an impressive job sending the Vitros to hell. They'd offered her a move from the information dissemination department to the bomb disposal department. She'd politely declined.

Sydney had told her, as they waited to be escorted to their rooms, that she was already formulating a plot for a new book. Fiction, she assured Lexi and Kess with a small, knowing smile.

"Hello, girls," Lark greeted them cheerfully as she walked into the room where they'd been told to wait. Black lipstick made her teeth appear very white. She wore skintight black pants and a plaid red-and-black bustier. Chains and piercings and lots of curly black hair completed the picture. "I'm to take you off to your chambers for a night of rest before Medical releases you in the morning." She indicated a door that hadn't been there before. "Shall we?"

"Is Alex—are the guys okay?" Lexi asked. Of course he was.

"They will be once my Caleb finishes with them." Lark indicated they take the elevator.

Lexi shot her a curious glance. "I thought he was married."

"Och, he is. To darling Serena. She's a bonny girl, that one." Lark exited and Lexi, Sydney, and Kess followed her like freaking baby ducks. Lark's high-heeled boots clacked on the hard surface of the floor.

"And he's your Duncan, how?" Sydney asked.

"Oh, he's my great, great—" Lark waved a slender beringed hand. "Many times great-grandson."

Lexi shot Sydney an amused look. Clearly, Duncan Edge was older than Lark by several years. "Hmm."

"That's some ring," Sydney said admiringly, changing the subject.

"It did its job," Lexi said dryly; knowing he only did it to save the day didn't help her hurting heart.

"It's more than that, surely," Kess offered as they walked.

"He figured out that being committed to me would amp his powers. That was the one thing Knight couldn't fight. The power of love." Lexi tried to twist the ostentatious diamond off her finger. She wanted to chuck it as far as it would fly, if she could get it off. "Or a close proximity of it."

Lark cleared her throat. "Sydney, my cherub? This is your suite."

Sydney accepted the keycard and opened the door. "See you guys later?"

Kess leaned over and gave her a hug. "Much later," she said straightening. "Much, much. *Much* later."

"Thursday good for you?" Sydney laughed.

"Make that Monday!" Kess called back, tucking her arm into Lexi's as they walked slightly behind Lark.

"You're not going to get the ring off unless he takes it off," Lark told her mildly, without turning around. Lord, did the woman have eyes in the back of her head?

"And you don't really want that, do you?"

"I want him to love me," Lexi's voice was tight and filled with emotion she was sick of trying to hide. "*That's* what I want."

Alex was practically chewing glass as he teleported to Lexi's suite. He'd given his report ninety-six ways from Sunday. Anything else they wanted would damned well have to wait until he'd seen, touched, and talked to Lexi. It might be a good long while before he got to the talking part.

He felt jubilant and ridiculously happy seeing Lexi seated cross-legged on the wide bed. She'd showered, and changed into shorts and a white tank top.

"You look better than the last time I saw you," she told him coolly, glancing up from a magazine as he arrived to stand beside the bed. "All done?"

"Yeah." He'd kinda been hoping she'd scream with joy on seeing him, and fling herself into his arms. They'd kiss and touch and make love fast and then slowly. And then talk. Then make love again. Then maybe a bit more talking. The look in her soft gray eyes wasn't telegraphing any of that. Not even close. "Want to go somewhere else?"

She cocked her head. "Like?"

"Bermuda? Spain? The Galápagos Islands?"

"This is fine." She looked down, twisting the ring on her finger. Alex was quite proud of the size and clarity of the diamond, considering his time constraints.

"I'll probably be given another op in the morning."

Then she was going to be disappointed. He'd requested a couple of weeks R&R for both of them. "The Council gave Knight's powers to us. Blackthorne and Fox were relieved. It shocked the hell out of them to discover we were less than Halfs."

Her eyes, her beautiful, dove gray eyes met his. "Didn't that bother you as well?"

Scared the crap out of him. "Yeah. Gotta admit, it was a relief to me too."

"So now you're all full wizards?"

"Yeah." If this revelation, and the monumental fix had happened at any other time in his life, Alex would be consumed with the size of it. Right now he was more concerned watching Lexi trying to unscrew her damned finger. "Got a problem with the ring?"

"Yes," she narrowed her eyes at him. "As a matter of fact, I do."

Alex's heart swelled with love for this woman. His warrior woman. With her soft mouth, golden, spiky hair, and spirit as big as the sky. He loved every smooth, rounded inch of her.

"Yeah?" he asked mildly, sitting on the edge of the mattress. Just out of arm's reach, because she looked far from loving right then, and capable of reaching out and punching him in the nose. "What's the problem with it?"

"Diamonds have dubious origins," she informed him, still twisting.

"Not this one. DeBeers all the way."

"It's too big and ostentatious."

He reduced it to three carats, saw by her expression it was still too big, and changed it to two. While looking between the ring and her lovely face he paused to admire her unbound breasts under the thin cotton of the tank top. Apparently the touching part of the program was being delayed some. Alex tried not to be too impatient. Lexi, being Lexi, needed things spelled out, apparently. He was good with that. He planned on spelling out anything she wanted over the next fifty to sixty years.

"Better?" he inquired politely, resting his hand on her bare knee.

"Eighty percent of engagement rings are diamonds."

"Ah. Much too common for an uncommon woman. Got it. Do you have a stone preference?" The skin on her leg was as soft and smooth as silk. And very sensitive; her pupils dilated as he smoothed his palm up her inner thigh.

"What I want—What I *want*," she told him looking him straight in the eye, her gaze steady, her color a little high. "What I want is to know your real intentions. Was the ring a means to an end?"

He snaked his arm around her waist and tugged her closer. For a moment he thought she'd resist all the way, but after a brief hesitation, Lexi relaxed against him. "The ring was absolutely a means to an end."

She let out a little breath. "Oh."

He pushed her down on the nice firm mattress, with its crisp white sheets. "The purpose was an outward declaration of how I feel about you."

"And that is?"

"I love you."

Lexi punched his arm. "Dammit, Alex, why didn't you say that in the first place?"

He grinned. "I thought it was fairly obvious."

"I didn't want to hope."

"I love you, Alexis Stone. From the bottom of my heart, with *all* my heart. From now until the end of time."

"That's good, because I love you, Alex Stone. From the bottom of my heart, with all my heart. From now until the end of time."

"Excellent. Before we get from the great part to the starting the rest of our lives really, really good part—What kind of ring would you like?"

"Emerald, incidentally the color of your eyes. Emerald cut. Two carats, platinum band."

Yeah, that was his Lexi. She'd probably started researching rings the day they met. Alex grinned.

"You got it." He materialized the ring. She held out her hand to admire it.

"Perfect."

"Yeah. You are." He had to freaking kiss her before he exploded with lust. His mouth covered hers, and her eager response made his heart swell. He'd never conceived of loving anyone this deeply. The depth of his love for her staggered him. After several minutes he lifted his head to capture her cheek in his palm.

"Emeralds are a very soft stone, as I'm sure you know. So you have to be very careful not to get shot at when you're working. I'd hate to lose on my investment."

"You know I love you, Alex. There's just one thing—"

Oh, Lord, what now? "Yes, sweetheart?"

"I'm not changing my name when we get married. That's non-negotiable."

Laughing, Alex shimmered away their clothing. "Fair enough, my love. Fair enough."

ACKNOWLEDGMENTS

If you are waiting for a sign—this is it!

ABOUT THE AUTHOR

New York Times bestseller Cherry Adair has garnered numerous awards for her innovative action-adventure novels, which include *Night Secrets, Night Fall, White Heat, Hot Ice, On Thin Ice, Out of Sight,* and *In Too Deep,* as well as her thrilling Edge trilogy: *Edge of Danger, Edge of Fear,* and *Edge of Darkness.* A favorite of reviewers and fans alike, she lives in the Pacific Northwest.